Andrearth

Andrearth

Quest For Kindred Spirits Across Galactic Frontiers

Satyajai Mayor

PARTRIDGE
A Penguin Random House Company

To order additional copies of this book, contact
Partridge India
000 800 10062 62
orders.india@partridgepublishing.com

www.partridgepublishing.com/india

AUTHOR'S NOTE

The photograph on the back cover was taken by me on a freezing full moon night in Stratford upon Avon just outside the Dirty Duck – the pub opposite the Shakespeare theatre. The silhouette of the girl is so prominent that it still gives me goose pimples when I see it. There was not a soul around when I took the photo and still haven't been able to explain the appearance of the silhouette. Stratford is where my uncle lived and coincidentally is known to have the highest sightings of UFOs and recordings of spooky activity. That's where I wrote most of this novel.

The beginning of my practice of meditation through Sahaj Marg (Ramchandra Mission), way back in 2001 set the wheels of writing this novel in motion. I wrote the first draft in 2003; literally a visualization or revelation, which led to penning this pacy mystical sci-fi novel focusing on spirituality, human potential, love, and the existence of human life on a more enlightened plane in another galaxy. Coincidentally, much later, the mission published several volumes of translations of the conversations between our late Master (Babuji) with a medium, where he talks about the presence of several highly evolved human civilizations spread across the universe.

Human aliens or our own souls evolving on another planet, is of course a strong probability, much stronger than a "Hole in One" in the game of golf. All it needs is an identical sun and the solar system. Our galaxy, the Milky Way, itself boasts of more than a million Suns, and there are more than a million galaxies beyond…

ACKNOWLEDGEMENTS

To my family & friends who have inspired and
guided me in my literary pursuit
&
In the memory of Uncle Kamm who was very much part of
my journey and hosted me in Stratford upon Avon

CHAPTER 1

D r. Masuda held his breath as he pressed the ENTER button. Suddenly, the screen was filled with concentric circles. His small round eyes reduced to slits and the lines on his forehead deepened as he looked at the image. He closed his eyes and began to scratch his bald head, feeling the moistness come off on his finger tips, still trying to comprehend the result of his patient's encephalogram – a signal so strong travelling faster than light. He sighed, letting out a loud hiss and removed his round gold rimmed spectacles, when he heard the door squeak open. He swiveled around and extricated himself out of his chair to welcome the visitors he was expecting.

"Alan! My Goodness," said Dr. Lowe stopping a few feet away from Dr. Masuda, "It's been...hmmm...," his large brown eyes with puff bags underneath, looked at the doctor as if seeking an answer. "Yes! The last time we met was at the Uppsala conference." He smiled; showing his set of irregular brown teeth. The portly doctor in his lab coat bowed, and then gave his hand out only to feel his small hands swallowed by the large but soft hand. There was a certain superior air about the professor because of his large nose pointed upwards at the tip; his unbuttoned beige corduroy jacket displaying the characteristic red and white striped tie that stood out against his plain white full sleeve shirt over grey trousers.

Dr. Masuda turned to Ray. His jaw dropped as he stared into the blood shot sleep laden dark eyes of his patient. Drooping shoulders and thinned out arms swimming in a faded blue crumpled T shirt worn on equally grubby jeans meant that this boy had slipped back into another bout of depression.

Stroking his several day old stubble, Ray scanned the capacious interiors of his psychiatrist's office. The polished stainless steel name plate: "Head of Department: Neurosciences' was still lying on the table since the last session. Red leather upholstery on the chairs brightened the room up; and the glass topped round table supported on polished steel tubes did not give the room an appearance of a hospital consulting. There were no papers on the table except for a plastic folder with his name written in red marker on the top.

Dr. Lowe hung his jacket on the stand, rolled up his sleeves, and loosened the knot of his tie.

"Arigato," said Dr. Masuda, bowing again.

"Always a pleasure," said Dr. Lowe, returning the bow, his prominent adams apple moving rather conspicuously, and sat down heavily on the chair next to Ray.

Dr. Masuda poured hot water from the kettle into three red mugs, and put them on the table. Ray rested his elbow on the table and supported his chin with his palm. He closed his eyes, but his head began to spin like a top; so he opened them quickly. His eyes smarted with the lack of sleep.

"So much work has gone into this program. Ray designed a special transmitter, and had just put it to test." Dr. Lowe took a sip from his cup, and looked up, "Green tea from your garden?"

Dr. Masuda bowed half heartedly and his red pouted lips parted into a faint smile. His small round eyes lighted up as he stroked his hand over his bald head, flattening a few long strands of graying hair over his head.

"It's not just the closure of the facility ---," Ray mumbled under his breath, not sure whether he wanted to get involved in the conversation, and looked at his professor.

Dr. Lowe gulped his tea down, the folds of his smooth skin deepening on his long face, as he opened his eyes wide and raised his long bushy eyebrows.

"Mister Robinson has something to share with us, Chris."

Ray looked at Dr. Masuda. "Err...."

"Haven't you told him about the signal?"

Ray straightened himself and looked at his professor; feeling a lump forming in his throat, he swallowed.

"The signal --?"

Dr. Masuda grunted, rubbing his palms together, and glanced at Ray.

Ray averted the gaze and turned to face his professor. "I thought I told you that we had received an unknown signal through our new transponder," he said and paused, as if waiting for an acknowledgement. "The wave forms were... concentric circles!" He almost whispered the last few words.

Dr. Lowe put his cup down gently, scratched his nose, and slowly turned to look at Ray. "I see," he said plainly, and continued to stare at him, attempting to put a stand of curly brown hair back in place on his otherwise neatly combed hair parted to the left.

"Let me---." Dr. Masuda raised his hand gesturing Ray to stop.

"Actually, I called the meeting for this purpose."

"That is?" said Dr. Lowe, emptying the contents of his cigarette rolling kit. He placed the tobacco sachet on the table, peeled out one paper strip from its box, then dug his hand into the tobacco sachet and took out some.

"For Miester Robinson to explain his findings."

The professor didn't bother to respond, concentrating on rolling his cigarette. He licked the open end and sealed it. Ray continued to stare at Dr. Lowe's thick but long fingers hold the rather thin and out of shape cigarette as he lit it.

Dr. Lowe looked at Ray, as he blew a puff of smoke into the air. "Why didn't you tell me?"

"You were still in America when I received the signal. I went to the facility the next morning, but was turned away." Ray paused to swallow. "That's when you called to give me the bad news. "From that moment, something inside me --- just --- switched --- off…," said Ray, as tears welled in his eyes.

Dr. Lowe shook his head and took a deep puff. "If only the grant's committee had given us one more year," he said and patted Ray on his back. "Son…! Life has to go on. Aliens or no aliens."

Ray coughed as smoke filled the room, and wiped his face with the back of his hand. Dr. Masuda handed him a glass of water, which he gulped down.

Dr. Masuda put on his gold rimmed spectacles, and turned around in his swivel chair to face his computer; only the grey strands of hair bobbed above the rim of the chair. "All these years, I searched for an answer to the readings of your encephalogram," he said, and the tapping of the keys became faster. Then Ray heard some beeps that sounded more like warning signals; the beeps stopped as soon as he heard the tap of another key. The doctor moved away to allow the two men full view. Concentric circles were flashing on the screen!

Dr. Masuda pointed a finger onto the screen. "When you told me about your signal, I connected the two." Dr. Masuda looked at Ray as if seeking validation.

"You got the transponder here, didn't you?" interrupted Dr. Lowe, almost crushing what was left of his cigarette into the ashtray.

"This is not from your transmitter. These are the abnormal signals that Ray's brain was receiving when he was a child."

Ray sensed a hint of irritation in the doctor's tone. He got up and held on to the edge of the table, feeling weak in his knees; he felt a flutter in his stomach, and sat down again. "This is exactly what came up on the transponder that night."

Ray's heart was beating fast, his mind in a whirr making a connection.

Dr. Masuda turned around, caught hold of the edge of the table and pulled himself closer. He opened the file and took out a page tagged with a yellow sticker.

"You kept repeating a name," said Dr. Masuda, turning the pages in the file, until he found what he was looking for. Ray leaned over and tried to make sense of the scribbles. "A-N-T-A-R-E-S." Dr. Masuda spelt it out.

Ray combed his fingers through his thick, black bushy hair, trying to remember what happened ten years ago when he was hit on the head with the cricket ball in school.

"YES!" he said rather loudly, as he looked at his professor. Dr. Lowe sat up straight and set his cup down hard on the table. Ray thought he gave a perfunctory nod as if to say he was listening.

"I think I remember: it started just before I was hit by the cricket ball."

Dr. Masuda's small eyes flickered. He adjusted his glasses, as he looked at Ray expectantly.

"Moments before the ball hit me; I felt I was transported into a different realm. Tentacles of gas and dust were spewing out from a shiny, bright central disc, resembling a spiral galaxy. I didn't even see the ball coming, when it hit me on the left temple." He massaged the area. "I must have blacked out, but the dream seemed to continue. I saw a reddish hue, which slowly transformed into a hollow disk and started to float towards me. As it came closer it began to elongate, and, then, suddenly, I saw a human form, like a projection in space; it was floating in the background of the stars."

Dr. Masuda nodded furiously, his frown intensifying, as if he had got the answer to his conundrum.

"Have you ever told anyone about this?" Dr. Lowe said in a plain voice.

"Nope!" Ray shook his head furiously. The heaviness in his chest seemed to have lifted.

Dr. Masuda went back to looking at the screen. "It's not just the wave pattern. A very powerful signal had resonated with your neural electrical impulses; this interference created repetitive wave forms of very high frequency." He punched some more keys, and the waveforms gave way to an array of alphanumeric tables and graphs. "We have managed to isolate the brain signals from the resonating wave."

"Hold on, Alan," said Dr. Lowe leaning forward with his folded hands resting on the table. "You are implying that Ray was subjected to an external neurological stimulus."

Dr. Masuda's eyelids flickered, and his eyebrows furrowed. "Someone was interfering with his thoughts."

"You mean, planting thoughts in his mind." Dr. Lowe sighed, leaning forward, and resting his hands on the table.

"I knew you would understand," said Dr. Masuda, continuing to concentrate on the screen. "The waves seem to be travelling much faster than our own neural impulses."

He paused and then swiveled around to face his visitors. "No man-made gadget or stimuli can generate such high frequencies."

Ray just stood listening to the revelations, aware of the fact that what was being discussed was about his own condition and experiences, but it was not making him nervous. On the contrary, he felt much better than when he had walked in.

"He was receiving a form of energy that travels even faster than light!" Dr. Masuda paused and looked at Dr. Lowe, whose gentle nod seemed to give him courage to continue. "It cannot be from anywhere on Earth."

"I was in communication with an extraterrestrial." Ray said, looking at his professor, and then at his doctor.

"I wish you were, now," said Dr. Lowe, setting out to roll his second cigarette. "I do believe that life exists in outer space. Enormous amounts of money are being spent on this search. Finally, these aliens end up communicating with a little boy. Sounds quite bizarre, Alan."

"But there seems to be no other explanation," said Dr. Masuda. "In my decades of consulting and research into the workings of the mind, this is the first time I have come across something so puzzling. I have also compared the CT scans at the time of the accident with those before his discharge. A slight swelling on the cortex region that was worrying us, had disappeared rather fast, which, under normal curative conditions, would take a minimum of two months."

Dr. Lowe and his student exchanged glances.

"The swelling was not because of the knock," Dr. Masuda's eyes seem to light up, "which fits in with my theory."

"Which is?" said Dr. Lowe.

"His brain seemed to have been subjected to an external stimulus, which swelled up the cortex. Once the signal ebbed in intensity, the swelling subsided, and then disappeared."

Dr Lowe just grunted.

"Could they be communicating on the thought level?" said Ray. "Probably, that's why the encephalogram worked; while the computer failed even to even recognize the signal."

"The Japanese people believe in after-life," said Dr. Masuda. "There are people who are gifted with special powers to communicate with a soul."

"You mean Clairvoyants; London's full of them," said Dr. Lowe, unfolding his long legs.

Dr. Masuda took his glasses in his hand, blew into each of the lenses, and wiped the mist off with a tissue, before wearing them. "Your search has just got more difficult."

Dr. Lowe frowned as if wanting an explanation.

"Ray was in telepathic contact right through his childhood, until the cricket ball hit him."

"Maybe it was a way to attract attention and make us aware of their presence," said Ray, stifling a yawn.

Dr. Masuda got up from his chair. "Some Green Tea?"

Dr' Lowe offered his cup, but Ray covered his cup with his hand.

"It is because of the knock that we found out about this signal," said Dr. Masuda, opening a new packet of tea.

"Shouldn't he get another reading done," said Dr. Lowe.

"Not in his present condition." Dr. Masuda shook his head as he began pouring out the hot water.

"Somehow I have to retrieve the transponder and see if the signal is still there," said Ray.

"That's if we get some funds to continue our research," said Dr. Lowe, getting up from his chair. "Last year, the US senate announced a budget cut on all scientific explorations. Only those projects, which, directly, or indirectly, had relevance to the Water Resource Mobilization Program (WARM), would continue to be funded."

"Wouldn't I have to switch to the new project?" said Ray. The heaviness in the chest was back, and his shoulders drooped as he somehow couldn't think of anything but the signal and now the connection with his own condition. He suddenly felt hollow in his legs and his hands began to tremble.

Dr. Masuda came around and massaged his shoulders. "Close your eyes. Take a deep breath."

Ray closed his eyes, but his head spun like a top, so he quickly opened them.

"You have to take charge of yourself and calm your mind," said Dr. Masuda from behind.

"Take a break," said Dr. Lowe, patting Ray on the back. "I will hold your seat for the new project." He looked at his watch and got up, "Gosh, it's late."

Ray hesitated, and then got up.

Dr. Lowe was already wearing his jacket. "I have a lunch meeting," he said opening the door.

Dr. Masuda bowed as the two of them stepped out onto the hallway.

Dr. Lowe reciprocated. "Arigato, Alan."

"There is someone out there," said Dr. Lowe, as the two walked down the hallway. "This maybe our only chance." He lit the freshly rolled cigarette, even as Ray nudged him to look at the NO SMOKING sign.

Ray stroked his stubble; a plan was forming in his mind.

CHAPTER 2

After dropping Dr. Lowe, he went up to his studio apartment on campus, packed an overnight bag and drove straight home. He reached Stratford upon Avon in three hours, just before the rush hour traffic.

Ray parked the car behind his father's blue Ford. His mother's car was not there, and he presumed she was at work manning the Shakespeare trust gift shop.

A shiny round bald head bobbed above the wooden gate that doubled up as the side entrance leading into the garden. The head turned and the bright green wooden side-gate opened. Dressed in a white, full sleeve shirt, neatly tucked inside his grey trousers, Ray's father looked as if he had just returned from office. The paunch was a little more obvious than the last time he had seen Paul; the red hair around his crown curled at the ends; all this made him look older.

"Hello Dad?" Ray said in a low voice, surveying his two – storied home; his nostrils twitching at the smell of fresh paint. The double glazed windows of the room on the upper floor, facing the road, were shut, and the curtains drawn. His parents had kept it locked ever since he could remember, and chose not to speak about it.

"Just the same, eh, except for a fresh coat of paint," said Paul, exposing his stained teeth, as he reached out to hug Ray. The whiff of paco rabanne after shave mixed with tobacco pricked his nostrils. "Master is coming on Friday."

"To our house?" said Ray, stepping back.

Paul nodded, stroking his head. "He's staying with us."

Ray frowned as if in deep thought and looked up into the sky. A red Cessna was returning from one of its training sessions. Far above a jet plane was leaving behind a trial of condensed gases in the clear blue sky. His mind oscillated from the nostalgia of his childhood and the coincidence of the arrival of the Master.

He stroked his stubble and looked at his father, "That's just what the doctor ordered," and then stifled a big yawn.

"Huh...You...," Paul paused pointing his finger at Ray, "...and meditation?"

"Come on Dad?"

Suddenly Paul's rosy red cheeks darkened. Ray felt a pang of remorse as he noticed his father's big blue eyes moistening. "When did I ever say I don't believe in it? It's not fair. We only try and find explanations."

Ray shivered involuntarily as he felt a draft of cool air sting his face, and looked at his watch. "Time for Mom to be back."

"Revti will be late. Master is a strict vegetarian, so she is picking up some greens from Oxtal farm."

He found the way his father pronounced Revathi very funny and smiled to himself. Ray paused to think of the people at Oxtal Farm where he had spent a lot of time when he was small. His mind wandered to the times when he spent nights there during his holidays; the scrumptious breakfast with farm fresh eggs, bacon and freshly baked bread made his stomach growl with hunger.

Paul looked into Ray's eyes, "You need a good night's sleep, I say," and walked towards the garden.

Before Ray went up to his room, he raided the refrigerator and gobbled a few slices of bread dipped in curry, washing it down with a glass of skimmed milk.

Washed and changed, he came down and settled himself in the garden, waiting for Revathi, stroking his smooth clean shaven face. He took a deep breath to take in the aroma of freshly cut grass, which was lying in small heaps at different places on the lawn. His eyes roamed the garden as he reclined on the deck chair. The lone pear tree at the far end was full of his favorite conference pears. The vegetable patch was also well groomed, neatly divided into individual rectangles, with tiny saplings on the rise. The tool shed also had been given a face lift with a fresh coat of green oil paint. At the far corner beyond the vegetable patch, he saw the dome under which his father had installed the telescope he had built; it was the only structure that seemed to have missed being painted. He looked up into the sky and squinted, as the sun emerged out of a large white cloud. Somehow his mind was at rest and the heaviness in the chest had lifted.

"Still dreaming of your friends up there," he heard his father say; he opened his eyes and pulled himself up from the comfort of the deck chair.

He found Paul pulling a chair next to him, sporting his khaki shorts and a light blue collared T shirt.

"I must have dozed off," Ray said and looked at his watch. Just then his mother came out of the kitchen with the tea tray. She still wore her work clothes – a cream full sleeved shirt on top of black pants, with the logo of the Shakespeare trust printed on the pocket of the shirt. Her oval face and sharp long nose over a wide mouth with thick lips proportioned well with her long neck that was more prominent as she had tied her hair into a loose bun.

"Can't remember when the three of us were together," said Paul, stroking his bald head, as Revathi put the tray on the table.

"It's so nice to have you back," she said, and looked at Paul. "This is all Master's work."

Ray was careful and chose not to respond.

"How is the telescope fairing?" he said trying to change the topic.

"Haven't been near it for quite some time," said Paul raising his eyebrows as he took a sip of his tea. "It was different when you were young, when you had your own dialogue with the stars."

"PAUL..."

The sharpness in her tone drew Ray's attention. "Mom, it's fine, we can talk about my 'rather eventful' childhood. Incidentally, I had a long session with Dr. Masuda about it."

Ray explained in brief the findings of the doctor. In the middle, Revathi got up and began clearing the cups. "*Chalo,* now, let's not talk about all this. It makes me very nervous." Ray looked into her black doe like eyes, and for a moment he felt they were moist.

"You two catch up, while I put some dinner together," she said. Ray watched his mother disappear into the kitchen. He admired her tenacity and forthright attitude. She hadn't changed much; she had maintained her lean figure, and had just the same dark, straight, shoulder-length hair.

ॐ   ॐ   ॐ

After dinner, Ray went straight up to bed. His room was being readied for Master, so he was put into the smaller bedroom – the one that had been locked up. It had just enough place for a bed and one chair. He opened the window above his bed to let some air in, wiping beads of sweat off his brow.

No sooner had he switched off the light, he heard his doorknob turn.

"Ray, are you asleep?" he heard Paul's voice.

"No Dad."

The door opened, letting in a stream of light.

"I just wanted to share something with you, rather, get something off my chest."

Ray reached out behind him and switched on the light. Paul squeezed in through the door, and came and sat at the edge of the bed. He handed Ray a neatly folded paper. It looked more like a page torn off a school notebook. He glanced at his father who was looking at him intently, and then, unfolded it.

Dear Mom and Dad,

I love you both very much, but I just cannot understand what happens to me. All of a sudden, as if I am tuning into a radio channel, a voice speaks to me inside my head.

Ray looked at his father. "I really don't remember writing this. I must have really lost my mind."

"You had left this in your room, ten years ago — the same night, after you had given that speech at school."

"You did mention something about an apparition you saw when I was just born," said Ray. Paul was in the process of getting up, but sat down again with a jerk.

"Oh!" Paul's eyes widened, and his cheeks darkened. "Who told you that?"

"It's important for me to know as it might have relevance to my work."

"Must have been Dr. Lowe," said Paul, massaging his head.

Paul got up and closed the door. He pulled the chair closer to the bed. "You were exactly a month old that day. It was the night of the Leonid meteor showers, and I stepped out sometime around three thirty in the morning to observe the shower. Fortunately, it was a cloudless winter's night; I drove out into the country off Banbury road, towards Long Marston."

"I know that place. Didn't we go there many times?"

Paul nodded. "I scanned the skies, waiting for the streaks of meteors. Suddenly, I saw a flash of fiery light streak across the northern sky. I was sure it was not a meteor. The fiery streak was now suspended in mid air as a ball of white light. It was beginning to take a human form. I just stood gaping. As quickly as it had appeared it disappeared, not into thin air, but onto the concrete jungle, right over our home. Then began a beautiful display of shooting stars; it was as if this apparition had ushered in the meteor shower. After the showers I went back home."

"Sure it was not one of those UFO sightings?"

Paul shook his head and continued in the same breath. Ray noticed sweat beads form on Paul's forehead. "I had just stopped the car in their driveway and switched of the headlights, when I was distracted by a bright light overhead. A blinding light — pure white — overflowed out of our bedroom window. Suddenly, it began to emanate from…," Paul paused. "…this window," he said, pointing to the window above Ray's bed.

Ray sat up and looked at the window as Paul continued. "It took a shape resembling the same apparition that I had seen from the observation site. Then, it turned into a ball and rose into the sky, as if a meteor was on its way up. I mustered the courage to go into the house and went straight up to our bedroom where Revti and you were sleeping. It was dark; the bedroom window was shut, and both of you were fast asleep. I remember Revti telling me the next morning that she was awakened by a gurgle, and then, a loud laugh. She opened her eyes, turned around and happened to glance at the window, when she saw a faint white streak of light flashing past it."

"Ray stretched himself and let out a loud yawn. "I really don't know what to make of this."

"Nothing," said Paul. "Better get some rest; we have a long day tomorrow." Paul yawned, and got up from the chair. Ray watched his father open the door. He knew this was the best time to ask the question he had avoided all these years. "Can I ask you something?"

"Huh…" Paul turned around, and shut the door gently. "I really think you should go to bed."

"This room…" Ray paused, not sure if he had done the right thing.

"I know it's a bit crammed." Ray sensed a hint of irritation in Paul's voice. "Couldn't put the Master in this room."

"That's not what I meant." Ray felt a bit embarrassed. "Good Night, Dad?"

CHAPTER 3

As the 10.05 Thames Rail glided into the station, the reception committee of around fifteen followers closed in. Ray looked around and walked towards a man dressed in a maroon Kurta and white pajamas, standing patiently on one side, near the exit, stroking his plastered down oiled dark hair and thick bushy moustache, alternately; he presumed the rather dark skinned man to be a follower of the mission as he sported a badge pinned onto the Kurta just below the button line that every *abhyasi* or follower wore; even his parents wore it when they went to any gathering of this Mission.

"I was expecting lines of people with garlands," Ray told the square faced short and stout man.

"Chha, Chha…Master does not like such *tamasha*." The pronunciation was so much like what he had heard when he was down visiting his mother's family in Kerala.

"That's him." The man pointed to a tall, broad shouldered man with a walking stick in one hand, alighting from a coach; he was aided by two people; one was Julie, and the lady on the left was his mother. He smiled to himself. His mother was after him to date Julie, or, rather, marry her. The Master was dressed simply, but elegantly; he was wearing a half-sleeve shirt and khaki trousers; he was clean shaven, contrary to what Ray had pictured him to be. He hurried out of the station, before the crowd reached the exit, and decided to walk home.

Crossing the park, Ray strolled along the riverside towards the old church. He laughed at his own thoughts; they were recollections of his own experiences during his rather eventful childhood.

Did it really happen? Did the ice cream really float into my cone, guided by a hidden force?

Dragging his unbuckled sandals along, he still remembered the incident of the ice cream cone in this very park he was walking through.

It was one of those days when his mother was summoned to school because of his weird bouts of talking into the sky. His mother had taken him to the park on the way back. He had already reached the counter, and was trying to chat up the girl manning the ice cream stall; she already knew what he would order and got it ready. Ray reached his hand out to take his ice cream. Just then, a grubby looking girl in her teens barged in front of Ray, and grabbed the cone. All of a sudden, the scoop dislodged from the cone and started to float towards him. The girl who was holding the cone followed the ice-cream scoop. She looked like a juggler, trying to retrieve it. The scoop floated towards his outstretched hand. At that moment, her cornet had been under the scoop, but her hand was blocking Ray's view of the scoop. In her moments of acrobatics to secure the scoop, it fell on her blouse. Ray beat a hasty retreat.

ॐ   ॐ   ॐ

The Master arrived home rather late in the evening, and was escorted straight to the dining room. Ray was expecting some more people, but to his surprise, Master was alone. He suddenly realized that this was, probably, the first time he had sat in their formal dining room. Seated opposite Master, all he did was gape, mesmerized by the magnetism radiating from the Master's eyes.

"Are you the one looking for aliens?" The Master broke the silence, making Ray almost choke on his food; fortunately, he swallowed the whole portion, and put his fork down. "Yes… Sir." He sat up straight.

"Don't call me, Sir," Master laughed; Revathi and Paul laughed half heartedly. "Have you found anything so far?" The Master smiled mischievously, continuing to look at Ray.

"No… Si –" Ray looked at his mother who hadn't even taken anything on her plate. "The facility where I was conducting these experiments is no longer available, as my grant has been withdrawn."

"Master, it's so unfair," said Revathi, as she served him with a large helping of the main course.

"It is all there," said Master, pointing a finger to his temple. Meditation is one way to open your channels of thoughts, beyond your comprehension, reaching into the depths of your consciousness, thus awakening the subconscious," the Master continued, much to the bewilderment of all at the table. Ray was transfixed staring open-mouthed at the Master. "Our thoughts travel at the speed of light or maybe even faster, and the brain is a living mobile phone receiving and transmitting signals into space. When you reach your higher consciousness, you are one with the cosmos. Everything within you is present outside. We all exist outside ourselves today and are moving further away. Meditation teaches you to look within, condition your mind, and bring about equanimity in one's life."

He looked at Ray and gave a faint mischievous smile. Ray smiled back. Not a word was spoken through the rest of the meal. After desert Revathi escorted Master to his room.

"Rather encouraging, eh," said Paul, as he came back to clear some more things off the table.

"I sure need divine intervention," said Ray gathering the unused cutlery and putting it on the side table.

☼ ☼ ☼

"Good Morning, Master," said Ray, as he walked into the garden. Seated on the wrought iron garden chair, in front of the wrought iron table, the Master looked up with a start. "Sorry, did I disturb you, Master?"

"No, not at all; in fact I had a feeling you would join me."

Ray paused for a moment. "I'll just get us some tea."

The Master grunted in his characteristic style. "Your mother is already preparing some," and looked towards the kitchen window.

"Did you not sleep well, last night?"

Ray shook his head.

"Restlessness is a sign of change and growth."

The Master took a deep breath, as if he were savoring the crisp and cool air. "Would you like to take three sittings while I am here?"

Ray looked at the Master and frowned. He was mesmerized by the mere presence of the Master. In step with his starched, white raw-cotton (*khadi*) shirt, matched with a cream colored, gold-bordered silk wrap around, Master's silver grey hair was neatly plastered down with not a strand out of place.

"What are sittings, Master?"

"What it means is the process of initiation into the practice of meditation? The first three '*sittings*' open your channels to receive energies from the higher power. It is necessary for you to take these sittings on consecutive days."

"No harm in giving it a try," said Ray, shrugging his shoulders.

The Master reacted with a faint smile. "I will tell you a secret." Ray suddenly sat up straight. "I am fortunate to have found the right person," continued the Master, "as it really is about reaching out to extra terrestrial beings. You will not need the tools of modern science."

Ray looked on in amazement, unable to react. As it is he was awestruck by the very presence of the Master. The softness, yet firmness in his voice; the humility; it was all so special; so very overwhelming; Ray had come to the conclusion that the Master was, indeed, an enlightened soul. Despite the excitement about Master's revelations, he felt a sense of peace and contentment.

Ray started, drawn out of his enthralled state, as Revathi came from behind and set the tea-tray on the table.

"He is ready to take three sittings, which I shall give him over today and tomorrow."

"But, Master! I have yet to decide," protested Ray.

"Do you want to know my secret?"

ॐ   ॐ   ॐ

"Imagine a light in your heart, like what you see at dawn just before the sun rises. Treat your thoughts like uninvited guests and ignore them," were the final words of guidance, as part of the first initiation session, which was being conducted in the bedroom that Ray was using.

Deep inside his consciousness Ray heard the word, "Over."

His eyes flickered open, rubbing them as if he had awoken from a deep slumber. He looked at his watch. "Wow, it's been an hour!"

The Master grunted in his characteristic style. "What did you feel?"

"I feel light-headed."

The Master raised his eyebrows and burst out laughing.

"No, no. That's not what I asked."

"I closed my eyes and imagined this light," began Ray. "I kept seeing stars, and then, darkness beyond. A flash of light crossed my vision; my eyes refused to open. Then it happened! I felt my extremities turn hot, as if there was a flow of energy out through my fingers and toes; I felt as if my body was on fire; I wanted to cry out, but was unable to do so. A sudden feeling of emptiness pervaded me. Awareness came back only when you said, '*Over*'."

Ray looked expectantly at the Master, as if seeking validation of his maiden spiritual experience. The Master's countenance gave nothing away.

"Meditation is a process of letting go of your thoughts," said Master. It is exactly opposite of concentration. Once you have attained the power to control your thoughts, rather than it dictating terms, you can concentrate on what you really should be doing. One's mind is like a wild horse. You harness it, it will do wonders; and if you cannot, it will trample you," he continued after gulping down a glass of water. "The most important aspect, or, rather, benefit, of meditation, is that it removes the impressions of the past; it's like reformatting a hard disk of a computer. You are practically wiping the slate clean, making you react to situations, not based on your past experiences, but solely in the present context; this, ultimately, is the most appropriate and unimpeded reaction. It also helps you to maintain your state of equanimity. These impressions, or sanskaras, could be, not just of your present life, but also the ones you would have imbibed over several lifetimes. I am only a conduit for this cleansing energy, which is received from my Masters, who in turn are in resonance with pure cosmic energy."

Ray just sat on the bed completely relaxed.

"Our next sitting will be this evening, before dinner. But let me explain the most important and critical aspect of our system."

"Everyday at dusk, you need to perform cleaning."

"Cleaning? What do you mean? I should sit for meditation only after a shower?"

The Master laughed half heartedly. "Cleaning is a process unique to this system of meditation. At the end of each day, cleaning is performed. When you sit in meditation, instead of giving a thought of receiving white light, you give a thought to remove the grossness and impurities from your mind. This prevents any new impressions to be formed, and removes the existing impressions that are brought forth during the morning meditation."

"Do I have to clean this evening?"

The Master shook his head, "Not until you complete the three sittings," and excused himself, leaving Ray quite unnerved and incomplete.

❦ ❦ ❦

Ray heard a car door bang. He rushed to his parent's bedroom and looked down from the window. He heaved a sigh of relief, and ran down the stairs. He opened the door just as the doorbell rang.

"Were you expecting someone," said Revathi as she stepped in followed by the Master.

The Master gave a shallow laugh. "He is only restless. His channels are so open that the effect of the first sitting is still there. I am sure the second sitting will ease some of his discomfort."

Ray looked at the Master and frowned. *Gosh, he can read my mind,* he thought.

"Dinner will be ready in an hour," said Revathi.

"So we better get on with the sitting," said the Master.

"Don't you want to unwind and relax for a while," said Ray, who was amazed at the stamina of the Master. What amazed him even more was that the Master looked as fresh as the time when he had left the house in the morning.

The two of them went upstairs into the small bedroom. Ray sat on the little cane chair while the Master chose to sit on the floor, facing his pupil -- *abhyasi*.

"Please start meditation," he said very softly.

But Ray had not heard him. He wanted to discuss his state of mind with the Master. He looked up to say something, but he found the Master already in his meditative reverie. He quickly shut his eyes and began meditation. Some time into the sitting, Ray felt a tingling sensation, followed by a jolt. He struggled to keep his balance. He opened his eyes and found the Master desperately trying to resist doing the same. The Master grimaced, as if he was in pain. Suddenly, his face relaxed; his equanimity seemed to have been restored.

Seeing him back to his normal self, Ray closed his eyes. A profound calmness pervaded his consciousness. But it made room for a disturbing thought, which persisted throughout the sitting.

Soon after the sitting, it was Master who broached the subject. "Were you trying to call a higher power?"

"Uhh..., what do you mean?" Ray thought for a moment. "Are you referring to the momentary disturbance that WE experienced during the sitting?"

"No. You were definitely in a deep meditative state throughout the sitting. But midway you were subjected to a very strong transmission. On the contrary, I received it from you. I was unable to clean the nagging thought in your mind."

Ray gaped at the Master.

"Don't worry about it. It will be cleaned out in the next sitting."

The Master got up and walked away, as Ray looked on. He had so many questions, especially now, when the Master had touched upon what he presumed to be something to do with the 'secret'

"But…" The Master didn't seem to hear him. All he heard were the creaks of the wooden staircase as the Master descended.

ॐ   ॐ   ॐ

The Master gave Ray his final sitting early on Sunday morning. Since Ray was driving back to London that evening, he was only too pleased to give Master a ride back.

When it was time to go, Ray took out a photo of the Master from his mother's drawer and put it safely in his wallet.

He picked up the Master from the hall, which was on his way out onto the motorway.

The Master still looked fresh; his hair neatly plastered down, and not a wrinkle on his spotlessly white Kurta. Ray kept glancing at the Master as he drove.

"I know you want the secret," said the Master, as soon as the car got off the ramp onto the Motorway. He gave a short throaty laugh. "While giving you the last sitting, I delved deeper into your sub conscious. It seems you have been subjected to a much higher transmission during your child hood, as if someone has planted a homing device in your brain. I experienced the same transmission, twenty years ago. You probably were not even born then. It kept repeating: *I need a guide to visit your world.* My Master – Babuji – was still alive. He seemed to know what was going on, but always avoided talking about it."

Ray felt a strange sensation in his head as if tiny bubbles were bursting inside. "Then what happened?"

"Nothing. It's for you to find out."

"Me?" Ray tightened his grip on the steering wheel.

"Yes. You are already on the right track."

They came to a toll booth, and once they were off, Ray suddenly realized what the Master had just said, and went on to describe his recent experience, beginning with the cricket ball episode.

"…Before the facility shut down, I did receive a strange signal," said Ray. His ears had become all hot, and he turned the air conditioning to full. The Master calmly redirected the flaps towards Ray.

"It was several orders of magnitude more powerful than any signal we know of, or even can perceive. It has to be a signal, which was generated consciously by someone out there. Strangely, my professor was contemplating the possibility of transmission of thought. No radio astronomy software could recognize what we had received. A similar wave pattern was recorded by an encephalogram."

The Master unfolded his legs, and gave a throaty laugh. "Your senses must have been numbed after the head injury, making your mind impervious to these signals."

"That's not all, Master. When I was small I could hear little insects as if they were talking to me. The whistling of the trees in the wind was music to my ears. And then, I felt as if a fairy is telling the story of the stars, planets and the universe. It almost seemed to be a message from someone out there who is trying to get in touch with us."

"You seem to be on the same plane as me."

"I don't quite get you."

"For the first time, in my practice of meditation, after becoming the Master, I had been drawn out of meditation by an external disturbance. As soon as I tried to get back into meditation, a silent voice pervaded my thoughts: *There is only one other soul on your planet that is receiving us,* and faded away." The Master shifted in his seat.

"You mean to say all this time they have been in contact, and I have ignored their messages?" said Ray.

"I have been able to open your channels once again. You may be able to combine your gadgets with the power of your mind and reconnect."

"Why can't you establish contact directly?"

"My job is with the mission, guided by my Master. I am only a conduit for transmitting this energy. I can help you in your pursuit to make contact, but will not be a party to it."

"How will we do it? You are in India, seven thousand miles away."

"Energy is all pervasive. It recognizes no physical boundaries."

"My sensitivity to human vibrations is strong enough to distinguish between a genuine attempt and a hoax." The Master stifled a yawn. "They must have some patience to have been in contact for twenty years."

Ray reduced speed as he saw a message on a road screen asking traffic to slow down to 30 mph. "Dammit," he cursed, and slapped the steering wheel.

"We must be approaching London," said the Master.

Ray nodded, his thoughts going back to what the Master had just concluded. "No human being would have that kind of patience."

The Master laughed. "I can see that."

"It's not even a millisecond on the universal space-time scale. It definitely would be an anticlimax. I would have imagined a far more intelligent being alighting from a space ship." Ray looked at the Master. "But, it could just be experiences in the mind within one's own self."

"Putting aside science and its rationality for a moment, we at least are sure that our body does have energy. The sum total of the energy, when we are born, and even after we die, has to remain constant. Where does this energy go, after we die?"

Ray shrugged and shook his head. "What has this got to do with our imagination?"

"The energy floats away into space. This energy is called the soul. It carries with it the impressions of the past and the directions for its future course. When a person dies, it is the soul that leaves the body. So coming back to the messages in your mind, it certainly can be generated within one's self, but not unless one's soul was exposed to some form of experience or stimuli, at any point in the course of its journey."

"Billions of dollars, maybe trillions, have gone into this program, but all that has come up is radio static. And now if you are right, there was no need for all this gadgetry."

The Master chuckled, "An expensive price to pay for tuning into a radio," he said, and then looked at Ray. "All we need is another Einstein to put the cycle of Birth, Life, and Death in the form of equations and formulae."

"Probably, we will end up with a constant, like the cosmological constant," said Ray, looking straight ahead, "and be able to predict our rebirth, liberation, and existence, from the value of the constant."

Ray changed lanes as the traffic inched forward. Luckily he was taking the first exit, where traffic was moving rather smoothly.

"I need to tell you another secret, before we arrive. It's something concerning your parents."

Ray shivered involuntarily and glanced at Master who continued to look straight ahead.

"When your parents came to me, I had just become the Master." The Master stroked his hair as if he was trying to recollect something. "Yes…! It was in Birmingham during the July 24th celebrations. For the first time I had planned it out of India." He paused again. "That's the first time I met your parents. They were still grieving."

"About what?"

"Your sister's death?"

"SISTER?"

"Revathi had a daughter, ten years before you were born. Tragically, she was kidnapped when she was five, never to be found again."

"Oh Nooooo…" said Ray, suddenly releasing his foot from the accelerator, only to be hooted on from the back. He quickly changed lanes. "They never told me. How could they do this?" He felt sick in the stomach, and heavy in the chest. He moved into the service lane and stopped the car.

"You should be grateful to them for not burdening you with their grief."

"How could they leave me out of their lives? It's not fair. I almost feel like an outsider."

"Tut, tut…," the Master clicked his tongue. "I am the one who advised them not to tell you, and if I had not told you now, you would never have known."

"Then why did you tell me," said Ray slapping the steering wheel with both his hands. Suddenly, he felt the Master hold his hand. A burst of energy as if someone had sent a mild electric current through him, flowed through his body. It took away the knot in his stomach, the queasiness eased, and his mind relaxed; he felt his muscles relaxing.

"There is a time and place for everything, and I feel that the accident, your childhood experiences and search for extraterrestrial life have a connection. Don't ask me what. Let it unfold."

"What do you --?"

Master raised his hand. "The ball is in your court. Not a word to your parents about this," he said, and closed his eyes.

By then Ray had entered the outer ring road, and was looking for the right turning as mentioned on the printed directions.

A short while later the Master awoke to find Ray meandering through a narrow road with trees on either side.

"Let me know how you progress on this. I sit for meditation at four-thirty every morning. If you can sit at that time, we can, together, send a message out to that lost soul," said the Master, as Ray drove up to what appeared to be the porch, where a dozen or so guests were gathered.

He didn't wait to be introduced, and headed back to his apartment in the college campus. A plan was crystallizing in his mind.

CHAPTER 4

Ray tossed and turned in bed, not having slept a wink since he lay down, wondering whether to go ahead with what he was thinking. He switched on his bedside table lamp and looked at his watch. The time was two fifty five in the morning.

Digging out his cell phone from under his rather thin feather pillow, he dialed Ross's number, but pressed the red button before it rang; he did this again, but the third time he let it ring. Hearing a recorded voice at the other end, he threw the phone on the bedside table and jumped out of bed.

He was soon speeding on the M3; his destination was Amesbury. Sleeping villages flashed past. The lights of a police car did little to deter him from reducing his speed, and the siren faded away in the distance. In fifty-five minutes, he was screeching to a halt outside the Radio Telescope facility, where he had received the signal. The main gate was locked. The headlights reflected a fresh coat of silver paint off the round steel bars. Ray honked twice before the sliding glass window on the watchman's cabin adjacent to the gate, opened; a round cherubic face appeared, and his round eyes were heavy with sleep.

"What do you think you are doing here at this ungodly hour?" asked the watchman, and stifled a yawn.

Ray stuck his face out and felt the crisp morning air on his face. "I am looking for Ross."

"It's his night off," the guard said, and, then, slid the glass down and disappeared from view.

"Damn!" Ray swore under his breath, slapping his hands on the steering wheel. He reversed the car and drove straight to an inn just outside Amesbury. He thought it best not to wake Ross in the middle of the night, lest he had company. He remembered how he had caught Ross, literally, with his pants down, one night, when he had wound up very late and had decided to camp in Ross's room.

From his window, Ray watched dawn break; he heard the milkman's knock on the main door, downstairs; and then finally he managed to slip into meditation.

He awoke with a start, and checked the time on his mobile. It was just after twelve. He shot out of bed, and got ready in record time. He didn't wait to grab a bite, and ran out of the main door. His calf muscles stiffened as he stepped on the gas; he switched on the air-conditioning as his ears began to feel hot. He hoped Ross would go along with his plan.

It was a good fifteen minutes before Ray was knocking at the door. A blonde haired boy dressed in just a pair of boxers opened it; he rubbed his eyes, and, then stifled a yawn. Ray's childhood, friend, Ross, whom he had met on their holiday to Maldives, almost ten years ago, was standing in front of him. He was a few inches shorter than Ray but much stockier and muscular, and looked like a bouncer of a night club guarding the doorway.

"Hey man," said Ross, and wrapped his tanned muscular arms around Ray.

"The room is in big mess, man! You should have called!" He led Ray into the small drawing cum dining room, and reached out for a T shirt slung over one of the chairs. The room was small, but bright as sunlight poured into it through a window above the kitchen sink. More like a studio, he had done well to fit in all the amenities under the kitchen platform. The bed fit snugly in the corner to his left, and couldn't be seen because of a wooden partition.

"I desperately need your help," said Ray, wiping sweat off his forehead, and went on to tell his story. Ross listened as he made some breakfast and coffee.

Before Ray could finish, Ross butted in, "Where do I come in? Maybe those guys, up there," he said, pointing with his finger to the ceiling, "want to be left alone."

"Ross! I am in no mood for your wisecracks. I know there is someone wanting to get in touch with us."

"Yeah, man," said Ross. "These radio signals must be very boring. Rock, Reggae, or even the Stones may excite them."

As he served himself to an omelet sandwich, Ray said, "I need to use the facility."

Ross turned around and gave a half hearted laugh, as he gulped down some orange juice.

Ray nodded. "Seriously!"

Ross put the glass down with a jerk. "I'm out of it, man," he said, throwing up his hands.

"Just one night," said Ray, getting up from the chair. "Ouch!" he grimaced as his knee hit the bottom of the table, making the half filled glass of orange juice wobble. Ross was quick to hold it in place.

"It's simple," said Ray. "You lend me your spare uniform, and leave the rest to me."

Ross just grunted. "The facility runs on auxiliary power, which is just enough to provide for outdoor lighting; the head office would need to authorize the electricity department to reconnect the main power."

A knot welled Ray's stomach. "Fine, then." He shrugged his shoulders. "All those years of work down the drain." He let out a deep sigh, and headed towards the door.

"No. wait!" said Ross, following Ray.

Ray stopped in his tracks, turned around and hugged him tightly. "When can we start?"

The silhouettes of the large antenna's rose like phantoms in the fading light of this cool and breezy summer evening, as Ray saw the facility come into view. A barbed wire fence ran around the whole area; and a flying saucer shaped building on stilts jutted out of the flat and green landscape. A chill ran down Ray's spine as he opened the car door. Dressed in comfortable grey cargo pants and a collared light yellow T shirt, he stepped out of the car and felt the same nip in the air that he had savored over his tenure here. He looked up the rather long metal staircase going up to the landing. As he surveyed the structure, he felt a knot tighten in his stomach. The dome shaped structure, raised on stilts, flattened at the top, forming a very shallow dish; this made the whole building look like a parked flying saucer. Large windows were recessed into the curvature of the wall that ran around the building. It was all stone, with glass windows more like port holes.

Ross parked the car under the building, and joined him. They both climbed the metal staircase, the loosely placed checkered plates clanging against their footfalls.

Ray took a deep breath and closed his eyes for a moment as he entered the very space that had been almost his second home for over fifteen months.

Both of them stifled a sneeze almost at the same time as a strong musty smell pricked their nostrils.

"Ross, make sure all the curtains are drawn."

"Done. And lights?"

"Wow," said Ray, as he scanned the oval shaped room that was about the length of a basketball court. The white walls were still sparkling, remembering that they had painted it just before it was closed. The array of electronic control panels were pushed against the walls taking up one whole side; he passed them stroking the switches and displays as he made his way to his work station jutting out of the adjacent wall. A dark and lifeless screen, about six feet wide, installed on the wall above his seat, stared into his face. His eyes focused onto the computer; a yellow post-it clipped onto the side of the monitor caught his attention. He wiped his sweaty palms on the back of his cargo pants and unclipped the paper. His hand shook as he read the numbers scribbled on it.

"ROSS." His voice echoed through the room.

"Shh….," said Ross, with a finger on his lips.

Ray held the paper up. "These numbers; they are the space coordinates from where the signal was coming."

Ray switched on his computer, and waited for the system to boot. The large screens, which were also connected to his monitor, flickered on.

Ray punched in his password, accessing the folder in which he had entered all the data. He studied the calculations and his eyes widened as he reached the bottom of the sheet.

He stood staring at the screen, and, then covered his face with his palms and closed his eyes. He felt weak in the knees, and sat down heavily in his swivel chair.

"What's wrong, man?" He felt Ross's hand on his shoulder.

"I just opened a file in which I had done some calculations. The signal was coming to us from a distance of over thirty thousand light years," said Ray, gaping at the figures on the screen. "Its velocity is several orders of magnitude faster than light, and is moving towards us. Do you realize what I am saying?" Ray looked back at Ross who was standing with folded arms and looking at the screen. He gestured as if he was clueless.

"This will shake the very foundations of our understanding of the cosmos." Ray sighed. "I should have taken this data back with me to show Dr. Lowe."

"You should get the Bell prize," said Ross. "That big prize, you know."

"Cut it out!" By the way it is the Nobel prize." Ray went back to staring at the screen, chewing his fingernails furiously.

"The object is headed in our direction. But, it would be impossible for us to know its source, at least in our life time. If it's a physical entity like a space ship, we would not be around to herald its arrival."

"Take it easy, man. You haven't even started searching."

"Now wait. Hold tight. I am feeding the coordinates."

Ray typed in the coordinates. After a brief pause he glanced at his friend, and then pressed the 'Enter' key ever so gently.

The experiment was underway. The innocuous tap on the keyboard had started off a sequence of actions, leading to the vast array of antennas repositioning themselves.

A human being asks for absolution or alms from the almighty; here, the array of wires and masses of steel were trying to reach out into the depths of the cosmos to ask only one question: *Is anyone out there?*

"Loud and clear!" shouted Ray. "We are receiving the signal. The coordinates are the same."

Ray's frown grew deeper with each tap on the keyboard. Concentric circles flashed on the screen and then steadied. Ray broke into a cold sweat. This was what Dr. Masuda had recorded on his encephalogram. *Could it be...?* Ray did not even want to give this thought any importance. Suddenly the concentric circles vanished, and a series of iterations came up on the screen. The numbers scrolled down rapidly, and then stopped

"It cannot be! Oh my God!"

Ray rolled his chair back and stood up, staring at the large screen in front.

"It's only a few hundred light hours away. In a few months it has travelled just under thirty-thousand light years, Ross!"

Keep trying; there is someone out there, it was his inner voice again.

Ross looked at his friend blankly. "I think someone is playing a big joke on us."

"It's impossible for some prankster to generate these signals."

"What happened to the meditation Master? Weren't you supposed to get in touch with him?"

"You are a genius, Ross! I had forgotten about it. Everything's happening so quickly."

Ray looked at his watch with renewed optimism; it was 10.30 pm.

"I am going to first try on my own; I do not know where the Master would be tonight?"

"Didn't you say he was flying back the next day?"

"Yes, of course, but he probably would be en-route to India."

Ray went back to his desk and just stared into his computer screen; his knees shaking.

"Ross...." Ray paused, looking straight into his friend's eyes. "Is it all a wild dream?"

Ray pinched himself on his arm.

"If you ask me. Let's get out of here."

"Let me check if I really can connect up with him by going into meditation."

"Are you really going to try and make telepathic contact with this Master?"

Ray closed his eyes, and gave a thought to accept white light — a process to start meditation. He began to felt dizzy and light headed. His thoughts switched between the Master's revelations and the signal that he was receiving. Then, all of a sudden, a thought came to him. *I want to know if anyone can read my thoughts.* It was coming in repetitive bursts. After a brief pause as if waiting for an answer, it repeated itself again.

Ray sent a thought. *We are from Earth. Can you read me?*

The reply came back. *Will you guide me to your world?*

Do you recognize the coordinate system?

No, the answer came.

Being in meditation, Ray was unconscious of the surroundings, the conversation seeming perfectly natural to him. It did not unduly excite him.

Now, what should I do Master," he posed a question while deep in meditation.

I need a pyramid; it has four sides at the base and then goes up from each side tapering down to a single point, came a reply, but it was not from the Master!

Finally, Ray opened his eyes; he rubbed them and blinked a few times to readjust to the brightness.

He looked at his watch. "Gosh! It has been two hours, Ross!" and looked around the room. He found Ross fast asleep; a strange whistling sound was coming from him.

Is this all a dream, or am I hallucinating? Ray asked himself.

"Ross! Wake up." His repeated shouts were futile. Ray finally went up to him; he pushed Ross so hard that he toppled off the chair.

"You must listen to this."

"Leave me alone!" said Ross, picking himself up from the floor. "What on earth are you so excited about? The screen was talking to me, man. These round round lines kept coming and going. Ooohhh… Eerie, man!"

"I am in no mood for your wisecracks."

"Hey, wait a minute: You conveniently go off to sleep on the pretext of meditation and expect me to watch you smile into nothingness for two whole hours." Ross shook his head. "You have lost it."

"I think I have made contact with the entity," said Ray and looked at Ross, but his mind was now trying to connect the spurts of concentric circles with the conversation. And then it struck him, *whenever it tries to communicate with me, the concentric circles flash.*

"Oh Jesus, save my poor friend from going mad," said Ross with folded hands, looking up at the ceiling. "What fun! Laser guns being fired at us. Their eyes popping out from gooey masses that palpate like beating hearts…Yuck," squirmed Ross as he gestured with his hands. "I'm going, man."

"Have you finished, Ross? Now, may I say something?"

"By all means."

"If she is Cleopatra reborn, would you stay?"

"You must be out of your mind, Ray. Just because you cannot find a girl on Earth, you have high hopes of a blue eyed blonde landing on your lap from Heaven."

"Jokes apart, Ross, I need you with me. If this *someone* has to come, it will be in the next three days if it maintains its current speed. Gravitational slingshot effects of Jupiter and Saturn could delay the arrival by a day, not more."

"Are you sure it is not a prankster?"

Ray did not respond; he was chewing his nails again. He suddenly stopped and gave Ross a nasty glare.

"Hey! I was just joking; I am there for you until my last breath… on Earth."

"I am nervous, Ross. It defies all fundamentals." He got up and walked to Ross, sweat pouring down his face.

"Just go by what your heart says," said Ross. "That's what Mom always used to say."

"I still remember what Helen told us before we went out on that fateful catamaran ride," said Ray, recollecting his first holiday in the Maldives ten years ago, when he and Ross had got caught in a storm on their way back from deep sea on the catamaran. This had marked the beginning of a very special friendship. Since then, Paul had helped Ross migrate to England, two years after their second successive visit to the island.

"Do not battle with nature. Flow with the tide and she shall hold you in her arms like her very own child." Both of them repeated these lines in chorus.

Ray went over and embraced Ross, giving him a tight squeeze. "Thanks Rossy!"

"Not me, man. Thank the dolphins for saving us."

"I guess you are right. If not for the three dolphins, we would have been gobbled up by that shark."

"And, we wouldn't be here today, looking for aliens," said Ross.

Ray walked back to his desk and peered into the screen, as if there was something more than what met his eyes. Instead of the flashing concentric circles, the signal had steadied, reaching a state of constancy.

"The signal is getting stronger. It's moving really fast. I wish we could see this mysterious alien on our screen."

"We have come this far, Ray. Even if it is not an alien, you may be interested in knowing who this prankster is."

"I need to make a call to Master."

"It's two in the morning, Ray."

Ray dialed his home. The phone was answered on the second ring.

"Mom, are you awake?" he spoke softly into the phone.

"Darling, are you all right?"

"Fine; don't worry. I just want Master's telephone number in India."

"At this hour?"

"But, in India, it would be around eight in the morning,"

"Hold on a second. I will just look for it," said Revathi. "Why this urgency?"

"It's regarding my work. By the way, is Dad asleep?"

"Paul's out at the telescope, I believe it is the night of the Perseid meteor showers."

There was a momentary pause, and then Revathi came back online with the number.

Ray repeated the number while Ross jotted it down.

"Thanks, Mom," he said and disconnected the line.

Ray tried Master's mobile several times over; it was switched off.

"I can't get him. I'll try meditating."

"Not AGAIN!" said Ross. "You can wake me up when you drift out of your stupor."

Ray didn't bother to reply, and closed his eyes.

ℬ ℬ ℬ

Ray opened his eyes; he couldn't see a thing, but heard the steady breathing of someone.

It must be Ross, he thought, and looked at his watch; the fluorescent dials showed four fifteen.

"I must have gone off to sleep," Ray said to himself.

He quickly got up from his chair and went to find the light switches, when his foot kicked something soft. It was reciprocated with a swift tackle; he fell flat on his face; his nose was just about saved, as he broke his fall with his elbow.

"Are they here?" he heard Ross scream.

"Who?"

"Oh it's you!" a sleepy voice of Ross echoed.

"Were you dreaming of aliens, or what?"

"You bet. I had a nightmare, Ray. The aliens had overrun us and we were being transported aboard a spaceship. Phew! Am I glad to be back on Earth?"

The ring on his cell phone alerted him, but he couldn't find it. Suddenly the lights came on. The humming of the air-conditioning broke the eerie silence of the night.

Both of them gathered themselves; Ray massaged his elbow and winced in pain as he felt a big swelling.

His phone was on his desk, and he checked the missed calls list. It was Master who had called. He immediately called back, and felt a surge of excitement when he heard the voice of Master.

"I am still in London. I leave later this morning."

"Can you delay your departure by a day, Master, and come to the facility?"

"No, my son, I have other important assignments. But, as I said, we could communicate, irrespective of where I am, like we did last night."

Ray froze, his eyes almost popping out.

"Keep your mind open," continued the Master. "You are on the right track and soon a miracle will change the course of your life. Follow the instructions from the Heavens. The pyramid should be constructed as soon as possible. Make sure it is from natural material such as stone blocks or mud."

The clear-cut instructions from the Master were actually answers to the question he was yet to pose. Shocked and speechless, Ray continued to gape at Ross.

"What happened? Has the Master hung up on you?"

"Hello, Ray; are you still on the phone. Hello…!"

"Yes…Yes, Master. I will certainly take your advice. About the pyramids, how did…." Ray didn't finish the sentence.

"What about the pyramids. I can barely hear you, Ray."

"Master, when are you sitting for meditation again? I need to talk to this alien creature to ask for the dimensions of the pyramid."

"I was about to go and sit for my morning meditation. You can sit in exactly fifteen minutes."

"Wow, what luck, Ross. Master is about to sit in meditation," announced Ray triumphantly as he disconnected the call.

"You bet!" said Ross, as he poured some coffee from the thermos.

"I have spent over a year at this facility; all in vain. Finally, it is the power of thought that has enabled us to communicate."

Ray pinched himself to make sure it was no dream — these mesmerizing thoughts from nowhere! For him, techniques of meditation and other forms of prayer were for the weak hearted -- for those who needed a crutch to hang on to. He had always been a rationalist in his outlook as well as approach to life, but the meeting with Master seemed to have transformed him.

"What's all this about pyramids," said Ross.

"Oh, the Master informs me that the entity needs a pyramid to be able to land on Earth."

"Then it must be some Egyptian King rising from the dead."

Ray shook his head. "Today, pyramids are used in harmonizing techniques such as, Fengshui, Reiki etc. to create positive energies in a given physical space or surroundings. Therefore, it may not be so bizarre that an alien is familiar with the pyramid shape."

"You mean aliens could have landed in the massive pyramids, which were supposed to have been monuments for the dead?"

"Probably," said Ray, and looked at his watch. He was again lost in contemplation; he began to pace up and down the hall, and kept looking at his watch.

"Patience, Ray. Why don't you just close your eyes and go to sleep," said Ross.

"It is meditation, OKAY!" said Ray and sat down on the floor, crossed his legs, and closed his eyes.

Do you receive me? Ray transmitted a thought. He paused for an answer. But, when he received none, he repeated: *Please answer me.*

He was lucky the second time. He had his answer even before he could ask the question.

I receive you. The base of the pyramid should be diagonally as long as my shadow at noon. But, take care that the tip is like a point of a star. This should be enough for you to build one fast.

Are you from another planet? Ray asked.

There was silence. That ended the dialogue and Ray drifted into a deep trance even beyond the reaches of his thoughts. He opened his eyes exactly one hour later and looked at the screen.

"Good Heavens! This is impossible. My calculations show that if an object a few meters in diameter hits Earth at such speeds, we would be in for another ice age."

He punched in some more numbers.

"You are scaring me, Ray. I do not want to die so young."

Ray swiveled in his chair. "It's not the end of the world," he said, "We do not know what this object is. It has not appeared on our radars yet, nor is it bouncing off laser signals."

Ross's eyes widened. "Who is sending lasers?"

Ray managed to give a faint smile. "Optical lasers are being used in the SETI program for several years. Lasers generate a signal of such high energy that for fractions of a second it even outshines our sun. This light would appear like a beacon in space, emanating from the vicinity of the parent star, thus giving a clear definition of the existence of an intelligent being in that region."

"How many galaxies have these lasers reached out to?"

"Galaxies! These lasers fade away beyond a thousand light years, where not more than five million stars like our sun, reside. All this is still within our own galaxy. And a mere five percent of these stars have been covered so far."

"This entity has bypassed all our technological gizmos, and reached straight into your mind."

Ray nodded. "Someone out there has a very powerful mind." He looked at Ross. "Have we really progressed, or has it been at the cost of regression of our own mind?"

Ross shrugged his shoulders. "That's for you scientists to figure out, but at this moment, the most important thing for us is not to be caught inside."

"Okay, let's not push our luck too far," said Ray as he shut down the computer.

Ross was already at the door, when Ray joined him. He stared ahead into the graying dawn at the pastures of grasslands that stretched far across; a lone star shone in the eastern sky was fast being swallowed up in the brightening azure.

"One of the wonders of the world spread out in front of us, Ross. One time, probably, an observatory, or even a landing pad for aliens," said Ray, as he gazed far into the distance towards Stonehenge. "I really wonder how those stones were transported three thousand years ago."

"Behind those clump of trees," said Ross, pointing in the south easterly direction, "and beyond the mounds of the dead, river Avon flows. It is believed that the blue stones, each weighing five to six tones and six meters high, were transported from the Blue Mountains, on the river; they were, then, drawn by over a thousand men who rolled them over logs of wood to the site."

"Anything is possible, I suppose," said Ray.

"Look Ross, do you notice that the sun is rising just above the hele stone."

"It's a day before summer solstice."

Suddenly, there was a flash of light almost at the horizon, a few degrees north of the rising sun. The sky turned red at the point of the flash, and got brighter. Then it took the shape of a ball, almost like the sun itself.

"It's rising with the sun, and getting larger!" exclaimed Ray, as he stood rooted to the spot at the top of the steps, gaping at the strange phenomena.

As quickly as it had appeared, the red patch cleared up. The sky resumed its original color and the sun was back in the limelight.

"Could it be related to the events of last night; probably, it could be a missile test?"

Ray smiled to himself. "I don't think so."

Ross looked out searchingly, hoping that no one would see them. He escorted Ray to the main gate and saw him off; he had to stay back to hand over charge to the day watchman.

"I will be here at six in the evening," Ray told Ross, and drove off to his little room.

Before he realized, he had reached the inn. He went straight to his room. Extremely tired, sleep came almost instantly, overriding his hunger pangs, despite not having eaten a morsel through the night.

He awoke only to find sunlight streaming into the room; he squinted, still adjusting to the sudden brightness. The alarm clock next to him showed the time to be 3.15, which meant he had slept for more than seven hours. He went down and got himself some tea. Sipping his cup of tea he stood by the window and gazed out. The sun was beating down on the bald pastures, drying the bales of hay readied for the winter; the glint of steel flashed as sunlight reflected off the fast moving cars on the motorway. All this appeared so trivial, as he looked searchingly into the clear blue skies; he wondered where this signal could be coming from, and what form would it have. The click of the lock disturbed him, pulling him out of his thoughts. Ross closed the door behind him, and went and stood next to Ray, by the window. "I am sure, before they can even enter our atmosphere they would be shot down by the stealth bombers. And that would be the end of our journey, gathering dust in a TOP SECRET and CONFIDENTIAL folder of the US military."

"I must tell you of my dream this morning," said Ray. "A beautiful girl comes out of a pyramid. Just walks out of a solid wall! And wow, was she beautiful! That was it."

"That's what I told you. It is Cleopatra!"

"Wait and watch. I have an inkling that we are in for a bigger surprise; I should say, shock," said Ray.

"Wow, this is becoming exciting. Not just a scientific experiment. But admit it, Ray! You, too, wish it to be a beautiful girl. Maybe you will find your match and get married to her. What fun; my sister-in-law will be from outer space!"

CHAPTER 5

Ray stood on the steps of the facility, and looked into the firmament. "So silent are the skies. One can only assume, *We are Alone*."

"All that might change, tonight," said Ross, leading the way in.

Ray looked at his watch as soon as he reached his seat. "It's almost eleven-thirty. Here goes, Rossy. Wish me luck."

Drifting into a meditative stupor, he immediately connected up with the Master; he sensed the presence of one more vibration in his thoughts.

I am coming to your planet in a form that needs transformation. The pyramid that I have described is in which I will transform. If you have made one already, guide me to the nearest star that shines directly above it. This will be enough to lead me to the centre of the pyramid, from which I shall emerge as my real self. I imagine that you have advanced sufficiently to be able to connect with me. Therefore I see no difficulty in transformation.

The thought signals were now coming as complete sentences.

Ray tried his hand at sending a thought. *I am Ray, from planet Earth. Please reveal your coordinates. I am tracking you down to declination 23 deg and RA 00 57'. Please confirm.*

He received a strange thought back, *Are they superior beings? Will they allow me to visit their planet? Or, will they annihilate me?*

Ray sent his reply: *we are peace-loving and want to welcome you on Earth.*

Ray received a strange thought, *suppose they do not have anything to cover my body? How will I get out of the pyramid? Would there be Masters to walk me through the walls?*

These are questions, which we will come to when we have to and if we have to. Ray presumed it was the Master who had responded.

I will make contact once I find a pyramid, Ray replied, and opened his eyes.

"Hey man: that look on your face. Did you connect up with someone?"

"I was actually conversing with the entity... I hope so."

"You mean you could hear voices? I didn't even see your lips move."

"They were telepathic transmissions."

"It's almost like one of those 'call the spirit' games. Suppose you end up calling one your ancestors."

"I just hope someone is really out there."

"When do you expect this thing to fall from the sky?"

"As a matter of fact, the ball is in our court."

"What about calling Paul?"

"It's between the heavens and us," said Ray, gesturing skywards. "No one else should know."

"Yes Sir! Whatever you say."

"Talking about security, I just have one fear. Suppose this alien is hostile? The irony of it all will be: when we are put away in a mental home for disturbing the peace of the universe, leave alone, *Earth!*"

"Make up your mind. One thing is for sure, if it is a girl, she is mine!"

"At least, I am relieved that Master is aware of all this. This voice has requested his presence, anyway."

"Got to obey orders from Heaven!" said Ross. "What if it's a gargoyle, a slimy monster, or an invisible creature, which spreads some deadly incurable disease?"

Ray ran his fingers through his hair and began to stroke his chin. "Search me."

"Is it really worth the risk?"

"No turning back," said Ray. "The pyramid is what we need to build. The alien said it should be as long as its shadow at noon. Considering the height of an average human to be around five feet five inches, the shadow at noon would be no more than three feet."

"You think this alien is a dwarf?"

"Well, it certainly has some idea of shape and size, from what I could gather."

"Why build one at all? Let us use one of the existing ones in the world. After all, we are not doing this for ourselves. It is the next most important issue in the world, after the water crisis."

"We don't have the money to fly down to Egypt or South America and use those pyramids," said Ray.

"Even when the president of Bogotá, or some such nondescript country, arrives here, he gets a royal welcome," argued Ross. "And for this poor alien, only three people in the world know about it."

"That's exactly what we need: Secrecy," said Ray.

"Suppose the experiment fails, or we run into trouble. There would be no one to come to our rescue."

"I don't think we have an option, nor are we sure whether we are really in touch with any extraterrestrial entity."

"What is in your mind chief? You are talking in riddles now."

Ray continued to stare at the blank screen; the signal came and then vanished. He was beginning to understand the nature of the signal. Whenever the entity spoke to them, it generated this wave form and since it was 'thought', it was only recorded by the encephalogram. His ears were burning, and he closed his eyes tightly. Everything was blank – no whirring thoughts whizzing through his mind. Then it dawned on him, *they have been in touch with me for at least ten years.*

"Are you meditating, again?" he heard Ross's voice in the background.

"Huh--- No. But I need to call Master now." He got up from his chair, clenched his fists and took a deep breath before he turned to face Ross. "If we do not execute and complete our pyramid in the next twenty-four hours, I have a strong feeling that the signal will fade away."

"Has it told you so?"

"I don't know why I have this nagging feeling of urgency. We do not know on what time scale these beings may be operating, if they have a time scale at all. The mind operates on its own scale, building up references and conditions, against which it operates. These may be completely different from our understanding."

"All this is okay, but what are we to do next?" said Ross. "Better think of something fast."

"Comprehending an alien civilization and assuming it to be similar to ours is a very utopian way of looking at the cosmos," Ray continued, paying no heed to what Ross had said. "It would defeat the purpose of the material progress that mankind has made today. But, of course, whether it has been good for us or not, is a matter of debate."

Ross sat down heavily on the nearest chair.

Ray leaned forward and put his hands on Ross's firm shoulders. "I have decided that we will make the pyramid ourselves." He paused to see how his friend would react, but Ross's face was blank, his eyes were red and laden with sleep. "It will be in and around the facility."

"You must be crazy. Go and get some sleep," said Ross, getting up from the chair. "Even in the Maldives, building a sand pyramid was next to impossible. It is not as easy as you think."

"I know who can help us. Dr. Menon, the curator of the museum at Salisbury, is an expert on ancient architecture." Ray had his network well in place, having learnt the art from Dr. Lowe.

A few quick phone calls, the next day, were enough to fix an appointment with Dr. Menon. Fortunately, Ray got the first appointment for the following day.

🦋 🦋 🦋

Precisely at ten, Ray knocked on the frosted glass door that displayed the sign, 'Museum Curator'.

It was answered by a sharp featured man in his late fifties of about Ray's height. Clean shaven, he had thick lips and small brown eyes, and had much darker skin color than even Ross. He had carefully plastered down his more red than auburn strands of hair to hide the baldness on his oval head. Dressed in a plain light blue half-sleeve linen shirt with beige trousers, he removed his thick plastic framed spectacles. "Come on in?" He ushered them in, still holding the door with one hand and his spectacles in the other.

"You must be Ray Robinson, and you are...?" he said looking at Ross.

"This is Ross, my colleague."

Dr. Menon shook hands with each of them. Ray was impressed by the firmness of his handshake — one of his key benchmarks to judge a person's character.

Dr. Menon gestured them to take the only two seats in front of his cluttered table. It had all kinds of artifacts, fossil like bones, and objects; and of course, a pile of files that looked as if they had not been moved for years. The legs of the table were intricately carved and the dark brown polish had dulled.

"This is the first time someone really wants to build a pyramid from stone," said the curator, with a gleam in his eye. "Dr. Robinson, are you by any chance a student of Dr. Lowe at Imperial College?"

"Yes Sir; I am doing my doctorate under him. But this is not an official visit."

He did not have any intention of pursuing the topic any further, lest Dr. Menon got the wind of their real motive.

Dr. Menon got up and turned around and appeared to be searching for a book on the rack. Almost the entire wall behind the curator's desk was covered with books neatly arranged on a dark brown polished rack of five shelves that ran across the cream wallpapered wall. He took out a rather thin booklet which had been just kept on top of some of the books. Ray watched the curator and found him so much like the Egyptian who ran the college bookshop.

"Building a pyramid from stone is not easy," continued Dr. Menon, putting the booklet on the table. "It needs stones cut to their exact dimensions, down to the millimeter. The accuracy of the right angles and the surface flatness will decide the quality of the pyramid, especially, if you have the limitation of building one with natural materials. Today, we have gone beyond using anything natural. Everything we use is synthetic, right up to the milk we drink."

Ray leaned back and put his hands on the back of his head. "How did the ancient civilizations manage to build such structures?"

"Look at Stonehenge, the Sphinx, or even the city of Persepolis," said Dr. Menon, leafing through the booklet. "They have been built out of stone pillars and blocks. Have you seen the stone pillars at Persepolis?" Dr. Menon's furious gestures almost cost him his antique lamp, but he continued without even blinking an eyelid while Ross lunged forward and managed to save the lamp from falling off the table. "They are a work of precise engineering and architecture; a real miraculous achievement even in the present context. Two hundred tones of stone were moved to heights of over thousand feet, way back in about 4000 BC. I have my doubts about it being made only by hand. Possibly, a more advanced civilization did exist at that time, which we see no trace of today."

"Sir, the Pyramids...." Ray was about to get on with his agenda when Dr. Menon tried to interrupt him again.

Ross was the one who completed Ray's sentence, before their host could interrupt. "Can we make the pyramid out of mud or clay?"

"Of course," replied the curator, looking at Ross. "Some of the smaller structures in the Mesopotamia and Egyptian civilizations were made from clay; they were fired and hardened, too."

Ray could see the earnestness in the curator's eyes, and was impressed by his knowledge of ancient architecture. It was apparent that Dr. Menon was indeed a prominent figure in his field.

"I am just curious, and hope you do not mind me prying into your affairs. Why do you want to build this pyramid?" said Dr. Menon.

"Sir, I am originally from the Maldivian islands," Ross began, "which are situated, further down south, off the Sri Lankan coast. I wanted to make a pyramid on the island we lived on. It was to be a gravestone for one of my relatives," continued Ross, as Dr. Menon listened patiently with his arms resting on the table. "He had worked most of his life in Egypt, and was fascinated by the pharaohs. We just want to fulfill his last wish, of being buried in a pyramid. Since we could not build it there, we want to build it in my back yard, in his memory. He was a very kind soul and brought a lot of luck to our family. It is said that the pyramid is a resting place for souls, and wherever they find one, they rest there and spread good luck."

Ray continued to look at Ross, rather perplexed at the sudden intervention. But what surprised him most was the reason he had cooked up, and was afraid that it would not hold water with the curator.

"That's interesting, and very thoughtful," said the curator. "I would be most pleased to help you. You seem to have a love for old architecture, which very few people appreciate nowadays. Why don't you both go to the library and see what you can find in our archives."

Dr. Menon got up from his chair and led them out of the room. "Go straight down the corridor, and when you enter the hallway, go across to the other wing. The second door to the left is the library entrance. Meet me back here after you finish."

The walk to the library was a long one, as it was located in the opposite wing. And when they entered, they were surprised how small the room was. It was cramped with around ten steel racks almost ten feet high, and every shelf was filled to the very last space. Two long tables with plastic bucket chairs placed along the tables was the only other piece of furniture. There were two computers set against the wall adjacent to the door. A sign said: *Digitized files of the contents of each book in the computer.* This made their search much simpler. There was no librarian or even an assistant to guide them, so they went in and began browsing through the contents. He found seven relevant books that mentioned pyramids. While Ray was browsing through the selected books and chapters on pyramids and ancient architecture, one particular piece of information caught his eye. It was related to the various combinations of materials used by the Egyptians to build their pyramids. He took Xerox copies of almost twenty pages of data and figures, for which he had to go down to the hallway where he had seen a sign: Communications.

By the time they were on their way back, it was the lunch break for the museum staff; they were relieved to find Dr. Menon still in his office. When they entered, an elaborate spread of sandwiches and fresh fruit greeted their eyes. The three of them ate heartily, finishing every morsel on the plate, leaving behind only the apple cores.

Dr. Menon went through the papers they had collected. He small eyes peered through his spectacles, as he turned the pages with his thumb and middle finger as his index finger was missing.

After a brief debate, they arrived at a consensus about the size of the pyramid, the recipe for the clay, and the rest of the finer details.

"I think this should be enough for you to execute the plan," said Dr. Menon.

Ray sensed a twinge of disappointment in Dr. Menon's tone. "Can we make a request, Sir?" Dr. Menon shifted in his seat and sat upright. "We need you to supervise the construction; and the work has to be completed tonight. I hope you do not mind."

"Why—Err – tonight?"

Then he looked at them thoughtfully. "Okay. Let's give it our best and see where we reach."

The boys exchanged smiles, and Ross gave the thumbs up signal.

Selecting the site was critical. It would have to be in an open ground with an expanse of barren space of at least five hundred meters on all sides. This was the first hurdle to cross, as they would be using public land. More so, it would definitely not be a backyard gravestone. They had no clue as to what to expect, a huge space ship, a blazing fireball, or a ghostly apparition that would float into the pyramid. Weird thoughts crossed Ray's mind while Dr. Menon was busy calculating the material quantities required for the construction. The site they selected was at the base of the hill on which Stonehenge was located.

They had chosen a spot out of the way of the tourist traffic, on the opposite side of the main entrance.

Armed with the list of materials to be gathered, Ross set off into town. By the time the material had been stacked up, it was evening. They had bought clay soil from a nearby kiln; it was filled in big jute bags and stuffed in the boot of Ross's car. Almost seventy-five such bags had been transported in twelve trips.

Both of them were in a mess with wet clay on their hands and feet, kneading furiously, like a baker would knead his dough. They kneaded until the consistency met the approval of Dr. Menon, who sat by the side watching them intently. A wooden mould of the size of the pyramid stood ready to receive the clay. It looked rather small with a base of five feet, even though Ray had decided to make the pyramid a little larger than instructed. He felt that if the alien did not fit, God knows what would happen. It might get angry and create havoc. Or disappear, assuming it was a trap.

They decided to take a break. Ray went over to where Dr. Menon was standing while Ross drove into Amesbury to fetch some food and drink.

"We will have to keep one side open to fill in the firewood and burn it from inside," advised Dr. Menon, as they both sat back and admired their architectural feat. "The heat of the fire will harden the clay automatically. Then, we can close the open end with a plank of wood, rather than clay, again. We will then finish the outside with a mixture of clay, lime, and mortar; this will give luster to the whole structure."

"Thank God for small mercies," said Ray, as he saw Ross approach them loaded with what appeared to be something to eat.

The three of them gobbled up the food in no time. Chilled beer added to the quality of the experience and they continued through the night, completing the structure by morning. A pyramid, that they could be proud of, stood as an edifice of perseverance; the real reason was unknown to the architect; for him the excitement was in creating a work of ancient architecture in modern times.

"I think it is best that we fire it in the day," said Ray. "The glow would be seen far away at night, alerting the townspeople; the last thing we want is to have a screaming fire engine come and pour 'cold water' onto our whole exercise."

Dr. Menon had camped out with the two boys. Being a bachelor, he seemed to enjoy the little adventure. Just before sunrise, the three of them trooped into Ross's apartment looking like mud wrestlers straight from a fight. They had dried clay stuck in their hair and almost all over their exposed bodies.

One by one they had a good scrub, thanks to Ross's arrangements of spare towels. Except for Dr. Menon, whose clothes were relatively unsoiled, the two changed into fresh clothes.

After breakfast, they went back to the site. Their next job was to fire the pyramid.

Ray and Dr. Menon succeeded in starting it off.

"OH NO!" both, Ray and Ross, shouted in chorus.

"The pyramid is crumbling from the top. It is giving way!" cried out Ross.

"Don't panic, it is just the beginning. We need to fill it in with much finer clay soil after it cools," said Dr. Menon.

In an hour, the fires had ebbed. All that remained was a black sooty structure -- a perfect pyramid with an opening of around six inches at the apex.

Ross had already carved out a miniature pyramid from wood at the behest of Dr. Menon. It was placed on the open end at the top; Dr. Menon insisted on giving the final touches.

"I forgot one instruction!" said Ray, suddenly remembering the mention of a pointed tip, like that of a star. "Is there a relationship between Pyramids and Stars?"

"I feel you are holding back something from me," said the curator.

Ray felt a pang of guilt, but quickly regained his composure. "I am fascinated with the leanings of ancient architecture towards astronomical events. Since we are talking of pyramids, I thought you might be able to shed some light on this subject."

"For the Egyptian civilization, a star symbolized the coming of floods," began Dr. Menon, "who looked upon Sirius as their time marker. The rising of Sirius — the Dog Star — heralded the Egyptian New Year, also their harvest season, and signaled the onset of the flooding of the Nile. Another star — Spica — in the constellation Virgo, represented Virgin Mary for the medieval Christians. She is Kanya, the mother of Lord Krishna, for the Hindus."

Dr. Menon's profound knowledge of the stars amazed Ray, but it did not solve his conundrum, and he chose not to probe the curator any further.

Finally, the pyramid tip was inserted, covered by clay and fired once again. The open side of the pyramid was sealed off with a wooden plank. The finishing touches of the lime and mortar plaster ended their crusade.

"I think our ancestors did a much better job, and definitely were less messy. It really does look like a mud hut rather than a pyramid," said Dr. Menon. "I hope it's not an insult to your relative."

"Will she like it? Hope she does not run away?" blurted out Ross; he got a sharp pinch from Ray, who was standing beside him.

Dr. Menon looked at them with suspicion, but didn't react, much to Ray's relief.

Well boys, I suppose you don't need my services anymore," said Dr. Menon.

Yes… err… We don't know how to thank you for your help," said Ray.

"It's me who should be thanking you for letting me into your plan and involving me in this very noble gesture. I just hope it doesn't get us into any trouble."

"Don't worry about that at all, Sir," said Ross. "It's only a memorial for my uncle. No one should mind."

"Anyway, I better get going. But, I am not sure that you guys have come clean with me."

That left both the boys rather stunned.

Ray was beginning to feel queasy, when Ross broke the silence. "Hey, Ray, just relax. You need to get some rest."

"I'll pick you up at ten tonight. I still hope Dr. Menon doesn't decide to snoop around."

CHAPTER 6

Hey man, I thought you wouldn't come," said Ross, opening the door for Ray.

"I almost didn't. Dr. Menon called me over, earlier in the evening," said Ray, and continued in the same breath. "The cops; they were nosing around and found Dr. Menon's visiting card near the pyramid. When they questioned him, he managed to convince them that it was an experiment; they, however, ordered him to destroy it by morning."

"Hope the cops leave him alone," said Ross, while on their way to the rendezvous point. The only thought on Ray's mind was the appointed time for the séance at twenty three minutes past midnight; he kept looking at his watch through the journey. By the time they reached, it was already midnight. Precisely, twenty-three minutes later, Spica would reach the zenith, right above the tip of the pyramid.

Sitting on the grass, beside the pyramid, Ross and Ray waited in baited breath. The full Moon rose steadily, casting an ethereal glow over the expanse. Every second seemed like eternity. The mounds of the dead in the eerie silence of the night gradually emerged from the darkness. Beyond them, the burly blocks of stone protruded out of the landscape, shimmering like ghostly apparitions.

Ray began to whisper: many a nights when the wind was in the trees, and the Moon was playing hide n seek with the clouds, a lonely intruder streaked across the sky, revealing a blazing fireball that hit the Earth with a thunderous roar.

"This couldn't have been only folklore; maybe, an alien landing," said Ray.

"Where will we hide this alien?"

"Let it come."

"I hope the police are not on the lookout, Ray? If it lands straight under their noses, it will either scare the hell out of them, or they will call in more forces and capture it."

Ray nodded and let out a deep sigh. He looked up into the sky. "Nothing else matters, Ross. It's a risk I... and, now, we have decided to take it."

"Just cover both your ears with your hands and listen," he said, and looked at Ross. "Do you hear anything?"

"Nothing at all, man. I think you need some rest. Let's just pack up and go home."

Ray had his ears still covered. "It is the silence that you can hear. It's deafening."

He looked up again into the moonlit sky. "Countless stars, some dying, some in mid life, and some just born; it is a new experience each time I look into the firmament. A vastness that our senses cannot comprehend, but a computer, that our own mind had created, could visualize. Lost is the glory of visual scientific exploration. Today we can see the entire universe as a grid of complex mathematical calculations."

Ray felt his hands been drawn away from his ears. "Hey, can you look at me, instead of getting all poetic and romantic."

"You won't understand the feeling, Ross," said Ray, and went back into his contemplative state.

"And tonight, the wheel is once again being turned back in time, to feel, to sense, and to see and experience something far beyond our comprehension; probably, what our science would call primitive — an alien landing without the excitement at Mission Control, without blinking lights and fiery winds."

"Okay, okay, but I think what I have to inform you now, is more important."

Ray looked at Ross, and then at his watch. "Why didn't you remind me earlier?"

He quickly got out his cell-phone and dialed the Master; before it could ring, he disconnected the call.

He began his séance and connected up immediately.

The pyramid is ready to receive you into our world, Master's thoughts radiated through space, which Ray received.

Ray also began his communication, *when Spica, the shining star of Virgo, shines above the tip of the pyramid, you must descend. The pyramid will be right below the star.*

Ray opened his eyes after a few minutes. "There is no reply."

"Maybe, it has switched off its radio, like we do during take-off and landing."

"Let's wait; it's countdown in the next thirty seconds," said Ray.

"After which, God only knows what will happen to our lives?" whispered Ross.

Ray was already counting, "Ten, nine, eight, seven, six...three, two, one ..." Nothing happened even after one whole minute.

Ray looked at Ross. Suddenly, a thought crossed Ray's mind, maybe it needs my thought signal as its guide. Spica may shine across many regions of the Earth; this could confuse this entity.

"What did I tell you? It must be a hoax," said Ross.

Ray did not reply. He had drifted back in meditation, and sensed that he had just connected with the entity, though no conversation ensued. Probably, it was using him as a beacon to guide it to the new world, he thought.

"It has come!" Ross exclaimed. Ray opened his eyes and looked up in the direction Ross was looking. Spica was still overhead, surrounded in a red halo. The halo became brighter and was approaching them at a tremendous speed. A reddish hue filled the sky; it enveloped the pyramid in its glow. A strange feeling swept through Ray's body. He felt cold, then hot, and then, a feeling of complete bliss pervaded him.

They gaped at the pyramid with their hands cupped to their ears, as if expecting a cataclysmic explosion. Ray was unable to grasp the implication of the moments of dancing colors in the sky. All of a sudden, the reddish hue disappeared. Spica had returned to its original state.

The two boys looked at each other questioningly. Ray got up and slowly made his way to the pyramid, almost crawling on all fours. He saw nothing, not even a trace of anyone having entered it.

"The alien is playing music. It sounds like one of the oldies," whispered Ross.

Ray answered his phone while continuing to stare at the pyramid. "Our visitor has landed," the Master's crisp and soothing voice came through. "Now, it is the ultimate test of your practice under my guidance. Access the pyramid and take in your charge, the visitor. Treat it like an important guest who brings good luck and harmony to the world and to your life."

The cell phone went dead. Ray was stunned, trying to come to terms with what the Master had just said.

"I think we should wait till morning, and then break open the wooden portion, said Ross, breaking the eerie silence. "We have to be careful not to scare this being away."

"It could be invisible and standing right next to us at this very moment," said Ray.

Ross turned to survey the surroundings. "Look! I saw something fly by in the sky. He pointed into the distance. "Over Stonehenge!"

Ray looked towards the array of stones that stood as ghostly apparitions over the mounds. His eyes fell on the full Moon, which had now reached the zenith. He looked harder, only to reaffirm what he had just seen. The Moon had turned bright red, surrounded by a halo, and before he could blink an eyelid, the halo elongated, turning into an inverted cone. As if a bolt of lightning had struck the centre of the monument, the distended halo extended right down from the Moon to the ground and disappeared. He was stupefied, unable to make head or tale of what he had just observed.

By then, Ross had also inched his way to the pyramid, attempting to take charge of the situation. "If no one's there, it is all over and out. We will go back to the inn and catch up on some much-needed sleep."

"If it's there?" said Ray in a low voice, still transfixed.

"Let's find out," said Ross, and took a shovel in one hand, while handing Ray the other.

"You don't need that contraption," said Ray, as he threw aside his shovel. "The mud will give way. Remember, it is not baked, so the door should come away."

Clawing at the mud with their hands, the door came away easily. It took a couple of minutes before they could adapt to the darkness inside. The pyramid was empty!

"Master couldn't be wrong, Ross! Didn't we see a halo travel down from the star?"

"Search me. You were the one in contact." Ross shrugged his shoulders.

Ray's thoughts switched back and forth, from the Master's phone call to the flash of light over the stones. He strongly felt there was some significance of the halo around the Moon.

Maybe she did not understand what Spica meant, and was more familiar with the Moon, he thought.

"Why don't you call your Master?"

Ray had already placed the phone to his ear. "There is no reply," he grumbled and gave up after the third try.

"Give up, Ray!" snapped Ross. "We are just scapegoats of a big hoax."

"It definitely is not a hoax. No one, even with the current advancement of science, can simulate such phenomena in the sky," said Ray. "Let me try sitting in meditation and see if I can connect up."

Ray tried to reach out through his thoughts, but there was just vacuity. He got up, shaking his head with defeat, but his brain continued to tick.

"Let's check out the area around Stonehenge. This is the best time, before morning light. The guards would not have started checking the perimeters."

"Yes Sir."

"Just a second, I'll just try the Master again."

His attempts were in vain, and sat down on the ground and dug his head into his knees. Feeling tiredness sweep over him, he shut his eyes. In the background of his stupor, he suddenly felt as if someone were calling out to him.

I have arrived. You must think differently from us, if this is what you call a pyramid, the voice echoed within his consciousness.

An anguished cry in the distance shook him out of his reverie. Startled, he lifted his head; he scanned the moonlit countryside, in the direction of Stonehenge, but saw nothing unusual.

He was beginning to doubt his own sanity; he felt that even the voice he had heard was a hallucination, knowing that a silent and eerie night could play havoc in one's mind.

He looked around for Ross. There was no trace of his friend; he inched his way, dragging his feet, across the undulating landscape, until he reached the outer perimeter of the demarcated land around Stonehenge. He hopped over the low stonewall, careful not to tread on a makeshift electric fence that had been put up around the wall, and crossed over a narrow channel dug into the ground that ran around the monument. Just when he was about to enter the inner circle, he felt a sudden jolt of current and was thrown back. He landed on hard ground, and yelled out in pain. Stunned by the fall, he lay on the ground for a moment, and, then, slowly picked himself up.

He heard the sound of labored breathing. His eyes fell on an object on the graveled pathway, and walked towards it, stopping every few steps to see whether it moved. His heart skipped a beat, when he recognized the still figure of Ross.

"Ross, Ross, get up!" He shook his friend vigorously.

"Huh... what hit me?" said Ross in a barely audible voice, rubbing the back of his head with his hand.

"Were you struck by a bolt of electricity?"

"Yeah, I think it was. I told you, this place is spooked."

"You stay here. I am going to enter the inner circle from the far side."

Ray broke into a run, but kept off the pebbled pathway. He experienced the same force field and was thrown back, but not as forcefully as before. Disappointed, he made his way back to where Ross was waiting. To his annoyance, Ross was nowhere in sight. He could not call out, lest the guards were alerted; he just hung around the area. He felt every muscle in his body protesting in pain, having reached their threshold. Fatigue was fast overcoming him. He started to feel listless and light-headed.

"Ray! Are you there?" he suddenly heard Ross shout. He forgot his aches and pains and scrambled up the slope; it got him closer to the periphery of the inner circle. He found Ross trying to peer through the breaking light of dawn, towards a gap between two large slabs of stone.

"I thought I saw a pair of eyes staring at me through that crack," pointed Ross.

"But that is within the circle. Nothing could have gotten there unless it has been resting through the night. Perhaps, it must be an owl or a bat," said Ray.

"It could it Cleopatra."

Ray burst out laughing. Suddenly, they heard a cough in the distance, and then the sound of lighting of a match.

"It's the guards," said Ray in a whisper. We better get out of this place."

"What about the alien?"

"It will have to wait." Ray shook his head. "What an utter waste of time and energy. I should have known listened to you."

"Don't give up so easily, Ray. Maybe the alien will make another attempt."

"I am dog tired, and desperately need some sleep. Please drop me off at the inn. I guess I have to get back into the real world."

Ross put his arm around Ray. "Call the Master once we get back to the inn; give it another shot."

🎜　🎜　🎜

Before going to sleep, Ray needed to communicate with the Master; he tried his cell phone; it was switched off. He decided to try and sit in meditation as he knew the moment he closed his eyes he would fall asleep. He sat upright in bed with his back resting against the wall, and closed his eyes.

Master, is the entity still there? Ray sent out a thought

You have not kept your appointment.

The reply didn't seem to come from the Master.

You mean you really came?

Yes. I will now transform on my own.

Where?

On top of a hill, inside a cave.

The whole conversation seemed to be so very natural and he didn't feel any excitement.

A cave? How will I find you?

I will

But…

He tried to communicate, but there was just complete silence in his mind. Then he tried to recollect the conversation. He thought hard wondering what it meant by 'you are familiar with it'. Did it mean it had come to Earth before? No wonder the doctor had recorded concentric wave patterns as long as ten years ago. He was now sure that the concentric circles were something to do with the entity. These were thoughts that came and went, giving him no chance to dwell on them.

The very next moment, as if he had tuned into another channel, he was seeing Paul in hospital; his body connected with all kinds of instruments and tubes. The doctors seemed to have given up, when suddenly the instruments began to malfunction. This went on for quite some time. The most bizarre thing was he heard his name being called out. "Ray," the voice was husky, but more feminine, "your father will live to see the dawn of another day."

Ray's eyes flickered open.

Thank God, it was a dream; he heaved a sigh of relief, as he got out of bed. His T-shirt was soaked in sweat. He looked at his watch, and found that only two hours had gone by.

He didn't wait to freshen up, and called home.

"Is Dad with you?" he asked his mother.

"Of course, Ray. Why?"

"Err... Nothing."

"Is something the matter? Just come back home."

"MOM, relax. I have not lost it yet."

"Do you need to speak to Paul?"

"No. it's OK."

He held the phone to his ear for a moment, and disconnected the call; then he jumped up on his feet. The dream or rather the nightmare was uppermost in his mind. Even after talking to his mother he had a nagging doubt about his father's well being. He suddenly made up his mind to go back home.

ॐ ॐ ॐ

Ray turned into the lane that led to his home. He was just in time to see an ambulance pull out of his driveway.

There were a few cars parked in the driveway. He checked his cell for any missed calls; he cursed his luck, as his mobile was switched off.

Darting in through the open front door, he found quite a few people in the drawing room; he looked searchingly into the crowd. His heart sank. He felt a knot tighten in his stomach, but before he could react to the situation, a soft but firm hand took him by the arm and made him sit down. It was their red head neighbor, Mrs. Arthunbott. Ever since she had lost her husband, last year, she depended a lot on his parents for emotional support. She was solidly built and just a few inches shorter than Ray. Dressed in a cream shirt with light blue flowers scattered, and a pair of black loose fitting pants, she seemed to have taken charge of the situation. The light make up and pale green eye shadow, and neatly combed auburn hair that was cut short, made her look much younger than her age.

"Son, it is the will of God to bring us to this blessed land and ONLY HIS WILL, to take us to Heaven," she said a shrill voice.

"Can someone tell me what has happened?" said Ray, as if appealing to the others seated in the room.

"It is your father," he heard a girlish voice from the back. "He has been taken ill and was rushed to hospital. Your mother has gone with him and I suggest you go, too."

"Julie, thank God you are here."

Her soft green eyes met his gaze. "I will drive you to the hospital," she said, while the rest looked on as she got up, straightening her short sleeved yellow top, under which she wore white jeans. Ray backed out of the room and rushed out of the front door, but couldn't help noticing her slender arms as she opened the car door. They had practically grown up together, went to the same school, and even lived in the same neighborhood for a few years. She was no more that chubby tom boyish girl who would be the first one to climb the wall and steal the apples from Mrs. Fenton's garden; she now had slim long legs, which seemed to be comfortable with her stilettos.

In less than two minutes they reached the hospital.

"I'll wait for you in the reception," shouted Julie, after Ray, as he slammed the car door shut and rushed in.

Ray didn't wait to answer, and went straight to the reception area, where he found his mother; he ran and put his arms around her. She looked at him blankly. Suddenly, she held her son's hand, and burst into heavy and uncontrollable sobs.

"Ray, it was my fault. I made him climb the roof to clean the windows. He fell off the ladder and has not moved since."

"Calm down, Mom. Let the doctors examine him and they will...." his voice was lost in the announcements over the Public Address system. He heard the name 'Robinson'.

When the announcement was repeated, he listened carefully. They were being summoned to the third floor to consult the doctor.

As they stepped out of the lift, a middle-aged man of medium height straightening his wavy grey hair with tinges of black was just coming down the corridor. His white coat was unbuttoned, flapping all around him.

Ray waited till he got closer. "Dr. Martin...?" he called out, and paused for an acknowledgement.

The doctor smiled, his green eyes opening wide. "Ah, so you must be the relatives of Mr. Robinson?" His accent was flat like that of a BBC news presenter, but heavy as if he had a cold.

Ray nodded.

"Let's talk in my office," he said, and led them all the way to the end of the corridor, his soft rubber shoes gliding noiselessly over the white tiled floor. He was broad shouldered and walked with an erect posture, his stethoscope carelessly slung over his shoulder. He ushered them into his small but neat, brightly lit office. Settling down, the three of them had cups of steaming hot coffee served to them by an attractive nurse.

He looked at them, and suddenly his square face darkened as he rubbed both his hands together, resting his elbows on the rectangular steel table. "He's had a stroke, and the fall has led to a clot in the left side of the brain," said Dr. Martin, his eyes fixed on Ray.

Tears welled in Ray's eyes. "Will my father live?"

"We will be keeping him under observation for forty-eight hours. Until then, I would like one of you to stay in the hospital." He looked at his watch, and gestured to get up. "I will see you on my rounds."

Revathi and Ray came out of the room. "I will stay tonight," said Ray.

"I want to be with him. All these years we have shared every moment of joy and sadness. God forbid, if anything happens to him, I want to be by his side." She stroked his face and hugged him tightly. "If there is anything, I will call you."

While leaving, Ray did not miss the distant look in her eyes, and suddenly felt very sad. The very thought of the eventuality numbed him.

As soon as Ray got out of the lift, Julie, who had been waiting down at the reception ran and wrapped her arms around him. "Oh Sweetheart…I hope everything is fine?"

She suddenly released her hold and looked at him with her hand on her mouth. "Uh…, I am sorry, Ray." She looked away and headed out, leaving him to savor the lingering fragrance of jasmine.

Ray was too preoccupied to react, and followed her out. But, he was beginning to take notice of her, and watched those long legs walk her to the car.

No conversation ensued, until they were well on their way home.

"Let's pick up a bite," said Ray, as they passed through the main street. After a debate over what to eat, they swung by the Thai restaurant in the Boathouse, and had a quick dinner. Julie dropped Ray, and drove off, rather abruptly. He looked on at the blue ford Mondeo that they had bought together from the dealership just outside Stratford; it turned off onto the main road and he went in.

In the comfort of his room, Ray still felt the emptiness in the house. Nostalgic memories filled his mind: How his father would take him on his astronomy sessions into the countryside; how proud was his father when he had completed the sixteen-inch telescope, and the very next day he recorded a strange object moving against the background stars. It was found to be a new comet with a period of over seventy-five years. The comet, now christened 'Comet Robin', had reached perihelion a few months later and then peaked in its brightness in a matter of days. It was a spectacular sight, even surpassing the brilliance of comet Halley.

Ray drifted out of his reverie, and wiped tears from his eyes. He was tired, but pensive, and decided to sit in meditation. It began peacefully with a prayer to Master for his father. And then, he was disturbed, but not in a way to draw him out of his meditation. It seemed like someone was trying to send a message to him. He felt the need to do some *cleaning*. In course of the transition from meditation to the cleaning mode, the thought faded away.

Soon, Ray drifted into a deep stupor.

꽃 꽃 꽃

Ray awoke to the sound of chirping birds, and looked at his watch; it was already past six in the morning, and he was relieved that there had been no call from the hospital. He quickly got into his beige trousers and light blue T shirt, and went downstairs. He desperately needed to get back to connecting up with the entity, and was trying to make sense of that last dialogue, as he opened the fridge to see what he could muster up for breakfast. Just then, his mobile rang. He looked at the screen, and was surprised to see the name of Dr. Lowe flashing.

"Come right away," his professor's voice came through, filled with irritation.

"You mean, now? But it's ---

"Please leave as soon as you can."

This was the first time Dr. Lowe had summoned him like this. He sensed that there was something terribly wrong. He didn't have the heart to tell him about his father's condition.

He drove at breakneck speed to the hospital. He found Revathi reading the newspaper; she didn't even bother to look up, when he entered the room. Ray walked over to his father's side and was surprised to see a calm and serene countenance, and on closer observation he noticed that his eyes were flickering, too.

"Mom...,' he hissed, "MOM?"

She looked up with a start and dropped the newspaper. "Uhh...," she looked at her watch. "Why so early."

"How is he?"

"The same,' she sighed, and got up to look at Paul. "He looks better."

Ray didn't know how to tell her of his necessity to go and see his professor. He felt a lump in his throat, and then turned the other way. Closing his eyes he covered his face with his hands and tried to get control of the thoughts racing through his mind. He felt dizzy. Suddenly, his mind went blank, and he opened his eyes.

"Just pray to Master." He heard his mother say, as she put her hand on his shoulder. "That's exactly what I was doing." He turned around, and looked at her. She appeared calm; there was no hint of lack of sleep or teary eyes.

"Oh! Did you read this,' said Revathi, picking up the newspaper and turning the pages, until she came to the right one."

Ray took the newspaper and scanned the page she had given him. He smiled when he saw the headline.

UFO SIGHTED OVER SALISBURY

As he read on, his smile widened. The newspapers, the Air Force, as well as Dr. Lowe who spoke for the scientific community, had passed it off as an atmospheric event. Dr. Lowe had gone on to explain that he had a foolproof detection device, which no UFO could bypass. The news item went on to describe the UFO as: *a blazing fireball that spun like a disc, landing somewhere in the vicinity of Stonehenge.... Did our Ancestors pay a flying visit to check on the structures they had built?*

"That explains it." Ray paused and looked at his mother in the eye. "Dr. Lowe rang me just before I left, and has told me to come immediately."

Revathi looked towards Paul. "Don't worry about him."

"Dr. Lowe was rather secretive about the need to meet."

"Obviously. It's not a thing that can be discussed over the phone."

Ray's attention was focused on another piece of news on the same page. His heart was in his mouth as he read the headline:

'Museum Curator found dead'

Sweat beads formed on his forehead, and his palms started to sweat, as he went on to read the contents:

Noted expert on ancient architecture, and curator of the Salisbury museum was found dead in his home yesterday morning. Police are investigating a report of a small pyramid shaped mud hut that had come up overnight on heritage land. The constable in-charge also mentioned that they had found the visiting card of

Dr. Menon in the vicinity, and had sent detectives to question him, the evening before his death. The curator had claimed responsibility for it and promised to remove it the next morning. That night he died under mysterious circumstances. Post mortem reports revealed that Dr. Menon was in perfect health; and surprisingly, all his systems were in order. But his brain seemed to have received an electric shock, whose source is a mystery. The doctors can find no other explanation for his death. Police feel that the curator might have been involved with some cult and was performing some dangerous experiments, which may have led to his sudden demise. The museum community is shocked at the loss...

Ray felt a shiver go down his spine; he staggered back, wondering if the meeting with Dr. Lowe had anything to do with this.

"Ray, what's wrong?" said Revathi, rushing up to him.

"Uhh... Nothing. Just wondering if I should go or not?"

"Go. But come back tonight."

CHAPTER 7

Ray had to take a long detour to reach the other end of London, on his way to Imperial College. But the traffic was light and he reached much faster than when he used to cut across Central London. Very soon, he was crossing the sprawling lawns of the college campus on his way to report to Dr. Lowe. By the time he climbed the stairs to the second floor of the building, his T shirt was soaked in sweat. He knocked several times, but didn't get any answer, so he opened the door and stuck his head in, only to be received by an empty chair behind the antiquated mahogany desk. The chair was at an angle drawn well back almost touching the wall; very unlike his neat and tidy ways, it seemed his professor had made a hurried departure. The window, behind, was open; and the opening of the door forced a gentle breeze to sweep across the table, ruffling a sheaf of papers on the desk. The cool draught unstuck the sweat soaked shirt from his body.

He stood his ground, holding the door open, as he surveyed the room. The room bred familiarity, having spent a lot of his time here in discussions; just the other day, he and the professor had sat here in despondency brooding over the closure of the radio telescope facility. The absence of Michael's picture on the professor's desk was a mute testimony to his strained relationship with his son. One of Van Gogh's lesser known works still hung on the wall – a surreal expression of solitude. In contrast, on the opposite side of the wall, to his left, was the classical map of the cosmos; the swirling masses of gas and dust strung across the cosmic string of time, slowly accreting into a cornucopia of objects, summed up the events from the beginning of time, spanning over thirteen billion years. A sudden gust of wind made some papers fly off the desk, scattering them all over. A soiled piece of paper landed at his feet, as if it were meant for him. He picked it up and crumpled it unnerved by the sound of the door banging shut. He glanced back, and, then, unfolded the scrap of paper, and immediately recognized the distinctive slant of his professor's writing. It seemed to have been written in a hurry. As he read it, he realized it was no ordinary scrap of paper; the message was meant for him.

I owe this discovery to my student who is more than just a student; we share a very special bond. I write this in hope that this note is passed on to Ray Robinson, to let him know what I feel about him. I can no longer take this pressure...

Ray read the note again; overcome with guilt; tears welling in his eyes. *What could be wrong with Dr. Lowe? Was he thinking of committing suicide?*

In a state of shock, he did not hear the door open.

"That was quick."

Ray turned around. He was staring into Dr. Lowe's face. He staggered back, still holding the piece of paper in his right hand; he just couldn't get his hand to crumple the paper.

"Err... Good Morning, Sir," he said, as Dr. Lowe coolly walked to his desk.

"I didn't expect you till afternoon?"

Ray was more concerned about what to do with the paper in his hand; his fidgeting drew the professor's attention.

"What's in your hand, Ray," he asked plainly.

That's when Ray snapped out of his flustered state. "Oh. Nothing. I was going to leave a note."

In a more composed state, Ray noticed that the professor suddenly looked old; his gaunt unshaven face and crumpled brown suit made him look even more haggard. He continued to observe Dr. Lowe, who was trying to put a pen back in its holder, but kept missing it. Ray noticed the trembling hands, and felt very sad.

"Give me that piece of paper," persisted Dr. Lowe, sitting down on his chair with a jerk.

Ray felt the note in his hand, and handed it. He gestured Ray to take a seat, and unfolded the note, his hands still shaking.

"What's all this going on?" said Ray.

Dr. Lowe pushed his chair back and swiveled around, and appeared to be looking out of the window.

"I have been receiving threatening phone calls," said Dr. Lowe, in a low voice. "It all began when I got the grant for this new water harnessing project. I thought someone was playing a prank, but next I was informed that the MI 5 had uncovered a plot to kidnap me."

"KIDNAP you, Sir?" Ray got up with a start, banging his knee under the table.

Dr. Lowe continued to stare out of the window. "A terrorist organization seems to be behind this."

"Have you confided in anybody?"

Dr. Lowe shook his head. Ray was sure that he would be the first person the professor must have confided in.

"If that's the case, the place should be swarming with security. I just walked into your office."

The professor stood up, and Ray heard the sound of paper being torn. He turned around and, now, some color had come back on his cheeks; the puff bags under his eyes still very prominent.

"I have just come back from Scotland Yard. I will be given a personal bodyguard; round the clock security will be posted outside the building and my home."

Dr. Lowe took a deep breath, and threw the shreds of paper into the dustbin under his table.

"It's bizarre," he said, his voice choked with emotion.

Ray embraced his professor and gave him a tight squeeze. "I am back, and nothing is going to happen to you."

Just then the door opened; Ray released his hold and looked back. A uniformed man stood at the door.

"Constable Santes from Special Branch, reporting," he said in his Spanish accent, looking at Ray inquiringly.

Ray returned the stare. The square jawed Santes came into the room; short and stocky, with closely cropped black hair, he looked a rather formidable adversary to encounter in a dark alley.

"It's alright, Constable, this is my student, Ray Robinson," said Dr. Lowe. "Now, if you may, please leave us alone. You can wait outside."

"I am sorry, Sir." He stood his ground, closing the door behind him.

"I am sorry, too," said the professor. "I need a private word with Ray; so PLEASE wait outside."

"But, Sir…," protested Santes.

"I SAID, PLEASE WAIT OUTSIDE."

The Constable staggered back, but stood at the door, and looked blankly at the two of them.

"Never mind; he is only carrying out his orders," said Ray, as Dr. Lowe excused himself to use the washroom at the end of the corridor.

Putting the kettle on for some coffee, Ray walked up to the window; his blue eyes peered searchingly into the azure, as if there was a message written across the clear blue summer skies; all his eyes met was a big black raven that had just flown in and perched itself on a branch in front of the window. He looked away, down onto the campus gardens. Everyone was going about their own thing. *I wish I could be just like one of them.*

A shuffle of footsteps drew him out of his rumination. He turned; he was now looking at a transformed Dr. Lowe, who had combed his graying hair, and changed into a well ironed tweed jacket, and was now clean shaven. His greenish eyes looked much brighter. Seeing the more cheerful Dr. Lowe, Ray mustered up the courage to probe further into the matter.

"Tell me all, Sir."

Dr. Lowe walked up to the sofa and sank into it. Ray pulled a chair in front of the professor.

"We have been exposed, Ray," said the professor almost in a whisper, looking at Ray straight in the eye.

Ray almost jumped out of chair. "What do you mean by exposed." He put his cup down on the table and looked at his professor questioningly.

"Last night, I got a call from the security agency of the Radio telescope facility, which you had so cleverly decided to use," began the professor.

Ray fidgeted, sensing a bit of sarcasm in his professor's tone.

"Ross has been suspended."

Ray's hands began to tremble, and felt weak in his knees. "NO!"

"And now they want me to appear before the Defense Secretary, here in London. The former director of the SETI project arrived yesterday."

Ray stared vacantly; the expose' still not having sunk into him, leave alone the repercussions.

"Despite it being a Sunday, yesterday, things have moved really fast; someone very high up in America is obviously taking this very seriously."

"Is Ross in serious trouble?"

Dr. Lowe grimaced, and raised his eyebrows.

"It's my fault," said Ray burying his face in his hands. "I feel terrible."

Dr. Lowe looked at his watch. "I have a meeting at the Ministry of Defense at one-thirty." He motioned to get up. "We have time for a quick bite."

Dr. Lowe hurried through his lunch, and excused himself. Ray took his time to finish his lunch, pondering over the turn of events. Just as he was leaving the dining room, his cell phone rang and he answered it after seeing the number on his display.

"I thought you went to your meeting, Sir?"

"Just reached home.

"The meeting?"

It's rescheduled to this afternoon. I want you here."

"Sure."

Ray didn't give himself time to think, and was pulling into Dr. Lowe's driveway in less than ten minutes. The clock on the dashboard displayed 13.14. The numbers were familiar. They were the same numbers scribbled on the slip of paper he had found when he had entered the facility – the coordinates from where the energy waves were originating from.

Before he could dwell on the coincidence, he was tying the main door; it was unlocked; he opened it slowly, and poked his head in, and then, put his right foot inside. Continuing to stand at the door, he surveyed the interiors. The door opened into a narrow passage way, facing the staircase that led up to the bedroom. Dr. Lowe's bunch of keys was lying on the mantle. He shut the door behind him, and entered into the drawing room to his right. It was a small but cozy space. Simple yet elegant furniture adorned the room and despite being a widower, Dr. Lowe kept everything in its appropriate place. Cream upholstery on the sofas with bright orange curtains lent a pleasant feeling to the room. He loved art, especially Hammershoi. The famous painting of the mystery woman with her back towards the viewer, hung above the fireplace. He shuddered, looking at it in a very different context now. He found it so very symbolic and relevant, considering the present state of affairs. He looked away as his mind was beginning to play tricks – he had a strong feeling that the mystery woman had turned and looked at him. He quickly turned away and walked to the far left corner into the kitchen. He opened the door that led to a small garden and sniffed the air, surveying the area. The small patch of lawn needed mowing; the lavender shrubs had overgrown.

"Ray, is that you," he heard his professor shout. "I'll be down in a second."

"Take your time, Sir."

Ray shut the door, and helped himself to some ice water; the nervous twitch of grinding his teeth had set in, and he bit into the ice cubes to counter that.

"There is some good coffee," Dr. Lowe's voice filtered into the kitchen.

Ray had already sniffed out the coffee tin, reading the label intently. He was just about to turn on the grinder to powder the beans, when the door-bell rang. He heard footsteps coming down the stairs, and chose to remain in the kitchen. His stomach tightened as a deep sense of guilt overcame him.

All this was because of me, he thought and his head began to spin. He held onto the edge of the counter and closed his eyes. *Master, give me the strength*, he pleaded in his thoughts.

"Good Afternoon, Sir," he heard a woman's voice come from the open door. "I am Commodore Susan Wooldridge, on deputation to the MoD from RAF; and this is Lieutenant Pollock from MoD who is assisting me on this case."

"Is he here?" he heard the woman ask. Ray took a deep breath and came out of the kitchen. He was quite surprised when he saw her. Dark haired, slim and of medium height, she had a small and pointy nose on a longish face, her cheeks were filled out, short of being plump. She was surveying the room while her colleague was taking out the papers from a rather smart well-polished leather folder. Her eyes met Ray's, and she looked at him questioningly.

"This is my student, Ray Robinson."

"Mister Robinson!" Ray couldn't stop looking at her as she walked towards him. She wore the RAF uniform, which added to Ray's attraction towards her.

She looked at Ray in the eye and smiled; her greenish eyes exuded a kind of softness and warmth, and, then, went back to where Dr. Lowe was seated. She seated herself on the cushioned chair opposite the professor.

She coughed, and cleared her throat, and then shot Ray a green eyed glance, before she began. "I have been a fan of yours through my growing years. An astronomy buff myself, I follow all your programs." She paused, and cleared her throat again. Her pen dropped to the floor, and she leaned over to retrieve it. Ray watched her intently, as she fumbled with her attempt, and motioned to help her. She gave up and straightened herself, and Ray pulled a dining chair and seated himself. Dabbing her brow with a tissue, she continued. "And, Pollock, here, knew Dr. Menon who died under mysterious circumstances. This is not all; rumors of a UFO sighting that night and an alien landing did not make matters any easier."

Ray raised his eyebrows, and glanced at Pollock. "I am sorry to hear that."

"The mystery still lies unsolved," said the square jawed Pollock, giving Ray a dark eyed glance; his boyish features and closely cropped hair confirmed his status as a service man.

"The press has cast doubts on Dr. Menon's character, accusing him of being involved in some cult worship."

Susan glanced at Pollock, and settled into a very business-like posture, sitting at the edge of her chair, ready to take notes; she obviously was widely experienced at her present job.

"The security breach at the facility was the last straw after Dr. Menon's death. The two security guards are in our custody." Her eyes were on Ray, who was visibly nervous.

Ray sat up straight. "I have a confession to make." He paused and looked at Dr. Lowe who gave him a puzzled look.

"I was working on the Search for Extra-terrestrial Intelligence (SETI) program; the facility in question was my laboratory. Just when I thought I had hit upon something very exciting, I was told to suspend the experiment the very next day. Dr. Lowe ran from pillar to post, to the extent of making two trips to Washington, in an attempt to convince the funding agencies to give us at least one more year."

Ray looked at Dr. Lowe expectantly.

"What do you expect," interrupted Dr. Lowe, "if decisions on projects involving complex scientific programs are taken by accountants."

Susan nodded sympathetically.

"I was frustrated and needed to corroborate my findings," said Ray; by now sweat was beginning to trickle down his side burns.

"Who wouldn't want to, especially, when it has such far reaching consequences," interjected Dr. Lowe.

"I bullied Ross, who is one of the security guards at the facility and happens to be a childhood friend of mine, to let me into the facility," continued Ray. "I spent two nights there, only to continue where I had left off. It was no big security breach. Please don't press charges on Ross."

"Utter waste of public money," chided Dr. Lowe.

Susan, who was furiously taking notes, stopped and looked at Ray thoughtfully. "So, did you find your answers?"

Ray shook his head. "Unfortunately, it was a waste of time, not worth the risk and all the mess it has dragged everyone into. What you should be concerned with is the threat on Dr. Lowe's life?"

"I need to be excused, Miss,' said Dr. Lowe in a low voice. "I don't feel too well."

"Just one more question, Sir," said Susan, her eyes popping out and thin lips trying to hold back a smile. "Is there life in outer space?"

"Carl Sagan was asked the same question by a little girl. His reply was: *if there is no life in space, it's an awful waste of space.*"

Susan looked questioningly, and smiled. "It has indeed been a great honor to have spent all this time with you? Of course, your student has all the signs of following your footsteps. He indeed is a charming boy, and I do appreciate his cooperation and frankness."

Ray blushed and quickly got up. "You can't go without some fresh coffee."

Susan looked at her watch. "Gosh! It's almost three?"

Dr. Lowe got up. "What about Ross?"

"In the light of Ray's revelations, I don't see any problem on that front," said Susan, moving towards the door. "I will file my report and submit it to the defense secretary. He'll be in our custody until we get clearance from MoD."

Dr. Lowe nodded half heartedly.

Susan took a deep breath and covered her nose and mouth with both her hands to stifle a sneeze. "Washington seems to have taken this very seriously. You don't seem to be very popular on the other side of the Atlantic?"

Dr. Lowe smirked. "Ray will see you off," he said, getting up.

"It's been our honor, Sir!" Susan bowed and shook hands with the professor. Pollock was already out of the door.

"Here is my card, Ray. Just call me on my mobile, if you think of anything. Every little piece of information, especially the truth, will help wrap up this investigation faster."

Just then her phone rang. "Yes, it's Commodore Susan Wooldridge," he heard her say. "Go on DCI, I can talk now."

Susan finished taking some notes, and then, looked up. "I have to tread on your territory, tomorrow. It seems there have been strange happenings over at Stonehenge."

"Anything specific?"

"It seems to have all started after you resumed your work at the facility."

Ray started as he heard the ring of his cell phone. "I was just going to call--."

"Come right away,' he heard his mother say. It was more of a nervous tone than one filled with anxiety.

"Is Dad --?" He stopped when he heard many voices in the background, as if there was a state of panic. A knot in his stomach tightened. He needed to get back, and rushed inside to explain the situation to Dr. Lowe.

CHAPTER 8

Unable to contact Revathi on the mobile, he drove way above the speed limit. In an hour and a half he was opening the door of the hospital room. The brightly lit room was empty. His mother's overnight bag lying on the ground, and her night clothes carelessly thrown onto the sofa, was an indication of a hasty exit. His heart skipped a beat, thinking of the worst. He turned towards the door as he heard it open. A rather petite, young nurse, probably, just out of her teens, entered. She had an elfin face with a pointy nose, her thin and small mouth drawn into a line.

"Are you Ray Robinson," she said in a shrill voice, straightening her white cap.

Ray nodded, unable to speak as a lump had developed in his throat. He looked into her round brown eyes, hoping to get an answer even before she would say anything.

"Your father's been taken to the fourth floor," she said, without any emotion, and brushed passed him, the smell of a floral perfume mixed with the smell of freshly washed laundry pricking his nostrils. Ray glanced at her and then hurried out. He checked the sign outside the lift, which directed him to the Intensive Cardiac Care Unit (ICCU) on the fourth floor.

As soon as he stepped out of the lift, the soft white luminescence that filtered out of the aquarium – a cylindrical glass column placed in the centre of the hall -- was soothing to his psyche. It was quite an eye catcher -- the glass column, around 2 feet in diameter and four to five feet in height, placed on a raised stone slab that made it almost touch the ceiling. A large orange fish was nibbling at the walls of the glass, while a silvery shark like fish displaying its menacing fangs circled just above. Family members of patients were seated on the chairs placed against the three corners of the wall. An elderly lady seated in one corner was knitting furiously, while another older man had extended the chair out and was fast asleep. Ray took a deep breath suffocated by the melancholic silence. A glass door to his right had a sign ICCU painted in red. He felt sick in the stomach, and closed his eyes tightly, squeezing out a few tears. Suddenly his mind went blank, and the whirring in his head stopped. When he opened his eyes, his fears only intensified, as he pushed open the swivel door. The inner door seemed locked and he pressed his thumb against the finger print reader, but it just beeped in annoyance, saying, Try Again'. He peered through the glass view hole, and saw a crowd collected around bed number three. A nurse was walking to the door, and he waited. Before she could shut the door, he just said, "Excuse me," and slipped in.

His mother stood by the side of the bed; she looked up and just gestured with her hand, as if to say it's all OK. His father had his eyes closed, and looked rather calm; at least the color had come back onto his face and his breathing had steadied. Ray looked up at the monitors; the readings on all the machines were displaying, 'ERR'. Then some lights began to flash and soon after, what he thought to be, the oscilloscope, began to beep loudly. Nothing was making sense.

"So you are finally here," a familiar voice spoke from behind – the oriental accent was so prominent. Before he could turn around he felt a hand on his shoulder.

Dr. Masuda bowed half heartedly, more like a reflex action than a salutation. He removed his round gold rimmed spectacles, and stroked his bald head, flattening the long strands of silver grey hair; he shook his head in disbelief. "Only when we connect the machines to your father, they malfunction."

The doctor turned and asked for the latest readings. His eyes reduced to slits bore into the hand held computer, the frown intensifying. Then he began to shake his head sideways. "He is fitter than all of us here --," he said and was interrupted by the beep of his mobile. He lifted his glasses and peered into the flashing screen. "I will see you in the room."

Relieved that the doctor had given a clean chit to his father, they headed down to the room, but before that, they stopped at the cafeteria. It was mostly full of doctors and nurses. The polished stainless steel tables, and oil painted white walls with bright fluorescent lighting was a welcome change. Ray got some coffee and settled himself.

"Are you sure Paul's alright?" she said, looking into Ray's eyes, as if trying to read the slightest change of expression. She had dark circles under her eyes; at the moment, she looked paler than Paul.

"Dr. Masuda is sure of it."

"All was not so quiet and peaceful at the hospital last night," said Revathi, sipping her coffee.

Ray's eyes widened, and he sat upright.

"The happenings have left the hospital staff completely at a loss. Shortly after midnight, I was about to leave the side of the bed and stretch out on the couch; all of a sudden, the monitor started to flicker and beep. The sound was driving me crazy. So, I called the nurse, who rushed into the room and tried to restart the machine. She adjusted the positions of the probes connected to the body. Paul continued to remain in a coma, showing no signs of movement. Nothing seemed to help to restore normalcy. Finally, the head nurse had to be called in. Even her attempts yielded no result, and then, came the emergency doctor on duty, followed by Dr. Martin, who had been woken up in his home."

Ray squeezed his mother's hand, which was resting on the table. "Why the hell didn't you call me?"

Revathi took another sip and continued as if she had not heard him. "Finally, Dr. Martin ordered the disconnection of the machines. He gave instructions to monitor Paul's condition, every hour, but with manual instruments. After a while, I was just about to doze off, taking advantage of the nurse being in the room. Suddenly I felt cold, and found a reddish hue enveloping the room. The white glow of the tube light also looked red. Then, I felt hot and began to perspire. I heard a voice echoing in my mind, but it seemed to fill the room. I couldn't make out the name, but it was something like *Den... will save you*. And, as quickly as the reddish hue had come, it faded away, so did the voice."

Ray looked into his mother's doe like dark eyes, which were now red; her face was flushed; he had a hunch that it was all to do with the entity he was in contact with, and had no words to pacify his mother, being in a quandary himself.

He put his hand on hers. "Why don't you go home and have a change."

Ray got up from the chair, expecting her to follow, but she continued sitting.

"I can't bear to leave him alone."

He did not argue further and escorted his mother back to the room. As they stepped out of the lift, they saw Dr. Masuda peep into the room, which was just near the lift.

"Ahh…," he said, when he saw the two exit the lift. They entered the room and Ray shut the door behind him. Revathi quickly went up to her chair and picked up the clothes from the floor. "Sorry for the mess," she said.

Dr. Masuda smiled, his eyes turning into slits. "My wife --," he paused, and sighed. "She also was very a very neat person."

Ray sensed the sadness in his tone, and went up to help his mother. Dr. Masuda took the file lying on the table next to the empty bed, and leafed through the pages. "I came back just to tell you that Paul's condition is stable. His vital functions have normalized, and should be down before dinner."

"Thanks doctor."

Dr. Masuda put the file down and scratched his head, as Revathi and Ray looked on. "It can only be a miracle that has brought about this sudden improvement in your father's condition. Not one of these gadgets has functioned through the night," he said, and scratched his head. "His brain activity shows significant improvement." He paused.

"Ray," he said, as if unsure of what he was going to say next, and looked towards the ceiling. "The encephalogram…"

"What about the encephalogram?"

"Dr. Masuda looked at Ray rather strangely, the color from his rosy plump cheeks suddenly vanished. "They are just like the concentric circles recorded when you were injured."

"Noo…." Ray felt as if his heart had really stopped and took a deep breath.

Dr. Masuda looked at Ray and frowned. "I am very sure. I can show it to you, if you want."

"No, no, I believe you."

"It's time you do something, Mr. Robinson. As I told you earlier, go and see a Medium. Someone is trying to get in touch with you. Reach out before it begins to haunt you for the rest of your life."

"Doctor…," Revathi almost whispered. "When will they discharge him?"

The doctor had reached the door and Ray opened it for him. "Hmm… Should be out of hospital in a day or two if he continues like this."

He stepped out of the door, leaving the two of them standing looking at each other. Ray noticed a faint smile on Revathi's face. He looked at her intently; her hair was still jet-black; she certainly didn't look fifty four; though, in the past few weeks, stress had caught up with her; her eyes were deep set, and had dark circles under them; but, she hadn't lost any weight, and ever since Ray could remember, Revathi had maintained her well proportioned figure.

He went up and gave her a comforting hug. "I will be back soon, Mom."

He reached the car park, which was now almost empty. No sooner had ne got to the car, his phone rang. He picked it up after seeing the number. "Ross! I don't know what --."

"No man. There is no need to be sorry. Tell me, how is Paul?"

Leaning against the car, Ray looked up into firmament. "Dad's much better."

The sky was clear on this warm sunny afternoon, only painted with the trail of a jet plane moving almost vertically up. He then went on to narrate what happened.

"I strongly feel this entity is behind the erratic functioning of the machines." Ray paused, when he saw a familiar face wave to him from a black Jaguar, and waved back when he recognized the face of Dr. Masuda which was barely visible over the wheel.

"It's begun to haunt me," he said.

"Ask your Master, what to do?"

"That's exactly what I was about to do," said Ray. "I'll call you right back."

He dialed the Master's number. "Thank God you are there, Master," Ray spoke.

"Revathi told me about Paul,' the Master interrupted.

"When did you speak to her?"

"Just a few minutes back."

"Oh. Then she must have told you everything."

"What do you make of this?"

"Don't dwell on it."

"Master, have you been in contact, at all?"

"It has been in contact with me since yesterday."

"Where the hell is it?" Ray bit his tongue. "Pardon me."

"It's on Earth."

"You mean it has transformed into a physical entity?"

"Yes. But it refuses to reveal its name and form until it comes in contact with you."

"If you connect up with it again, just tell it to go back and stop messing with my life."

The Master laughed. "Ray, you have not been doing meditation. Just do your cleaning daily."

Suddenly, Ray recollected the news item of the strange happenings at Stonehenge. He immediately dialed Ross. "Hey Rossy, we have to make a trip to Stonehenge."

"When?"

"We need to get there before nightfall."

"We ought to be on our way."

"Yes, I'll pick you up."

"Man, I can't come with you."

"What do you mean?"

"I am leaving for home, tonight. I thought I would take some time off, and see my parents."

Ray paused as he held his phone against his shoulder, trying to get the key into the ignition." I have been so selfish. I didn't even think about you and the fact that you have lost your job, and all this because of me."

"Hey man, come on, but I can help you." Ross's voice did not have his usual bubbly and excitable tone. "I know a security officer at Stonehenge. Maybe he can shed some light on the strange happenings there."

"That will be great," said Ray, starting the car.

ॐ   ॐ   ॐ

Ray pulled into the side road leading to Stonehenge. He inched forward as a big tourist bus pulled out of the gate onto the road. Ray slapped the steering wheel. *Damn, it is closing time. I don't think I'll ever find my way in today,* he mumbled, as he looked at his watch which read six twenty five.

He anyway decided to try his luck and parked his car and got out. Hands dug into his pockets, he felt the chilly wind bite into his flesh. His bare arms bore the brunt of the cold. He jostled amongst the masses of humanity that were flowing out of the entrance, and finally reached the security guard.

He enquired about Julian – Ross's friend -- and was directed inside. Walking down the stairs, he went through a tunnel, and again up another stairway.

Each time he saw Stonehenge, it left him awestruck, unable to comprehend the fact that those massive stones were moved to the site without the aid of any machines. This time his thoughts dwelled beyond just admiring the magnificence of the structure. A blonde haired boyish looking guard was seated on one of the benches just outside the office.

"I am looking for Julian."

"You must be Ray?"

Ray nodded and they shook hands.

"I have heard your name somewhere. Were you in the newspapers recently?"

"Err…probably in connection with my work. I am working in the SETI program."

"Ah… now I recollect, the investigating officers from special branch had mentioned you in connection with the dancing lights."

Ray was stunned. "Did you see them?"

Since Ross is a good friend, I can let you in on this, but please keep it to yourselves."

"Mum's the word." said Ray, as he was led into the office.

"A strange phenomenon is observed every night. It all started on the night of summer solstice, that's what I was told. The other night-shift guards have been taken ill after they observed the strange happenings. Probably, spooked out of their wits."

"You mean the dancing lights, as what was reported in the papers last week," said Ray.

"I really don't know, said Julian, shrugging his square shoulders. "If you are lucky, you will see the spectacle tonight."

"You mean I can stay?"

"I'll smuggle you in. You must avoid talking to the other guards. Anyway they are all new, except for my boss who comes in late and settles down for a snooze."

🜚   🜚   🜚

Large floodlights, almost three feet in diameter, came on as the sky darkened. Julian and Ray watched patiently, their eyes focused towards the centre, where the monumental blocks of stone were piled. Ray wondered whether anyone would walk into this obvious trap. On one hand he feared the capture of the alien, and on the other hand he was apprehensive of the events to come.

All of a sudden, the yellowish incandescence began to acquire a reddish tinge, which only deepened as they watched.

"Let's get closer," said Ray.

"Are you out of your mind?"

"I am going."

"You'll have to put on the company overcoat."

Ray slipped on the overcoat, which fitted him perfectly, and walked out of the office. An icy cool draft of wind slapped his face;

"For God's sake, shut the door. It's freezing outside."

Ray shut the door behind him and ventured out into the open vastness. The fully illuminated Stones didn't exude the same enigma that they did on a full moon night.

He stopped in his tracks when he saw a silhouette in the centre. He was now only ten meters from the periphery of the inner circle. Then he observed something very eerie. The ruddy hue was taking the shape of a human form; an erect, ghostly apparition hovered a few feet above the ground for a few seconds, giving no time for Ray to react. Suddenly the searchlights went out, plunging the area into darkness.

"You are lucky, tonight; it seems that the ghost came for you."

Ray jumped out of skin, hearing a voice behind him.

"I'll get the searchlights checked in the morning," said Julian, as he put a hand on Ray's shoulder. "Isn't all this bizarre?"

"I just felt a draft of warm air," said Ray. "Look over there. The hele stone is glowing as if it's on fire!"

"OUCH," Ray heard Julian cry out, and then he heard a thud. He turned to look; and his eyes fell on an object that resembled a gun; it was glowing bright red as if it was on fire, just like the hele stone. In the dull amber glow he also saw Julian sprawled on the floor; he was clutching his right hand and wincing in pain.

Ray went up to him and picked him up. "What on earth happened to you?"

"When I tried to cross into the inner circle, I was thrown back by a strong electrical field."

"Maybe the electric fences have been turned on?"

"I swear I haven't turned them on."

"Strange," said Ray, stroking his chin, his frown intensifying. He looked again at the hele stone. There was no sign of anything odd; the glow had disappeared, too. He turned back to look at Julian.

"Why are you clutching your hand?"

"That's what is so puzzling," said Julian, flicking on his flashlight. "That gun, it almost roasted my hand."

Ray knelt down to pick up the gun; he felt it with the tip of his finger, and then carefully picked it up. "Jesus, the handle has melted!"

"No wonder," said Julian, and looked at his hand, showing the torch on it. "It hurts like hell."

"Let's get out of this place," said Ray.

Is my mind playing tricks? Ray wondered, as they trooped back to the office.

"I must say it was a near miss. How the hell do I account for my gun?"

Ray removed his overcoat, and placed it on the coat hanger near the door. "Search me. I guess report it lost."

"My palm is singed. Look at it," said Julian spreading his palm out.

"Hmm…," Ray nodded, looking blankly at Julian. "Do you think I can use the couch for a snooze?"

"Sure, but I want you to slip away before five-thirty."

Ray looked at his watch. "It's three -thirty now. Maybe I'll scoot right away."

"I am new around here, and with great difficulty I managed to get this job. Can we just say that nothing happened; rather, we never met."

"Suits me," said Ray, finding a way to wriggle out of the situation more than easy.

He had envisaged being interrogated all over again, with a lot of explanation to give. He very much wanted to go and snoop around on his own, but was a bit apprehensive to go back to the inner circle, lest there was another burst of fireworks. This would certainly arouse suspicion of Julian however disinterested he appeared.

"Give my regards to Ross," said Julian as Ray closed the door behind him.

Ray was not finished with his work around Stonehenge. He had a strong feeling that the alien was trying to get in touch with him, and needed to sit in meditation to see whether he could connect up with it. He walked up to his car; instead of getting into the driver's seat he got into the back seat.

Confused and befuddled Ray just couldn't get into meditation; finally, after half an hour he got a strange sensation – the same feeling of a gust of cold air followed by warm air. Soon after, he drifted into deep meditation.

I come in peace, but it seems your species are out to harm me a thought reverberated in his mind. I have been waiting to make contact ever since we made contact the first time. Where have you been?

There was danger from my own people. I do not want you to fall into the wrong hands, Ray transmitted.

I must warn you that if you try and use force against me I will either return back or will be forced to retaliate. I am running out of energy and will have to transform and connect with you very soon. Be connected with me and I shall use that as a guide to reach you.

How will I know who you are?

That you shall see when I stand before you.

Deep in meditation, Ray still felt the goose pimples, as a feeling of foreboding was creeping in. The alien was being very insistent, almost controlling him.

I cannot transform around all these stones. I have found the place I was looking for. There is no need for any pyramid.

How will I find it?

My Masters will guide you.

How will I get in touch with them?

Through your Master.

And then there was silence as vacuity filled his mind.

CHAPTER 9

"Did you see that flash?" Ray heard his mother exclaim, and felt her grip tighten on his hand. No sooner had they taken another step, a loud explosion filled the air. The ground beneath them shook, bringing the trio of Revathi, Ray and her cousin Chandrasekhar to a halt. It could not have been thunder as the sky was unusually clear, though it was the peak of monsoon in Kerala. Ray's eyes roamed, scanning the landscape. To the right and left of them, along the straight and narrow road -- the main road of the village -- were square plots of waterlogged fields. Strands of large bladed grass skimmed over the top of the water, forming a loosely woven carpet, which merged in with the coconut trees in the distance. Way over the top of these green palms, he fixed his gaze on the silhouette of the temple perched on the summit. It looked more like a pyramid than the one they had built at Stonehenge – the memory of that still so vivid. He wondered whether this visit to his mother's home was connected to his search. He began to piece together the events that made them decide to come to his mother's village in the southern state of Kerala.

Just before he had left Stonehenge he had communicated with the entity who had told him to wait for his Master to tell him where to find it. He didn't even know what he would see in front of him if he were to encounter the extraterrestrial entity. As days passed, he continued his meditation, attending the group sessions, taking regular sittings, or, recharges, as he put it. The Master only knew that the entity was very much on Earth. When Ray had confronted him about being in contact with the entity, the Master had just laughed it off. All he had said was, "Be regular with your practice."

Ray's attempts to connect with the entity again, were unsuccessful. He finally confided in his mother, who was rather impressed with his experience in meditation and said people practicing for decades haven't been able to reach his level. She admitted that even after so many years of practice, her mind was full of thoughts when she drifted into meditation. Paul had been discharged and had never felt better when he came home, going straight to work. It was one telephone call from Revathi's cousin in Kerala that had set the ball rolling. Though his mother forced Ray to accompany her, it was the Master who finally convinced him. Paul remained behind, wanting to catch up with work.

It took Ray a few days to adjust to the rather rural lifestyle; his mother was busy with her cousins and a constant influx of guests. Among them was the local astrologer who visited her at least once in a day. He did not know what it signified, but he did overhear hear the words exorcism, removal of spirits, and some such mumbo jumbo, when Revathi had spoken to Paul over the telephone. Ray was still clueless as to why he had come, having just drifted into this 'mission' that his mother kept calling it.

"RAY!" he heard his mother calling out, but the voice was rather distant. He shook his head and rubbed his eyes, and looked ahead. His mother and her cousin were at least fifty yards away; he broke into a fast walk and joined them.

"Sorry! I was just ---."

"Are you alright," Revathi asked, resuming the journey. Ray just followed; his mind still full of questions.

He looked up again, and was just in time to see a flash of light lacing the coconut grove with a pinkish hue. A dull boom followed, which seemed to have come from the same direction.

"Tut...Tut... Quarry work," said Chandrasekhar, clucking his tongue and shaking his head with an air of finality. His long pointed nose, with big ears that resembled the ends of a trumpet, overflowing from the sides of his small unshaven face, he was a splitting image of grandpa elf in a movie that Ray had just seen before leaving England last week. His hands were also so thin that they seem to come out of his white half-sleeved kurta (an Indian style shirt) like little hands out of a wooden doll.

"Oh! I suppose it is okay to carry on?" said Revathi, straightening her gold-bordered, white wrap around.

Chandrasekhar nodded, seemingly lost in his own thoughts. "We need to hurry."

"Do I really need to come," said Ray.

She pursued her thin lips, and took a deep breath, shaking her oval head covered with shoulder length straight hair tinged with a streak of brown. "This puja is necessary," she said.

Ray noticed a twinge of sadness in her voice. "I know. But at least tell me what it is for?"

"I cannot explain now." She quickened her pace. "Let us get to the top."

"How far do we have to go," Ray asked, looking at Chandrasekhar.

"There, there," he said. "Only a few minutes' walk, now." He pointed in the direction of the temple, as if he were shaking hands with someone much taller than he was. The silhouette of a temple like structure had become clearer. Loose cobblestones' grinding against each other powered by their footfalls was the only sound that fell on Ray's ears. Pockets of grey translucence lingered amongst the thick foliage fuelled by the cooking fires from the houses ensconced in the depths of coconut and areca nut plantations. He took a deep breath as he filled his lungs with the fresh air laced with a smoky aroma.

A minibus roared past, making quite a racket. Ray gasped at the sight; pulled down to one side by a mass of humanity clinging to almost every part they could get their hand on, he feared the bus would topple over as it rounded the bend.

The trio turned off onto a narrow pathway surrounded by water logged paddy fields on either side, heading into the wooded slopes. They made their way, slowly, through the cashew trees that lined the narrow treacherous pathway up the hill, passing by small thatched homes ensconced between the lean and tall palm trees that shot up into the sky. The sound of gushing water on the sides, and an occasional view of flowing water streaming down the hill slope, was so invigorating that the tiredness in Ray seemed to have vanished. He was now leading the expedition. Chandrasekhar stopped when they came to a clearing, and suddenly hopped onto a boulder around two feet high.

"I'll just come from the namboodiri's house," he said, and disappeared into a thickly wooded patch. Revathi quickly disappeared into the foliage.

She emerged, trying to remove a prickly stem from the back of her blouse.

"Is this puja something to do with MY sister?" Ray said, unable to hold himself back.

She stopped in her tracks and looked at her son; her mouth half open, and her doe like eyes with that extra bit of kajal, almost popping out. She swallowed as she wiped her eyes with her sari, and suddenly turned her face away. Ray thought she was about to cry, and clenched his fists cursing himself for broaching the subject.

"Master told me about her," he said, without even thinking.

"Oh...," she paused, looking the other way, wiping her eyes with the loose end of her sari. "Tomorrow is her death anniversary."

"Did you ever find her body?"

"No. The police closed the case ten years later," she said in a calm voice.

"You mean she just walked out of the house and never came back?"

"I don't want to talk about it, please. We are trying to move on; for us she died the day we lost her."

He heard rustling in the bushes, and turned to look. Chandrasekhar appeared from the woods trying to push away branches and vines that blocked his path. "He must be in the temple."

His rather noisy return dissolved the tension in the air, at least temporarily, as he led them to a flight of steps carved into the rock face. Ray counted twenty-four steps when he set foot on to the summit. He scanned the expanse of flat rocky land, which was about the size of a tennis court. An enormous tree-trunk rose above the ground from one side of the cliff; the winding branches, sprouting small leaves, covered almost half the ground. The temple like structure had a square base with a verandah running right around; the top was like a pyramid with images of Gods and Goddesses carved out of black rock into the sides. The sun that was now fully visible, halfway down the hill over a carpet of coconut palms in the valley, shone like a searchlight illuminating the polished metal tip of the pyramid, as if it were sending out a beacon into space. He shivered involuntarily as a draft of cool moist air blew across; and hurried to catch up with his mother who had reached halfway to the temple.

A bare-chested man emerged from inside the temple, bending low to avoid hitting his clean-shaven head on the wooden beam. He was carrying a brass pot in one hand and a brass plate with a complex looking lamp in the other. It had a multitude of individual lamps all connected to each other.

"Hey, I want those tattoos, Mom," said Ray, trying to lighten the atmosphere between them, when he saw the man plastered with some creamy paste, applied in streaks on the side of his bare thick arms, his forehead, and on his chest.

"Shhh...," she put her hand on her lips. "He is the temple priest, and it's not a tattoo. It is sandalwood paste applied as a mark of respect to God."

As he neared, he smiled, exposing his stained teeth. Hair overflowed from his ears, and a white tuft of hair covered his chest. He had an unusually large stomach, and it shook as he walked. The man came up to them and exchanged some words in Malayalam – the local language—with Chandrasekhar. In the middle of their conversation, Chandrasekhar pointed his finger at Ray as if telling the priest who he was. The priest nodded, and looked at his watch. Then he gestured to Chandrasekhar, who in turn signaled the duo to stay put. Ray's gaze followed the man to a small pond near the steps where they had come up.

"You can come here," Chandrasekhar called out from the verandah.

Ray continued to watch the namboodiri. Despite the large paunch, the priest bent down and dunked the brass pot into the pond, rather effortlessly.

"Say hello to Vishwanathan," he heard his mother say.

Reluctantly, Ray turned around, and sized up the thin, lean figure standing next to his mother; it was the village astrologer he had seen at the house. Vishwanathan tousled his long flowing beard, and in the same flow, put his hair up and tied it into a neat bun.

"Namaskaram, namaskaram," Vishwanathan greeted Ray, looking at him keenly. "Verrrry tall, now," he said, and clicked his tongue, and giggled.

"Is everything ready?" she interrupted.

"We must wash feet, first," said Chandrasekhar, as he walked past them towards the pond, gesturing them to follow.

They crossed the namboodiri who was on his way back with the gleaming vessels. Ray was quite disappointed when he saw the pond -- a collection of water in a well of rock that resembled a shallow frying pan. A coconut shell lay beside it, which Chandrasekhar took and filled it with water. He gestured to Revathi to remove her slippers and get onto a flat rock next to the pond. She lifted her sari above the ankles and rubbed her feet together, as Chandrasekhar poured the water. Ray had already figured that the pond overflowed over the brim at one corner, and the trickle flowed down the hill just to the left of the steps from where they had come up. After Revathi, it was his turn to wash his feet. He followed suit, but did it himself, and rubbed his feet together. Even after washing his feet, they were stained red from the color from the soil. He sat down on his haunches, beside the pond and peered into the clear water.

"Can you hurry up, Ray," he heard his mother say, but he was engrossed, peering deeper into the water. At first tiny little tadpoles scurried around; suddenly he felt as if his eyes were out of focus; an image was forming on the surface of the water. First, he thought he was seeing his reflection, but as the image became clearer, it certainly did not look like him. When it steadied, he let out a gasp. A pair of deep-set brown doe-like eyes set over high cheekbones, and a full mouth, stared at him. Her golden curls over a perfectly cutout oval face, and round head, fluttered, as if the wind was causing it. Her lips moved in slow motion as though she was speaking to him. Then he began to hear garbled and incoherent chatter as though someone was playing a tape at a faster speed. He looked over his shoulder, wondering where the sounds were coming from, and, then, looked down again; the water was still and the tadpoles darted around; the mysterious image had vanished.

His knees became hollow and felt goose pimples forming; he turned around and looked towards the temple. He saw his mother scurrying towards him. A wailing sound carried forth by the wind laced with the aroma of moist ferrous earth filtered through the tendrils; rustling in the leaves just below him, brought out only a large cat, which he assumed to be of the priest. He was scared to look again into the pond, and was about to run towards the temple, when he heard as if someone had sucked water out with great force -- like a sink emptying out when you pull the plug. He turned to look; his heart skipped a beat, and his mouth went dry. The pond was empty; he slowly extended his hand out and felt the surface. It was bone dry!

Ray turned around and ran towards the temple. He hopped, trying to avoid the small sharp pebbles that pricked his long feet, having forgotten his shoes near the pond. As he stared into the clear cloudless sky, and looked over the horizon, the ocean of green coconut palms interspersed with buttons of red tiled roofs was growing darker as the sun was ready to take its final plunge; and the hues of pink began to fade into the deepening azure.

The verandah floor was cold, but the stone was so soothing to his feet, more like a cushion, after the run across. He put his hands on his hips and waited for a moment to regain his breath, scanning the interiors. Light brown rectangular timber beams interlocked with slotted crossbeams, ran around the verandah. Two perfectly round beams carved at their ends, stood erect at either side of the open doorway, resting on a three feet high parapet that ran around the temple. An eager, yet patient spider lurked above the door that led to the sanctum sanctorum. It was a large one, the size of his palm, possibly, reflecting sort of a complex weave of his own life now.

"Right foot first," he heard his mother say, as he entered.

"Na, na…," the priest said, gesturing him to stay out. Revathi, who was seated cross legged on the floor, opposite the priest, got up and came out.

"I completely forgot. You need to wear your mundu. It's lying over there," she said, pointing to the parapet on which a plastic bag lay. He quickly got into his mundu, which he had been practicing wearing since morning.

Revathi entered with folded hands chanting something under her breath. Ray followed, careful to put his right foot first.

"Aaa... chooo...," he sneezed. The smell of burning oil mixed with incense and camphor seemed to be the culprit. His eyes smarted as he tried to survey the interior.

"Good sign," said Vishwanathan with a giggle and stuck his tongue out. He sat, cross-legged, to the left of the deity, and went back to chanting some incoherent words, continuing to stroke his long flowing beard.

Chandrasekhar nodded as if seconding the inference. He sat beside Ray looking quite pleased with himself with that fixed smile on his face. Ray looked at the statue trying to figure out the form. As his eyes adjusted to the dim light, the figure became clearer. The deity was made of black stone, carved into a shape of a menacing looking female, with eyes popping out as if she were about to spew fire out of them, and her tongue was stretched out with menacing ferocity. Pink and white flowers, which he had seen while climbing up, lay at the deity's feet, and streaks of red paste lined her forehead. The flickering flames coming from the two oval shaped stone cups – oil lamps -- carved into the stone on either side of the deity, bathed the room in a dull eerie glow. Ray looked at the priest who was engrossed in filling water into each of the polished brass bowls, arranged in a semi-circle in front of the deity. Tiny beads of sweat had formed on his bald head and were now trickling down his sides. With a wave of his hand, he gestured Ray to come and sit next to him. Ray looked at his mother, but she had her eyes closed, hands folded in prayer. Vishwanathan, too, sat with his eyes closed, as if in deep concentration, and had cupped his right palm to the ground as if he were hiding something under it. A chessboard like pattern drawn out of white chalk was on the floor in front of him. Suddenly his mouth began to twitch, and he started talking to himself, as if in conversation with someone. His eyes opened, and eyeballs disappeared, leaving behind fiery red pupils. Then his cupped palm began to rotate; the sound of rustling marbles being ground against each other grew louder as his movement picked up speed. The whole scene was hypnotic, as Vishwanathan's head began to shake, and his neck stretched out as if he were in pain. The head began to shake even faster, his torso remaining quite stiff; there was some synchronicity in the two actions – the shake of the head and the rotation of the palm. The priest had started chanting some prayers, which was familiar to Ray. He was now adding different colored powders into their respective bowls; red one first, followed by orange, yellow, saffron, and lastly, white. After every spoonful of powder, the priest took some water in a spoon from each of the bowls and put it into a steel plate next to him. The grinding sound was now lost in the din of the chanting, which it seemed to have reached a crescendo. Vishwanathan's thin and bony structure began to perspire, glistening in the yellow incandescence; now his upper body was gyrating. The cupped hands suddenly stopped rotating; with lightning speed, he grabbed a handful of the contents and set them aside. The marbles turned out to be pea-pod sized shells. The chanting also stopped. The priest removed five incense sticks from the packet, and lit a match to light them. Once lit, he placed them on the deity, tucking them into spaces between the hand and the torso. He adjusted the wicks on the lamps, and suddenly the room became brighter. Vishwanathan was busy counting the shells that he had set aside. He muttered something into Chandrasekhar's ear, which he seemed to have acknowledged with a furious nod. He placed the shells one at a time on the checkered board, and then appeared to be talking into the board; he opened his eyes for a moment, looked towards Ray, and gave a blank stare. Suddenly Vishwanathan rattled off in Malayalam, directing the words to the priest, who sat up erect, and then leaned forward as if to catch what the astrologer was saying. He kept nodding in acknowledgement, each time Vishwanathan paused, and towards the end, he frowned deeply and his eyebrows furrowed. Then he responded, as if it were an answer or a solution to something Vishwanathan had said.

"Do whatever has to be done," said Revathi, and turned to Chandrasekhar. "Tell him, please."

"There is no remedy!" said Chandrasekhar softly.

"But didn't the namboodiri say something just now?"

"Oh, that is only a '*mana shanti homam*' (a ritual performed for mental peace)"

"Well, then at least do that," she said.

Ray felt very sad. He realized how desperate his mother was, but he chose to keep quiet.

"Vishwanathan says that there is no evil spirit inside your son. He was born with some past-life karma, and a soul from that life is in contact with his soul. It will vanish on its own. The next puja is for Anahita that has been pending for many years."

Ray assumed that Anahita was his deceased sister's name. He seemed to understand what Chandrasekhar had just said and looked at Revathi as if to say, *see I told you, everything is all right.* It made sense with what was going on in his life, but the explanation was nowhere helping him in his quest for making contact!

The priest discussed something with Chandrasekhar, and then all three of them looked at their watches.

"Let's finish it now," said Revathi.

First, the priest asked Ray to extend his hands out onto the brass plate. He poured three spoons of water over his hands and then tied a red cotton thread around Ray's right wrist. He did the same for the two others. Then, he dipped the finger, next to the little finger, into the five different colored powders and applied it on Ray's forehead while chanting some *mantras*. The same he applied to Revathi and Chandrasekhar. The chanting continued as the ritual progressed. The room was becoming stuffy. Sweat poured down Ray's face; Revathi's face glistened in the fading glow, and she kept wiping it with the end of her sari. The whole thing lasted for more than an hour. The bowls of water were now full of Tulsi leaves. To Ray's astonishment, when he took out the leaves, the color of water in each of the bowls was brown. The priest showed it to Revathi and Chandrasekhar, and began to fill water from each of the bowls into a stainless steel container of the size of a cup. He added some of the leaves and colored powder into it, and shut it tightly. An exchange of words between Vishwanathan and the priest marked the end of the ritual. Ray's eyes oscillated between the priest and Vishwanathan, as Vishwanathan reached out for the container, his hands shaking so vigorously that Ray thought he might drop it. His flaming red eyes were almost popping out; instead of the effeminate and affable look, his face was contorted. He quickly took the container and set it down as if he had held something very hot. The priest sprinkled some holy water onto Vishwanathan, a bit of it falling on Chandrasekhar and Revathi. They bowed in prayer. Ray thought he heard the little container rattle!

CHAPTER 10

A gentle breeze, carrying the delicate scents of rich infinitely sweet distillation of the monsoon night, vaporized the sweat beads off Ray's hands and face, as he stepped out of the temple. A symphony of crickets filled the air; fireflies flooded the foliage impregnating a silvery sheen onto the rain soaked leaves. The moon was conspicuous by its absence, making the night even darker, and the glowing diamonds to glow even brighter. Under the blanket of countless stars, they made their way towards the steps. Ray's knees felt hollow; he clutched his mother's sari, tightly, as he looked into the dark stony bowl where he had seen the image. Led by Chandrasekhar with torch in one hand and the container in the other, their descent was much faster. As they got off the narrow path onto the main road, Chandrasekhar turned left.

"But we have to go that way," said Ray, pointing in the opposite direction.

"A small puja needs to be performed," said Chandrasekhar, and cleared his throat. He lifted his mundu and wiped his face with one corner. "This has to be sprinkled inside," he said, showing the container that now hung from his hip having tied it to his mundu.

"Can't we do it tomorrow?" said Ray.

"We must follow the orders of the priest," said Chandrasekhar, his voice filtering through the gurgle of the stream that flowed beneath the bridge they were crossing. "Under Vishwanathan's prescription..."

"Isn't it strange, Chandrasekhar-etan," (etan, being the suffix when addressing an elder brother or even an older person) said Revathi, "that they call it a prescription. So scientific."

"Oh yes," he said. "We are very lucky, you know; Vishwanathan is a very busy man."

Except for the sound of the water flowing through, into the paddy fields, it was impossible to make out what was on either side of the road. Very soon, they turned right, onto a narrow footpath. An outline of a large tree was visible, and it became larger and larger as they neared. The long and sinuous vines hung low, almost touching the ground. The Milky Way streaked across the sky lacing the sky with its effervescent tendrils of plasma. Ray continued to feast on the sight as he stared into the moonless cavern.

"This is the Panniyur temple," Revathi said.

"Your father, Mr. Paul Robinson, came here on Wednesday, 27th day of February 2000 at 7.05 p.m, on his thirty second birthday," said Chandrasekhar.

"2500 years old, isn't it?" Ray said, continuing to stare into the firmament. "How do you know?"

"Why, on our morning walks, Rajan uncle brings me all the way here. He prays and then turns back."

"So you know it has one of the few Varaha idols in the country?"

"You mean the pig Avatar (life form) of Vishnu," said Ray.

"I didn't know your morning walk was more of an educational tour," said Revathi, as they came to a stop. The large tree was to their right, while the main gate of the temple was in front.

"Careful, there are thorns," said Chandrasekhar, when he saw Revathi turn right. The dull beam of his torch guided her along a narrow pathway towards the tree.

Ray watched his mother, as she stopped in front of the base of the tree. She crossed her feet, then she crossed her hands; with the left, she held her right ear; with the right, she held the left ear. The scene became funnier as she began to bend her knees and then stand up, almost like half-hearted sit-ups. He counted five sit-ups.

"She is praying to Lord Ganesha," Chandrasekhar said, as he gestured Ray to follow him.

The narrow wooden, wicket gate creaked as Chandrasekhar pushed it open. The chirping of the crickets stopped, and an eerie silence pervaded this dark, moonless night. Only when the kirr…kirr… stopped did Ray realize how quiet it could get. Chandrasekhar hopped over into the compound; Ray tried to copy him, He fell forward through the gate, and sprawled onto the ground, face down.

His head began to throb as if someone was beating drums into his ears. *You are following my Masters;* a voice filled his mind. A sudden burst of warm air replaced the cool air and the throbbing also stopped.

"Ouch," said Ray, rubbing his forehead, as he tried to get up. Revathi and Chandrasekhar were looking down on him. He suddenly got up, brushing the mud off his mundu, and looked at his mother.

"How can you be so careless?" said Revathi, sharply. "Didn't you hear what Vishwanathan said? You are prone to head injuries."

Ray chose to keep quiet, as he was not sure whether he really heard the voice or was he imagining. He touched his forehead as if to reaffirm that he had really fallen down. A little bump had formed, but the pain seemed to have disappeared as if it had come with the voice and gone away with it.

The sound of a dog howling seemed to have given some sort of signal to Chandrasekhar, as he started. He quickened his pace soon after he heard the last of the seven howls. The dull white of the walls filtered through the darkness. The three-storied pagoda like tiled roof sprung out from behind the wall, which presumably was the sanctum sanctorum.

Chandrasekhar stopped, turned towards a small temple-like hut, and bowed in obeisance. Revathi followed suit, and then they carried on. They came to the front of the temple, which had a large patch of open-ground in front. A large wooden gate somewhat similar to the front gate seemed to lead out of the compound. To the right, within the compound, was another temple structure, larger than the one they had passed. The square structure with sloping tiled roof had a small porch in front covered by a tiled roof supported by round wooden columns resting on a parapet. The main wall blocked off the inner sanctum, from which a platform ran across the whole breadth of the courtyard. A sloping tiled roof supported by round wooden columns covered the platform. Outside was an open courtyard, demarcated by a black stone parapet, and in-between was six-foot high structure, which Ray assumed to be a multitude of lamps carved from black rock. In no time, he counted 108 lamps. The door to the inner courtyard was shut, and the dark grey shadow of darkness did not help in revealing any more detail. Chandrasekhar moved on to the temple to their right. Instead of a covered porch, a parapet lined the sides in front, with an opening in the middle. In the centre, there was a lamp, much smaller than the main one, and it had sixty-three wicks. The last few wicks flickered in their dying moments, as if waiting for the trio, and, then went off. Thin wooden bars placed across the opening into the sanctum, cast a checkered pattern on the grassy patch as the orange glow from inside became brighter.

"Someone is inside," Ray whispered.

"It must be the temple priest," said Chandrasekhar, ducking his head repeatedly trying to get a glimpse. Mumbling under his breath, he went to the back of the temple and appeared very soon from the other side, and repeated this a few more times. Ray joined him for the next four rounds, and found nothing exciting in the whole process.

"Now what do we do?" said Revathi, who joined them in the last round, and seemed to be thoroughly enjoying the temple tour.

"Never mind, we'll do the puja," said Chandrasekhar, as he gave one last bow and retreated out of the narrow courtyard.

Just in front of the main temple, towards the far corner near the gate, Chandrasekhar pointed to a mound that resembled a ship's deck narrowing down to almost a spike at the end. Like a sore thumb, it emerged out of the backdrop of whispering trees shooting out of boulders of igneous rock. Almost ten feet high, and twenty feet long, the mound of mud and rock lay frozen in time with battered slabs of stone lying scattered beneath. They walked to it, only to find it even more dilapidated. A jagged terraced slope extended almost halfway along the length; and the mound had caved in after that, giving it the deck like appearance.

"You guys go up," said Revathi, staring at this crumbling edifice.

"No, no, no, only Mr. Ray can go," said Chandrasekhar, clicking his tongue with a vigorous shake of his head, as if the mere suggestion was sacrilegious.

Ray took a step, which seemed to have set off a mini avalanche as a football sized stone along with mud and gravel came rolling down, landing near his feet. Undeterred, he clawed his hands into the soil and began his climb.

"Here, take this," he heard Chandrasekhar shout, but refused to look back having established a firm foothold.

"But what does he have to do up there?"

"Just *springle* this water on the ground."

"That's hardly a puja," said Revathi, and sighed.

"Sometimes it is better not to question the higher power," said Chandrasekhar. "Look at this boy."

Ray reached out his hand, and his right foot slipped. Suddenly he felt a jolt, as if someone was pushing him up; his loose hand regained the grip of a piece of rock firmly embedded into the ground. Aided by the firm foothold, he was literally hoisted up. For a moment, he lay sprawled on his stomach on the high platform while he regained his breath. He got up and tried to dust his mundu, but found himself slapping his bare thighs. He looked down, and saw Chandrasekhar still holding the urn out.

"I've lost my mundu," he shouted.

"Shhh…. I'm not deaf. Do you want your pant?"

"Just give me that pot," he said feeling quite relaxed after the climb. He positioned himself at the edge flat out on his stomach, and leaned over, stretching his arm out and to his surprise, Revathi managed a foothold and reached out the urn to him. He felt the steel handle and clenched his fist, securing the handle. Getting back onto his feet, he turned around and surveyed the deck. He shivered involuntarily as a wisp of unusually cool air blew across the mound.

"It's so cold here," he shouted down. The wind seemed to carry his voice over the top into the mysterious contours of the landscape through the quivering vines, over the top of the heads of his two relatives as he surveyed the landscape from his vantage point. He had this strong feeling that someone was watching him, following his every move as he looked beyond the gate and over the crumbling boundary wall. Scattered amongst the black patches of rock embedded into the ruddy remains of volcanic dust, were tall lanky trees with large leaves. Climbing steadily into the distance the landscape was lost in the cover of darkness. He quickly looked away, and his eyes fell on a black patch at the far narrow end of the mound; tightening the grip on the urn, he walked towards it. Suddenly the air around him turned warm, and he began to sweat profusely. As if in a trance, he made his way to the black patch. As soon as he reached there, he saw it was a little pool of water filled into a concavity. So perfect was the roundness that it was completely out of place on the dilapidated mound. Again he shivered as he felt a blast of cool air, as if he had just walked into the cold section of a supermarket. He looked down into the water, and only saw his own face staring back at him. But, the next moment, the face began to morph into that of a girl. The same image that he had seen in the pond on the hill was staring at him—those golden curls, the button nose and large doe-like eyes. Then a beacon of light began to radiate from the mirror, and shot up into the sky as if one had sent up a laser beam. A piercing pain ripped through the centre of his head, right down to his feet. He suddenly found himself immersed in the translucent tunnel of light that now flowed in constancy from the mirrored pool of water up into eternity. A white ball of light was hurtling towards him. Blinded by the glare, he covered his face. The ball seemed to hit him, but nothing happened. Suddenly, he felt an unusually cold draft of air sting his face, and then a burst of warm air replaced it. He saw tentacles of gas and dust spewing out from a gleaming white central disc, which slowly transformed into a hollow disk, acquiring a reddish hue, and started to float towards him. As it came closer, it began to elongate, and then, suddenly, a human form confronted him, like a projection in space floating in the background of the stars. Then he heard the words reverberate in his mind, *open your palms and hold them out and ask Master to release me to your world.* It had a tone of finality and accomplishment. He followed the instructions and did just that, his words swept away by the whispering wind that now was building up speed. No sooner had he straightened his palms out, he felt a sudden draft of cold air and he squeezed his eyes shut, as if to avoid the cold draft. When he opened his eyes, he looked straight down into the pool. The mirror was just a puddle of still water and the yellow sheen of the urn bobbing in the water caught his eye.

He tried to turn, but his whole body was numb; his limbs just didn't respond.

"Ray, Ray, Ray…," he heard Revathi's anxious voice echoing through the eerie mist of darkness. It was lost in a loud gurgle, as if a sink full of water was emptying. This time, he managed to turn, and then dragged his feet to the wider edge and jumped off. Landing on soft ground, he was fortunate not to have hurt himself. He didn't find anyone around and ran to the other side, where his mother and his uncle were gazing in pregnant silence towards the top of the mound.

"I saw a gho…st," he said, burying his face in his hands. "I…I… swear I saw ---."

He suddenly hugged his mother tightly and whispered into her ear, "Did she have golden curls, and eyes like yours?"

He felt her body stiffen and heard her take the name of Master. Then she wrenched herself free. "RAY, are you alright?" she almost screamed, her words swallowed by the gathering storm.

"Where is the vessel," he heard Chandrasekhar say, as if he were least concerned about the happenings.

"I don't know."

"Now we should proceed for home," said Chandrasekhar. "We'll collect the vessel tomorrow."

Without looking back the trio walked back home. The memory of the event seemed to fade away by the time they reached the house. Not a word was spoken; even Chandrasekhar didn't mention the *vessel*.

CHAPTER 11

Lights still went off frequently, like tonight. The old inverter, which Chandrasekhar so proudly maintained and controlled, had used up its four hour quota of battery life by the time Ray went to bed. He climbed up onto his bed, which had four round carved posts and a wooden frame holding them together at the top. The yellow glow of the hurricane lantern cast an eerie shadow of the bottle of water that rested on the bedside table. He gazed at the shadow falling on the ceiling, pressing the small of his back on the flat and hard cotton mattress; every bone in his body ached; he didn't even have the energy to turn, but his eyes refused to close.

"Creee...aak...," he heard the solid wooden door close, downstairs. Continuing to stare at the ceiling, he could make out the hairline cracks in the yellowing plaster. Just over the wooden door, something moved. It was a spider, as large as his palm. Wrapped in its own web it was moving with careless abandon, as if it were spelling the state of Ray's own situation. The aroma of moist earth suddenly pricked his nostrils. He turned over onto his stomach, and looked out of the large window. The long and thick round bars of the window, weathered over time, danced in and out of focus as he gazed into the dead of night. The wind was in the trees, rippling the large oval leaves of the jackfruit tree, stirring the branches that kissed the sloping tiled roof outside the window. He got out of bed and tiptoed to the windowsill. Pushing his face between two bars, he looked up into the sky searching for the stars, hoping he would recognize some of them – always a favorite pastime whenever he was in a new place. A graying translucence hid the spectacle from view, and was an intimation of the rain gods. Taking a deep breath, he swallowed volumes of the fresh and fragrant air filled with the essence of moist earth mixed with a faint smell of cow dung. Through the humid moistness, he surveyed the surroundings, below. Nothing seemed to have changed as if time had stood still since his last visit almost ten years ago. The century old mango tree, as old as the house, still stood solidly, its branches kissing the sloping Mangalore tiles that formed the roof of the verandah running all round the house. Weathered under the harsh summers and violent storms, the roof of the haystack, made from intricately woven leaves of coconut palms supported by wooden logs, stared at him with careless abandon. Straight ahead on the slope, to his right was a little hut, which everyone called the temple, where a cock was sacrificed every year to ward off evil spirits. An involuntary shiver went down his spine as he continued to gaze into the dense tropical foliage interspersed with tall and lanky palms of coconut and areca nut. He went back to his bed, but a lingering doubt of something not so right prevented him from shutting his eyes. The face in the pond, the voice that spoke to him, the spooky events on the mound, all this was just too much for him to digest. He lay on his stomach with his chin resting on the back of his palms. He bit into his lower lip with his two rather large front teeth, and raised his eyebrows as if he were looking out of the window. The sound of the moments ticking away became fainter and fainter, as his mind wandered through the events of the evening. The bars of the window erupted into a sensuous dance of sinuous grace, and the next moment he was staring at a shimmering ball of light. Once his eyes were accustomed to the brightness, he made it out to be a perfect sphere. He stood on the opposite side of a lake, admiring this piece of perfect architecture. Somehow, it was alive, charged with energy about to take off. The shadow of the sphere fixed itself onto the calm and placid waters of the lake. He looked up again, and was just in time to see someone enter it; the golden curls was all that he made out of the silhouette, which was now swathed in a ruddy incandescence reflecting off the sphere. A blinding flash of light, and it was gone; a cool spray of water slapped his face carried forth by the whining wind. As if someone had wiped an image off a screen, the blackened bars of the window appeared before him. He got up on his knees and threw his duvet off. Staring through the cast iron grill, he wondered whether his mind was playing tricks as rain poured down in thunderous abandon. He got up and walked up to the window, and held the bars with both his hands, just to feel that they were real. Squeezing his face between the bars, his eyes wandered into the blurry night, as if searching for the sphere; and then he reached out to get a grip on the wooden shutter. Before he could do get hold of it, an ominous rumble followed by a thunderous roar shook the very foundations of the house. He cupped his ears and staggered back from the window, feeling the rain soaked sleeves against his face. The steady sound of falling water over the tin awning just above the window was his only source of comfort. And then, lightning lashed down like a whip, gorging its way through the bars. He blinked, expecting the blazing night to come back to its original calm. The flash was still there but an orange hue tinged the whiteness. He waited for the thunder, which did not come, and the orange glow faded away. As if someone had turned off a tap, the steady stream of water was reduced to a trickle and then to drops. He still waited for the thunder; the drops even had stopped as he gazed outside, standing a couple of feet away from the window with his hands on his hips. His bare feet were now feeling the moistness on the floor. Quickly stepping back onto his bed he lay down in the same position, and shivered involuntarily. The contours of darkness and the 'kirr...kirr' of the crickets filtered in through the bars. The dream still uppermost in his mind didn't seem to frighten him, but the absence of thunder was more bizarre.

$$\mathcal{D} \quad \mathcal{D} \quad \mathcal{D}$$

"Creeeee...aak," the familiar sound stirred him out of his morning meditation that he was struggling to get into, as he sat on his bed with his back resting against the head rest. Numbed by the connection he was making with the face in the pond and the spooky happenings at the mound, he just could not get himself to move from his position. A heaviness in the chest, and a lump in his throat persisted as the image of the girl was becoming more and more engrained into his mind. The sound of the metal knockers hitting against the polished jackfruit wood doors with greater force made him open his eyes. Slowly he got himself to sit at the edge of the bed with his legs dangling down. He looked at his watch, and, then, out of the barred window; it was still quite dark; plop...plop..., the first sounds of raindrops falling on the tiled roof indicated the coming of another heavy downpour. He tried to stand up, but his ankle really hurt, and sat down heavily on the bed, again.

Was it all just a dream, he thought, but the face of the girl was just too vivid, for him to discard it from his mind and pass it off as a dream. Above the din in his mind, he heard animated voices coming from the stairwell, followed by fading footsteps down the wooden stairs. He hobbled to the clothes stand in the corner and put on his collared white T-shirt and a grey cotton track pant that he had earned when he had played Tennis for Oxford while doing his Masters in Astrophysics. Flicking the switch, the tube-light flickered, and then suddenly the room was filled with a white incandescence. He straightened his stiff, thin, hair with his hand; slightly curled with a reddish tinge, his hair had never encountered a comb. He stroked his face and felt his three day old stubble. His large blue eyes were bloodshot, but he was even more appalled when he saw the color of his skin. The rosiness had given way to pallor, and dark circles had formed under his eyes. He shook his head to ward of the disturbing thoughts as he looked at his muscular hands -- the more red than wheatish complexion had also dulled. He quickly switched off the light and made his way downstairs for that much needed cup of tea, tiptoeing down the wooden stairs, lest he disturbed his aunt who slept on a cot under the staircase. Exiting the room at the bottom of the stairs, he walked into the central open courtyard -- a traditional architectural feature of a Kerala family home called the 'Nalukettu'. Some larger homes had two such courtyards, which was called the Ettukettu'. The Nalukettu was surrounded by the dining room to the right and the eclectic wood fired kitchen was straight ahead. On the platform, to the left of the courtyard, the small oil lamp still glowed, as if it had never got extinguished since his last visit. The framed photo-painting of Goddess Saraswati playing the Veena, was exactly in the same place, bathed in the dull glow of the sooty flame. Shanta – Chandrasekhar's wife -- was putting the cups and a thermos full of tea onto the rectangular dining table made of solid jackfruit wood. The clock struck five times, and he headed to fetch his cup of tea. He towered over her looking down onto her loosely plaited grey hair; he got the whiff of soap and freshness. Dressed in the traditional two piece clothing, pure white with a green border, and her forehead anointed with a ritualistic grey powder called bhasmam, she was all set for the long day ahead. Her hands were steady as she poured out his tea; and said something in Malayalam, which was difficult to catch; he acknowledged it with a smile and a nod. Taking his cup, he stretched out on the parapet-- a wooden platform with a backrest that formed the sides of the courtyard. He leaned against the intricately carved round, wooden pillars that extended from the platform to the sloping tiled roof. As the grey light of dawn funneled into the courtyard, he craned his neck out to look up into the sky. Dark clouds were gathering, moving fast; in no time they covered the courtyard, and it was dark again. A bolt of lightning lashed down as if it were lunging for him; he tried to shield the flash with his hand. He forgot he had the cup, and it fell into the courtyard.

The sound of breaking china was swallowed by the roar of thunder -- the loudest he had ever heard. He literally jumped off the seat. Then it poured with even greater ferocity, funneled through the four channels that sloped down from the roof to bring all the roof water into the courtyard. Ray put his hand out to feel the gush of water as it fell off one of the channels. It was as if a ton of weight pushed his hand down, and he quickly withdrew it. He got up to help himself to another cup of tea, when he looked out. To his surprise, the water level in the courtyard had risen, threatening to come into the house. "Don't worry, Mr. Ray; water will not overflow," he heard Chandrasekhar say as he walked into the dining room.

Dressed in his white kurta and mundu, he too had anointed his forehead with bhasmam. The closely cropped hair, almost to the point of baldness, exposed his round cranium, and made his cheek bones and jaw line even more prominent on his elf like face. His hands were very thin like two sticks sticking out of his oversized kurta. Ray was amazed at the way he walked so fast, as he shuffled his feet over the polished black stone floor. Chandrasekhar stopped at the far end, opposite the dining area, and began to pray in front of the platform. Kneeling down he uttered some prayer under his breath, then continued his walk, still muttering his prayers. Ray helped himself to another cup of tea when the clock struck again. Soon after, Shanta arrived with an aluminum pot, sat on the parapet, tucked the urn between her folded legs, and began to churn the buttermilk. The daily routine seemed to revolve around the strikes of this clock, which must have been as old as the house. Chandrasekhar scurried out, chanting his prayers, without even an acknowledgement. Ray found it odd; he continued to sit on the parapet, and watched the level slowly fall as the rain began to slow down and then abruptly stop.

"By the way, when you go for your walk, don't forget the namboodiri's urn?" Revathi said, as she came out into the courtyard. She was wearing a simple green bordered white cotton two piece mundu. "And please get me one dozen coconuts."

"One dozen!" said Ray.

"Yes," said Revathi, and disappeared into the kitchen. Ray collected his thoughts and went out to join Chandrasekhar for the morning walk.

Chandrasekhar, with his umbrella tucked under his arm was plucking Tulsi leaves from the shrub that was, probably, as old as the house. It was in the centre of the six inch wide, square platform, which Ray had helped to white wash.

Ray took a deep breath as he gingerly set foot on the soft moist ground; the lingering aroma of jasmine flowers that lay scattered on the ground was so refreshing.

"Let us go; otherwise we'll be late. Your mother wants us to collect the vessel also."

He lifted his mundu and folded it just above his knees, and climbed back onto the verandah. He appeared from the portico, which jutted out from the verandah eastwards. Its open doorway was exactly in line with the long driveway that led to the gate.

"The coconuts!" Revathi shouted from inside, as Ray hurried to join his uncle.

Walking down the gentle slope Ray looked up, only to find Chandrasekhar almost halfway up the drive, near the narrow gate that led to the pool on his left. The driveway was lined by crumbling blocks of porous stone that was actually once a five feet wall. Moss and weed grew out of the crevices. On the right were coconut palms, other tropical fruit trees, including Ray's favorite star fruit tree. They were planted on raised ground, in line with the top of the wall. Ray looked over the wall to his left and his eyes fell on the *madham* or puja room. He shifted his gaze as the house gave him the creeps after hearing the story of one of his mother's uncle shooting himself in this place. The branches of the tamarind trees from the right and the jackfruit trees from the left leaned over the driveway forming a rather decorative ceiling all along. Ray reached the point where he loved to lean over the wall and look down into the pool. It was a drop of around fifty feet, and had jumped from this point, many a times. The pool was actually the quarry site from where the stones for building the house were taken. A natural spring kept the pool filled with fresh water, and the fishes inside were the natural scavengers doubling up as filters. It was so refreshing to swim in this water; it felt much lighter and the absence of chlorine gave that sense of freshness.

Ray looked down into the greenish haze, and saw the fish rise up to the surface to scout for their morning snack. A silvery blue and white kingfisher waited in pregnant silence on the makeshift diving board much nearer to the surface, twitching its neck ready to pounce on its equally alert prey. The diving board was a narrow block of stone that sprung out of the murky waters from the west bank to the centre; this divided the pool into two zones – the far end was for the ladies and the one nearer to the wall was where the gents bathed. The deep green waters looked so inviting, but he was distracted by a splash in the pool. The ripples of green water radiated outwards from the ladies section. The familiar sound of clothes being bashed around on the stones laid out especially for that deterred him. The ripples moved forward and a body floated face-down with flailing arms, the head bobbing up for gasps of air. He didn't have the energy to face any strange faces in pools of water. He felt a bit sick and climbed down. He turned to see a girl, probably a few years older than him, dressed in a green blouse and a cream mundu, which may have been white, originally, walk past. She looked over her shoulder, and giggled, her thick jet-black hair with tiny curls, falling like a curtain right down to her knees. Holding a rather full load of clothes in a bucket tucked under one arm, she must have been heading for the pool. It was not really a swimming pool but a place where few select villagers connected with the house, and the inmates, had a bath, swam, as well as washed clothes here. The sound of the battering of the clothes started echoing through the valley, and the Kingfisher flew up onto a coconut palm. Ray broke into a run and caught up with Chandrasekhar, who had just stepped out of the gate. He was in serious conversation with a much older looking man. Bare bodied, his dark skin was wrinkled and his breasts sagged. His jaw moved as if he were chewing something, possibly because he had no teeth. He lowered his checked mundu and adjusted his turban made out from a rather dirty piece of cloth. Their chatter stopped as soon as Ray reached them; he looked at Ray and gave a wide smile. His round dark eyes widened looking into Ray's, eyes; and the wrinkles became even deeper. He somehow sensed that the man knew of his agony and turmoil and was trying to read his mind.

Ray quickly looked away, and started off. "Who was he?"

"Oh! That was the 'Pattra'."

"What's that?"

"The village soothsayer!"

"What was he saying?"

"He was talking nonsense."

"I thought he said something about me;" Ray paused, "Or was it about Anahita?"

Chandrasekhar did not to reply, and they choose to walk in silence down the slope.

"What exactly happened? I know she was kidnapped and was never found." Chandrasekhar stumbled, but Ray caught him in time. "Your mother has not told you anything?" He looked at Ray who saw the flushed look, and shook his head furiously.

Though it was five thirty in the morning, the village was quite alive. Men and Women were rushing for their baths to the temple tank, which was a similar pool as the one at the house, but twice as large.

"Didn't you hear thunder, last night," Ray asked, looking down at the ground. He decided to leave Anahita's topic for the time being.

"Ha...ha...; sometimes these pujas create illusions, and bring out bad dreams."

Ray was not satisfied with the explanation. "I thought these rituals are supposed to heal us."

"You mustn't think of these things. The more you go after it, the more you'll get influenced."

A passerby stopped Chandrasekhar who just nodded in a non committal fashion and continued onwards. They turned off onto the main arterial road that ran from the entrance of the village on the south to the other end on the north leading to the river bank. His gaze wandered over to the hill in front, where they had gone yesterday. The outline of the temple looked rather skewed, and was more black, than grey. Like a kaleidoscope, the deep azure lightened; the scattered white cumulous clouds, just over the hills, turned deep purple, merging in with the greenery dispersed across the hill slopes. The early morning freshness percolated into his senses, lifting the veil of confusion. By the time they reached the Panniyur temple turning, the hills were bathed in an orange glow. Ray looked away and turned his attention to getting into the temple. He was relieved there was still no one in the temple grounds, as they reached the mound.

"What's happened here?" said Ray, looking at the debris of stones lying scattered on the ground. The mound was now just a small rectangular piece, as if someone had cut through the centre and detached the tapered portion. A neat slope was all that was left of the deck that he had stood on, last night.

"The ground has given way," said Chandrasekhar, in a flat voice. "The vessel?"

"It must be buried under these stones." Ray halfheartedly kicked some of the debris with his shoes. He shivered at the very thought, that it was to do with him.

"That old man we met; I think he was telling you about all this."

Chandrasekhar clicked his tongue and nodded noncommittally. "I'll get Vaman namboodiri," he said and walked towards the small temple to their right. Ray looked on, and saw him disappear through a narrow wicket gate recessed into the shrubbery. Minutes ticked by as Ray continued to search for the urn that must have lain buried beneath this debris. Just then, he heard footsteps -- urgent ones— as if Chandrasekhar had something very important to share.

"We must leave this place," he said, looking deliberately away from the mound of debris.

"You look as if YOU have seen a ghost," said Ray.

Chandrasekhar didn't respond, and bowed with his hands folded in prayer in front of the main temple. He turned around after he finished his prayer. The fear in his sunken eyes in deep sockets was apparent. Ray, for the first time was afraid. He always thought of Chandrasekhar to be unaffected by all what went on, barring an incident which he so vividly remembered, when he had visibly shown his anger towards the women of the house, calling them lice breeders. He just followed him meekly.

"Tell me, no; what's the matter?" said Ray halfheartedly, as they stopped at a small temple on the way out.

"This is the Varaha murthy -- the pig faced form of Vishnu, the God of preservation. He saves the world from drowning by holding it on the snout." He bent low and looked inside. "Can you see it?"

Ray also peered through the barred doorway, and just about recognized the form. "But you are not telling me why you are so upset."

"EVERYONE IS CRAZY," Chandrasekhar shouted at the top of his voice, at decibels far higher than he had ever heard before from anyone in the village. He shook his head furiously, and suddenly prostrated himself in front of the steps of the little temple. It was humid and the sun had made its way up over the horizon, though still shaded by the hills. Ray was sweating profusely, numbed by what was going on, especially Chandrasekhar's behavior.

"Vaman Namboodiri has fractured his leg," said Chandrasekhar, as he got to his feet. "Last night there was a very big noise and he saw sparks fly on the mound. He climbed up to check it out. When he reached the edge, the whole thing just crumbled beneath him." Chandrasekhar seemed to deliberately avoid looking at Ray. "That mound is specially made for Yakshi puja."

"What is Yakshi?"

"Bhootam – ghosts!!"

Ray's knees became hollow as they reached the gate. He was dripping with sweat, and wiped some off his brow with his fingers, creating quite a spray. "You really mean it?"

"There is something funny going on. The priest is saying the spirits are angry."

"Does he know we came here last night?"

Chandrasekhar shook his head, much to Ray's relief. "He also said that there was damage to the Bhagvathy temple."

"The one we went to last night?"

Chandrasekhar gave a perfunctory nod.

The sun was up, over the hill, tinting the fields with a yellow sheen, as they treaded back empty handed. Seven in the morning was late for this hamlet. Girls, women and boys, some dressed for school, some for work, were waiting for their respective means of transport. Girls in their traditional blouse and long skirt like a petticoat, with their hair falling loose down their backs, were watching Ray with amusement. As he passed them, they giggled, and began talking amongst themselves. An elderly lady emerged from the centre of the crowd of girls. She was wearing a plain white, sari. There was a brief exchange of words in Malayalam between Chandrasekhar and her, and then, they headed back. Suddenly, it struck Ray, that wherever they had tread last night, there was damage. Could it be sheer coincidence? He desperately wanted to go there, but it was an important day for his mother – the last major ritual after his sister's disappearance, that had been pending ever since he was born. His mind was oscillating between the events of last night and getting to the bottom of Anahita's disappearance. Twenty five years was too long a time to expect any miracles, and he was sure his mother had accepted the fact that her daughter was dead.

CHAPTER 12

It was only in the evening that Ray could escape from the house. During the day, Revathi had arranged for a feast for almost the whole village. They came in groups, ate the food served by Revathi herself, and left. Some seemed to commiserate with her, as what was evident from their facial expressions.

Dong, dong, dong…The clock struck five times as Ray was putting on his sneakers sitting on a wooden bench outside on the verandah. Clad in a pale yellow collared T shirt, on faded blue jeans, which looked as if they were about to slip down, Ray felt much fresher and clear minded, after a busy day without having time to think about the entity and its whereabouts. In no time he was out of the compound, using the back exit, down the narrow pathway. He carefully maneuvered his footfalls, hopping across sharp stones and slippery rock. Sliding his left palm along the soft carpet of moss that covered the rock face on the sides, he considered it a means to gather his equanimity. He knew where he had to go, and very soon he was climbing the arduous pathway that led to the top of the hill where they had performed the puja, last night. He reached the base of the summit where the namboodiri's house was. He didn't want to face anyone, and looked up to climb the steps. To his horror, the entire front portion had fallen down, and a heap of rubble was lying behind a clump of bushes to his right. It seemed almost impossible to reach the top, now. He surveyed the terrain, and set out to the back of the hill. It took him almost halfway down, and then a steep climb up. By the time he reached the back he was completely out of breath. He sat down on a stone and caught his breath. He looked up into the sky as he felt a wisp of cool moist air brush the sweat beads off his face. Dark menacing clouds rolled out intimations for a stormy evening. But having come so far, his resolve to climb up was there. Somehow he made it up and arrived right behind the temple. He walked around, to the front verandah. To his horror, it was in a mess. The ceiling in front had collapsed, and charred remains of the beams lay buried underneath, poking out of the broken and blackened tiles. The main wooden pillars that supported the ceiling on the doorway had been reduced to ashes. He turned around, feeling the chill as a strong breeze had begun to blow. The surroundings darkened as the first drops of rain fell on his outstretched hands. Then a sudden roar of thunder rocked the valley, and Ray stepped out of the verandah, but stopped to inspect the big stone lamp, which was as tall as him. Each of the sixty three lamps that radiated from a central post giving it an appearance of a Christmas tree, were filled with oil, and the wicks blackened at the tips. The wind became stronger and he began to shiver, his damp and soiled clothes sticking to his body. He looked up into the sky and was surprised to find cracks in the cloud cover. Walking over to the front end of the summit facing the temple, he looked over. The steps had fallen, collapsing in a heap; the mud and rock around had also been eroded, exposing a perfectly round bowl of around two feet diameter, elevated to what was presently ground level. This brought forth the image of the little girl he had seen in the water. He stared at the curvature and knelt down to feel it. It was as smooth as glass as he moved his hand over it. A knot tightened in his stomach and he felt his heart beat quicken. He got up and turned around. Over the western horizon, laced with a deep purple pink the cumulous hovered just below the emerging evening star. Suddenly, he realized that the temple was bathed in a yellow glow, and he found the source right in front of him. His knees went hollow, and his heart skipped a beat; the blinding glare of the orange flames made him stagger back. A girl in a white sarong, and a round necked white top with her back towards him seemed to be lighting the last wick of the lamp in front of the temple. Her closely cropped hair reflected the orange glow as if she had just oiled it, exposing her long slender neck that rested on rather broad shoulders.

She must be real, he told himself, and took a few steps forward. Everything of her was so perfect and alluring to him, as he stood staring, his heart beating fast. Wiping the sweat beads off his forehead with the back of his hand, he moved closer, but she didn't even flinch, which he found rather odd. He shivered involuntarily, as the wicks burning at full power flickered in the strong wind. The girl turned around. Soaked in brightness of the flames she looked unreal as if she was just a projection from the lamp. Her light brown skin glistened contrasting with the blue of her doe like eyes. She help a puja tray in one hand and had cupped her long thin fingers over a small lamp in the tray; her slim but proportioned long nose twitched; and her thin moist lips parted, as if she were about to speak. He shook his head furiously, completely befuddled by the experience

Suddenly the lamps flickered, and, then, as if someone had turned off a switch, all the wicks blew out. He looked away as his nostrils twitched at the whiff of burnt oil mixed with the scent of incense. He wiped his smarting eyes and looked ahead, only to find the girl walking to the temple. He took small but quick strides and followed her.

"Hey! Wait for me."

She spun around, and dropped the puja plate. The dull thud with a short clang made Ray stop in his tracks. And at that moment he felt a draft of cool air sting his face, and then a wave of warm air replaced it. He turned, and stared into the face of a girl; her long blue eyes had no reaction, except that her eyelids were flickering as if it was a nervous twitch.

He still felt he was dreaming. He closed his eyes and the face disappeared. Squeezing his eyes tightly, he opened them again. She was still there; there was something in her look that set her apart. He mustered the courage, and went closer. The white sarong like wrap around and a simple white top was made from a fine woven fabric, finished to perfection. Her arms were slender but muscular; the taut unblemished skin added a glow to the captivating radiance that emanated from her.

"Who are you?"

"I used to love doing this," she said in a soft but coarse voice, bending down to pick up the plate.

"What do you mean?"

"When I was here."

"No. No…" Ray was fumbling for words. "Just hang on. This cannot be?" He closed his eyes and buried his face in his hands. "Master --,"

Ray removed his hands and looked at her; the closely cropped black hair, sharp features, high cheek bones on a longish face, was completely uncharacteristic of this area.

"I told you to make a pyramid, but you went and collected large stones and scattered them across the countryside." Her thin lips parted into a smile.

"Well, we did make the pyramid," said Ray, and then he paused and looked at her, still unsure of who she was.

But, then how did she know of the pyramid? Ray's ears became hot, and tried to swallow a lump that was developing in his throat.

"A…re you really …?"

"Yes, I am really from another planet. I have come from Andrearth."

Ray stretched his hand out and felt her arm. "Aaa…" He got a strong electric shock, and withdrew is hand.

"I am sorry; I must turn off the force field around me." She set the puja plate down on the parapet, and rubbed her palms vigorously against each other.

"I had energized an area around me, for protection. We turn it on before transforming in a new place."

"Transforming?" For a moment Ray thought she would change into some other form.

"When we travel through space we convert ourselves into energy waves, and transform back to our form on ground."

Ray reached out again; this time nothing happened, but quickly withdrew his hand.

"The force field around the inner circle--" Ray paused and waited for some sort of acknowledgement. "And also the melting of the gun--"

Ray was beginning to realize that all this made no sense to her, noticing the disinterested look on her face; her light blue doe like eyes kept fluttering.

He was about to pose another question, but she interrupted his thoughts.

"I was able to sense your vibrations, as you are the only one," she paused. 'Umm… There was one more person I could make contact with."

Ray looked aghast. She had answered the very question that he was going to ask.

"Your frequencies resonate with mine, and as I came closer, the vibrations became stronger."

"Then why didn't you land, or appear, or whatever ---."

"Amongst the stones?"

Ray looked at her. "You can read my thoughts."

Her lips parted and she laughed loudly. "I don't mean to."

"You mean you were able to influence my decision of coming here.

"I told you that my Master will make it happen."

"Then, what about the face in the pond; the dream?"

"That's because I was in contact with you ever since I left. This became engrained in your mind, and got projected in certain spaces which were in resonance with my vibrations."

Ray looked at her, completely in awe, mesmerized by her beauty and radiance. "But there is no resemblance."

"With whom?"

"The face I saw."

"All that is controlled by my Masters."

"From that distance?"

"Yes. Thought has no boundaries!"

Ray looked up into the star studded firmament, and locked his fingers into one another, as if pleading with a higher power. "Master, give me the strength to deal with all this."

She laughed, drawing him out of his prayer. "Antares, my father, had visited this planet twenty-one years ago, and connected up with you."

"Did you just say Antares?" Ray's voice was reduced to a whisper.

She nodded. Ray shook his head sideways, his mind trying to make a connection with the name. Then it struck him; just the other day Dr. Masuda mentioned it in connection with him visualizing an apparition while in a coma.

"OH MY GOD!" he exclaimed loudly, loud enough for the whole village to hear; the words echoing across the valley. "The apparition…," he paused.

Deneb reached out for his hand. He moved a few steps back, more out of reflex than wanting to avoid her.

"Yes. Antares saw your father."

Ray's mind was on overdrive.

A noise overhead distracted her. "What's that?" She pointed into the sky.

He shook his head in disbelief, and went and sat down on the remains of the steps of the temple, finding it difficult to deal with this moment of truth.

"It's called an airplane. For you this might be very primitive."

"We have evolved beyond such frivolous objects of desire and conveniences. Transformation of the basic elements is not allowed."

So this is Ross's Cleopatra, Ray mumbled to himself, mentally drained and physically exhausted, to probe any further. He had many questions in his mind, except that he didn't know which one to pose first. The most baffling of all was: *how did a human form have the ability and the resilience to just float down from interstellar space?*

"Who is Cleopatra?"

A shiver went down Ray's spine. She was intercepting his thoughts.

"My mother would very much like to see you?"

"Of course not!"

"It's Okay!" said Ray.

"It is the absence of resonance among your own, which is keeping the energy levels so low."

"Then why take all this trouble to visit us." Ray got up and dusted his trousers at the back. "By the way, how long do you plan to stay?"

"I don't know." She shrugged her shoulders. "My Masters will decide."

"Why me?"

"You were the only one to have responded to our messages."

"Must be a mistake. There are so many people searching for aliens."

"My Masters don't make mistakes."

Ray noticed the firmness in her tone. To his surprise, she had started to light the wicks again; and not with any matches, but as she put her index finger close to the wick, it lighted up. He began to walk towards the lamp whose light was becoming brighter as she lit them. As he came closer, she began to walk around the lamp, but very slowly. A gentle wind was beginning to blow across, carrying forth the aroma of moist earth. The *kirr* of the crickets became louder. She began to adjust the wicks to increase the flame as Ray watched her bathed in the orange glow of firelight against the backdrop of a dark grey sky. Suddenly she held up an index finger. To Ray's horror, the finger was on fire. She held it out and giggled, like a child when it sees something new.

"Watch out. You will burn your finger," said Ray, rushing to her side and trying to get hold of her finger. She just brushed him aside with her left hand. Even the gentle push was like a hard shove, and he staggered back.

"You must be crazy. Isn't it burning you?"

She giggled and put the finger in her mouth.

Ray looked on, staying where he was, wondering what he was going to do with this girl. "Can I see your finger?"

"She removed it from her mouth and just held it out.

He came closer but stayed a good two feet away from her and inspected her finger. There was not a bruise leave alone a burn on her rather long finger. He tried to see if there were any unusual marks or characteristics that would set her apart from the Earthly humans, but he couldn't spot anything, and only noticed she had well manicured nails; her unblemished skin glistening in the firelight.

"Please, for Heaven's sake," Ray pleaded with folded hands, "do not try such stunts, here. I don't even know where to take you if something happens."

"We can heal ourselves using our internal energies!"

Suddenly a strong gust of wind, followed by lightning and then almost immediately, a thunderous roar rocked the valley and shook the ground under him. Deneb held her index finger to one of the wicks; and to Ray's amazement, that was the only one alight. Her white outfit looked as if it were dyed deep orange in the light of one wick that she had kept going with her finger placed on it. Then Ray felt a big drop of water fall on his cheek and run down. The next moment, rain fell with thunderous abandon, as if someone had turned on a tap.

"Yeeeeeeeee…aaahh…," Deneb's squeal ripped through the curtain of rain. "It feels so much like home?" her words just about audible to Ray, now as it rained harder, the drops really stinging his face. He ran into the verandah, and took shelter under a portion of the roof that was intact.

"HEY!" he called out, but she paid no heed, enjoying every moment. Suddenly he realized that the wick was still alight, but with so many shocks and surprises in such short span of time, he found it normal. Her face was bathed in the orange translucence, the drops of water running down her face were like shimmering diamonds; her closely cropped hair was golden. He just watched her. What baffled him was her familiarity with the space she was in and the fact that she seemed to have taken to lighting the lamp and arranging the puja plate as if she had done it before. He still had a nagging doubt whether she really was an alien.

What was he to do next; should he just leave her and go? Take her home? Or stay with her and extract as much information from her? His stomach churned and an involuntary shiver ran through his body. He realized he was soaking wet. He sneezed loudly, and his eyes met Deneb's; she let go of her finger and the area plunged into darkness. Only then did he realize what difference the glow of that one wick had made. The rain had reduced to a light drizzle, but the sky was almost alight with a series of bursts of lightning and thunder, illuminating the area in a white incandescence as Deneb approached him.

"Tell your mother, the locket is in the room with lots of photos. I need that."

"Huh…." Ray just stared at her, making room for her to come under the shelter, but she chose to stand out.

"What locket?"

"The one your mother gave me."

"What the hell are you talking about?"

"Your mother will know. It's behind a photo in the prayer room."

"Tell her I was destined to leave Earth."

Ray couldn't believe what he was hearing.

She turned around and walked away towards the far end, to the right of where the concave bowl was, and suddenly disappeared over the edge. He ran across, and strained his neck to look over the edge. His heart skipped a beat as his foot almost slipped under the loose earth. He caught hold of a branch and steadied himself. Adapted to the darkness, he again looked over the edge; all he saw was a rock jutting out, and below was a straight drop down into blackness.

"DENEB, Deneb," he cupped his hands around his mouth and called out. But the words seemed to be swallowed in the well of darkness.

Shivering with cold, numb in the mind after the experience, which so abruptly had come to an end, he made his way back home. The scene at the temple faded into a vague memory as he reached the bottom of hill. Doubts of it ever having taken place crept into him. Her disappearance over the cliff was also a mystery. He was sure she had not fallen over, and with her powers she could have even vanished into thin air. His stomach churned and his head throbbed, thinking about all this. He suddenly felt her presence and strained his ears to catch any noise. A shiver went down his spine and he stopped and looked back. The sound of gushing water through the narrow channels and the croaks of the frogs was all that met his ears. He looked into the sky as if seeking an answer and stared at the blanket of curdled black and grey clouds. Sniffing into the humid moistness of this surreal monsoon night, he wondered if she were right next to him. He started off, and as soon as he turned onto the main road, the faint glow of the yellow streetlights in the distance brought some equanimity back. A light moved towards him at high speed; and as it came closer he was heaved a sigh of relief; the cyclist rang his bell several times giving music to the popular film song he was singing; the tune was familiar to Ray being having heard it on the loud speakers in the village centre. The whiff of the local brew pricked his nostrils as the cyclist passed him; and the familiar sight of the village shops in the distance brought back some semblance of reality.

He turned off the main road onto the road that ran along the village temple. The sight was so breathtaking; tiny oil lamps formed a ribbon of orange incandescence all along the temple wall, resembling a string of glowing beads. He vaguely recollected his mother saying she had made the offering and he should be back well in time for the puja. All this was for celebrating the memory of his sister on her death anniversary.

Her last words reverberated in his mind, "Your mother will know," which literally made his mouth go dry.

CHAPTER 13

The porch light facing the driveway was shining like a beacon as if guiding him in as he set foot into the compound. The multitude of nocturnal sounds was just a distant murmur as he made his way into the house.

The first to greet him was Chandrasekhar. "Your mother is very concerned because of your inordinate delay." He said it as if he were reading out a letter. Then, he just resumed his walk down into the dark end of the verandah, and Ray went in to the house.

By the time Ray came out of his bath, the house was dark, except for a zero watt bulb lending a dull yellow glow to the wash basin area outside the dining room. On his way up, he put the towel on the banister to dry, and ran across the large dark hall in the centre. This portion of the house had three bedrooms, one to the left where his mother slept, the larger room in the middle was where family members who came with children, occupied; and the one to his right was another bedroom. Both had individual double wooden doors, but one could only come out into the hall from the middle room, where Ray slept.

He glanced to his left towards his mother's bedroom; a thin stream of light streaked across the black stone floor, coming through the cracks in the wooden door; he hesitated, stopped and turned wondering whether he should ask about the locket now. Before he could react, his mother opened the door. His heart missed beat as he stood staring at her. She seemed to be waiting for him, still wearing her two piece sari. Her doe like eyes were moist and red as if she had been crying. As soon as he entered she hugged him and dug her face into his chest and began sobbing. He held her tightly not knowing how to react.

"I shouldn't have ---," she said and wriggled out of his embrace.

"What's the matter?"

She wiped her face with the edge of her sari. "Twenty five years is a long time, Ray. I shouldn't have kept this secret from you," she said, looking into his eyes. "See this chain," she said feeling the gold chain she was wearing. "I had kept it to give Anahita on her birthday, but ---." She sighed as tears welled in her eyes again.

"Wasn't there a locket?"

Huh…," Revathi looked at him and then at the chain. "What locket are you talking about?" She had a faraway look in her eyes, as if she were trying to work out something. "Who told you about the *taviz?*" Her words were almost inaudible, as if she wasn't sure if she wanted him to hear this.

Ray's heart was beating fast. "Someone I met."

"Impossible," Revathi said, shaking her head. "This was the chain I wanted her to wear with the locket, instead of the black ---." She sobbed lightly, and then swallowed. "-- black threa…," she said in low voice.

Ray dug his hands into his face. "Why did I even bring this up,' he muttered to himself. Deneb's last words rang through his whole body and he felt his ears turn hot.

"Someday I had to tell you," she said, gathering her composure.

"I know what happened," said Ray, still wondering how to handle this awkward moment. "What I wanted to tell you now was about the locket."

"Even Paul doesn't know about it. I was given the locket by the police, long after she disappeared." She paused and sat down, hard, on the bed; the wooden planks under the thin mattress creaked. "What's going on, Ray?"

"Let me tell you the whole story. Maybe, then you will believe me," said Ray, seating himself on the ledge of the window sill.

"You've become so dark. And where did you get those bruises from," she said pointing to his hands. He looked at his arms, which were now much darker and thinner. There were cuts and scratches on them. One of them on his elbow really smarted.

"Must have been the fall from the Yakshi mound?" he said.

"Put some dettol."

"Forget about my bruises, Mom. Just listen." Then he thought for a moment. 'Didn't Master tell you anything?"

"He doesn't say much. I was surprised how much you both talked." She let out another yawn, and then motioned to get up, when the lights went. The room was dark, illuminated only by the faint glow of the night. Suddenly, an eerie silence settled onto the night as the whirr of the pedestal fan faded away. Even the crickets were silent. A shiver went down Ray's spine as a cool draft blew onto his back. He turned around and looked out of the barred window;

he could hear the steady drops of water falling off onto the sloping tiled roof that was in line with the window; the outline of the trees and foliage outside stood still as if frozen in time, soaking in the moistness of the monsoon night.

"I keep asking Master when I can get a closure. There was no dead body; she just vanished without a trace. Master told me it will happen." She sighed and wiped her face with her sari. "Anyway, what's your story?"

"No Mom, just get it out; let us talk about her."

"The locket issue has brought back everything, anyway." She paused and took a deep breath. "Come, sit next to me." Ray obeyed and she held his hand and squeezed it tightly.

"My first marriage was with Shashi Menon – an arranged marriage. Anahita was our first child. But Shashi used to drink a lot and my Uncle who was against this marriage brought me back home with Anahita. Shashi never bothered to come to even see us. He went off to Dubai and my Uncle took me to England for a visit during one of his lecture tours. He was a famous philosopher and Sanskrit scholar. He had also got trained in Astrology from one of the most respected teachers here. That is where I got introduced to meditation and met Master. I met Paul there who was already an abhyasi. We fell in love, and Master got us married in a couple of year's time. Paul came to spend some time here as well. Even after our marriage I could not go to England and stay; it took two years for the visa to come. And during this waiting period all this happened. Shashi had come home that day to see Anahita, for the first time after he left. I had gone to the temple. No one knows what happened as when I returned I could not find Anahita. We searched everywhere and finally informed the police. Shashi also went back to Dubai. Later I got to know he also moved to England having got a job as an archeologist."

"Where is Shashi now?" interrupted Ray.

"The last I heard he was working as a Museum curator." She took his hand. "I think he died recently."

"Relax Mom!" Ray stood up and hugged her. "Deneb will have all the answers."

Ray was surprised at what he just said. "I mean there must be some connection for the Master to facilitate and approve of this séance and encounter."

"I just need closure, and that's what I came here for. I know she is dead! I consulted my Uncle also."

"It all started after Master came home," he began, and then went on to narrate the communication he had been having followed by their arrival at Verkath.

When he finished the part where he saw her face in the pond, she interrupted, "Are you absolutely sure you went through all this?"

"Ask Master, if you don't believe me."

"That's not the point."

Ray then completed the story without interruption. By such time, his night T shirt was soaked in sweat. The lights also had come on. Revathi got up and went to the room without saying a word, but she was back rather quickly. Holding a bottle of water in one hand and a book in another she came and sat down on the bed. Ray got up and took a large gulp of water from the bottle, and almost finished the bottle.

Revathi held out a photograph. Ray took it and looked at it. It was a color picture of a little girl in jeans and a pink T shirt with a picture of Cinderella embossed on it. But there was some familiarity, not just familial, but the golden curls and the small button nose looked so much like the face in the pond. He felt heavy in his chest as a well of sadness enveloped him. He wanted to cry but managed to hold back his tears when he saw his mother so composed.

"This is Anahita a week before she died… I mean disappeared," said Revathi in a tone that frightened Ray, because it was so distant, and emotionless. "The locket is on the black thread."

Ray looked at the picture closely and saw what his mother was describing. A golden capsule hung close to her neck, and it looked just like one of those accessories teenage girls wore.

Then he thought of Deneb, but couldn't relate her with the picture. He shook his head warding off any more thoughts about the connection.

"So the locket does exist," he said, wiping his eyes with the back of his hands, and, then, slipped the photo into his pocket.

"I still cannot believe that you came to know about it from a third person." Revathi emptied the contents of the bottle into her steel glass.

"She wants it back."

"What?" The glass fell to the floor making a loud noise, and Revathi motioned to pick it up.

"Wait!" said Ray, bending down and picking it up.

"Bring the girl to me," said Revathi in a low voice. "It's Anahita, Ray." She held his arms tightly. "Take me to her, now.... Please," she pleaded, looking at him expectantly.

Ray looked out of the barred window wondering what he should say. *Would Deneb agree to come?*

"At least let us get the locket." Ray looked at his mother, whose eyes were red and laden with tears.

"I don't remember where I kept it."

"It's in the puja room, behind a photo!"

Revathi walked out of the room. Ray followed. The house was dark, except for the funnel of grey that bathed the four sided inner courtyard. A night light glowed under the staircase where Shanta slept. She was snoring lightly and turned when they passed her. They stood outside the puja room and looked at each other. Ever since Revathi's father died, an oil lamp was always kept lit in the room, which was her father's study. Their shadows stood still and small in front of them. He watched his mother touch the foot of the door of the puja room before entering it, her shadow extending into the dark narrow space. Another wave of sadness overcame him; a lump was developing in his throat as Revathi readjusted the wick in the oil lamp that lay on a brass plate on the puja table. The dull eerie glow was replaced by a bright orange incandescence. Revathi wrapped her sari around tightly and knelt down. Ray waited in baited breath for Revathi to make the next move, coming nearer to the entrance. A fairly tall, almost three feet high, photo frame with the picture of Goddess Saraswati sitting cross legged and playing the Veena (a musical instrument similar to the sitar} filled almost half the puja table. Revathi took it in both hands and lifted it. Drops of sweat rolled down the side of her neck and the sweat beads glistened in the orange glow. Ray also wiped a slick of sweat off his forehead and dried his hands on his shorts. By this time the photo frame was resting against the window sill and Revathi was sitting on the floor on her knees, struggling with what looked like a key she had inserted into a dark brown wooden panel. Unless someone knew about the existence of this hiding place tucked away behind the photo, it would have been next to impossible to locate it.

So Deneb maybe right! Ray said to himself assuming that Revathi had put something away here.

"I hope so?" said Revathi between her puffs and grunts in trying to turn the key in its lock. She tried another key that was lying on the table, and finally dipped it into the oil lamp and inserted it. Revathi turned the key, tugged at it and pulled it outwards; and the door opened, taking along some flakes of whitewash with it.

Her face glistened in the bright orange glow, as she wiped off the sweat with the end of her sari. Stopping and arching her back, she looked at Ray who continued to stand outside the door. "Can you get the torch from the table?" she said pointing somewhere behind him. He grabbed a sleek black cylindrical torch about six inches long, but was amazed at the number of different types of torches from pen flash lights to regular sized torches and large searchlights lying on the table.

Revathi took it and flashed it inside the opening, and squeezed her clenched fist into the hole. After a few tries he saw her muscles tighten as if she had grabbed onto something. She wriggled her hand out and looked at him, her fist clenched, tightly. She came up to him, held out her fist and opened it. He looked down into her open palm. A gold capsule, similar to the one in the photograph stared into his face. He glanced at his mother and their eyes met. Her frozen stare made him uneasy; she was looking at him, but it was more like looking through him. She was holding it out as if offering it to him. Her glazed eyes didn't even flicker when he looked at them. Suddenly, he felt his stomach churn.

"Mom," he hissed. She continued to stand in the same position, her eyes flickering but showing no sign of connecting with him. He closed her palm around the locket and held her by her shoulders. "MOM!" he hissed loudly. "Is this the locket?"

"Take it and give it to her!' she said in a slow but sure voice. She opened her palm again and held it out. Ray took the locket and heaved a deep sigh. "I need --." Revathi raised her finger to her lips. Then she turned, went to the window and put the frame back in its place. She looked at Ray as she knelt down on her knees. "I need to be alone."

He held the locket in his palm and rubbed it against his shorts to dry it. He stood his ground watching her; she folded her hands in prayer and shut her eyes. The movement of her lips showed that she was reciting a prayer. She kept glancing at Ray and finally when she finished, she touched her forehead to the ground and then got up.

"Give me the photograph," she said.

Ray dug out the photo from the right pocket of his shorts, and handed it to Revathi. She looked at him blankly, and knelt down.

"What are you doing?" Ray said sharply, watching her stick the photo into the flame of the oil lamp. She did not answer and continued to hold the photo in the flame. As it burned, Ray went inside and tried to save it, but Revathi blocked his way by holding her free hand out, continuing to concentrate on what she was doing.

He stood next to her and watched the picture turn into ash. The lamp flickered as soon as Revathi stood up. It struggled to keep alight as if exhausted after the burning of the picture. Suddenly a strong gust of wind blew through the window. Ray shivered, and Revathi wrapped her sari tightly around and walked out. Ray went in and tried to recover what was left of the photo but it just crumbled in his fingers mixing with the bhasmam. Ray continued to watch the struggling wick till it gave up. The room went dark. Suddenly lightning ripped through the bars, illuminating the room in white incandescence; thunder thumped down onto the house and rain pelted down with raging ferocity. Somehow Ray felt it was a celebration of some sorts the heavens were having. The very next minute the deluge stopped. He wondered if this was characteristic to this area or something connected with what was happening.

He realized he was alone and ran upstairs. By the time he reached the room, it was dark, but a sliver of light streamed out of the loosely shut door of the inner room. He went up to the door, but hesitated to open it. Instead, he peered through the crack. She had lifted her mattress. Under that he could see a large poster with a face on it. She pulled it out and it came into his view. It was a pencil drawing of Anahita, on a chart paper. He continued to peep through the crack watching tears flow down Revathi's fair unblemished cheeks but her eyes were sunken and her thin lips quivered as she tried to hold back the tears. Her small ring less fingers held the poster on both sides as if she had lifted a child by both its arms.

"I knew you would come," she said, talking to the face, loud enough for him to hear. "Master was right, no?' She paused as if waiting for a reply.

All of a sudden she crumpled the drawing and held it close to her chest. Ray moved away from the line of sight as Revathi turned to look towards the door. And he quickly went back to his room.

He lay in bed, half expecting his mother to come and talk to him. A nagging feeling of not encountering Deneb, again, kept him awake. He realized he had not done his cleaning, and sat up in bed and did it. Finally, he shut his eyes and gave himself up to the peace of this century old family home whose inheritance had been preserved for this very reason.

CHAPTER 14

The sound of the metal knockers hitting against the polished jackfruit wood doors with greater force signaled the beginning of a new dawn. Somehow he just couldn't move but he felt he was wide awake. When he, actually, opened his eyes he tried to stir, but his back ached, and legs were stiff. Slowly he managed to raise himself halfway, and sat at the edge of the bed with his legs dangling off the rather high king sized bed. He looked at his watch, and, then, out of the barred window; it was still quite dark, and plop...plop..., the first sounds of raindrops falling on the tiled roof indicated the coming of another heavy downpour. It was five minutes to ten in his watch, but it did not seem to concur with the darkness outside.

Was it all just a dream, he thought, but the face of Deneb was just too vivid, for him to pass it off as a dream. It was as if he had had a bad hangover; unsure of even the time of day; everything around him seemed so transient, leaving him completely disorientated. Above the din in his mind, he heard animated voices downstairs, followed by someone climbing up the wooden stairs. He hobbled to the clothes stand in the corner and put on his collared white T-shirt and wrapped a mundu around. A face slowly emerged from the well of the stairway. "Kannee," said Shanta, in Malayalam, gesturing as if it was something to eat. Ray smiled and looked at her blankly; he was certainly hungry, and followed her down, but a lump in his throat was growing as the events of last night haunted him. As he entered the dining room, he was not sure what he would say to Revathi. He heaved a sigh of relief as the dining room was deserted. The rest of his actions were purely mechanical even as he dipped the spoon made out of a special leaf into the gruel of rice and its starchy water spiced with a slice of marinated raw mango. He ensured he got the last of the fast disappearing blob of white butter into the spoon. Taking the Stainless steel bowl in both his hands he gulped down the remaining portion. Customarily, he washed up his bowl in the sink outside, which had running water now, but the drain was still an open channel flowing out into the farm. The sound of the steel bucket falling into the well adjacent to the hand wash area indicated that someone was drawing water out of the well. These simple sounds were a pleasant intrusion over the turmoil in his mind. As soon as he stepped out, a flash of lightning illuminated the surroundings; he shielded his face as if it were about to strike him, and walked straight to the outer portico that formed the entrance to the house, jutting out from the verandah. The entrance was exactly in line with the pathway leading to the gate. He folded his arms and moved away from the strong breeze that carried forth a fine mist of rain. The large square screens of matted coconut leaves that surrounded the portico were beating their sides against each other adding fury to the storm.

"Listen to this," he heard his mother's voice.

"Uhhh…." Ray froze as he had not noticed her.

Revathi was sitting on the wooden bench with her legs folded and leaning against the plastered brick column, engrossed in reading a rather thick hard bound book. Dressed in a red bordered white sari, there was a certain freshness and vigor that had come back to her. Her hair was wrapped in a towel and folded up into a bun

"Did you say something?"

She adjusted her plastic framed spectacles. "Brighter worlds are scattered across the universe. It is only a matter of time that the chaos and havoc that nature and man is bringing upon the Earth will force those worlds to reach out to us."

Ray came closer. "What's that tome you are reading?"

She unfolded her legs and turned to face him. Inserting the bookmark, she closed the gold bordered navy blue book.

"These are whispers from our Master's who have passed on."

"Whispers?" he paused.

Revathi's thin lips opened into a smile. "A medium gets messages from them every day. These are her translations." She took the book in her hand and leafed through the first few pages. "Babuji is in touch with those worlds," she said, and looked at Ray, "and from time to time escorts them to Earth for specific purposes."

Ray thought for a moment; adjusting his mundu he sat down on the wooden parapet next to Revathi.

"Did you really mean it, when you told me to give the locket to *her?*"

She removed her spectacles and rubbed her eyes. "Didn't you understand Guruji's message?"

"That means --." Ray stopped and looked at his mother.

"All that guilt, sadness." Revathi spoke in a very composed tone. "It's all gone. She has made it happen! Twenty five years; to live with such a feeling; it has been hell, and now....." She put her hand to her chest and heaved a deep sigh.

Ray thought Revathi was about to cry as she took her handkerchief and blew her nose. "And please give her the locket. It is hers!" She crossed her legs and went back to reading the book. This nonchalance left Ray even more shocked. He shook his head and sat there staring blankly.

She thinks it is Anahita, he told himself, and got up, and glanced at his mother; she seemed a picture of serenity, resting the big fat book in her lap and reading intently. He wondered what else the Guruji had said about extra terrestrial life.

He made his way outside, looking intently at the brightening background of dense and freshly washed foliage against the sodden red soil, noticing the sparkle of the droplets that were slowly dribbling off the deep green leaves of the Champa (magnolia) tree. He wiped the sweat with the end of his mundu, and wondered what he should do. The locket had to be given to Deneb. How was he to find her? He could not even connect with her in meditation.

ॐ ॐ ॐ

He tried hard all afternoon, choosing to remain in his room, but had no luck. He couldn't even connect with the Master. A heavy downpour just before tea played spoil sport to his plans of setting off to the hill. After dinner when everyone retired to their rooms, he got into a black round necked T shirt and jeans, and set off. He reached the base of the summit very fast. The deep green carpet of coconut palms far below contiguous with the horizon was laced in the deep yellow sheen of the after-glow of the sun. The humidity was soaring and his T shirt was soaked; the absence of any breeze, added to his discomfort. He looked at the lamp in front of the temple; it appeared unused, the cups were completely dry with no trace of last night's oil and wicks.

"Deneb," he called out softly. "DENEB." He waited for a few seconds and then headed into the temple. He took deep breaths hoping to catch the faintest scent of her presence. He went up to the other end of the summit; the empty pond stared into his face.

The nocturnal sounds filled his ears -- the howl of a dog in the distance, bashing of clothes against the steps of a bath, and an occasional shout of a woman, probably, yelling at her drunken husband. The moon had risen, peeping through from behind the luminescent puffs of clouds that still lingered in the eastern sky, illuminating the surroundings. Laced with a wisp of gentle breeze, his bare arms began to sprout goose pimples as the sweat evaporated. The reddish glow of sodium vapor street lights illuminated the skyline to his left, while, to the right of him, the wooded slopes looked even darker. His eyes scanned the tableau bathed in the bronze light of the waning moon, shivering involuntarily as the wind picked up speed. As soon as he stepped onto the verandah, his legs just folded and gave way under him: he managed to hold on to the wooden pillar and settled down on the floor. Resting his back against the wall, he dug his head into his knees, and closed his eyes. His head whirred and he felt as if he was spinning like a top. *Why does this have to happen to me?* He told himself, shutting his eyes tightly, and felt the moisture of tears trickling down from the sides. Suddenly his mind went blank. *We have been in contact ever since you were born.* A voice reverberated in his mind. He tried to open his eyes, but went deeper into his reverie. Suddenly the familiar scent of jasmine incense filled his nostrils, and he forced his eyes open. First, he thought that dawn had broken as the surroundings were illuminated with a yellow glow, but when he lifted his head and looked ahead, all 108 wicks of the lamp were burning. Deneb was there in the same white outfit, standing in front of the lamp with her back towards him.

He sprang to his feet, and took a deep breath. "What the hell is going--?" He stifled a sneeze as a sudden burst of the smell of incense mixed with that of burning oil tickled his nostrils.

She didn't bother to turn around, but continued to adjust the burning wicks.

"I thought you had disappeared," he said, standing up to his full height. She finally turned around. Her white top had an orange tint, and her face glowed even redder. Her eyes flickered in quick succession as she looked on at him. She wiped her hands on the scalp of her closely cropped hair. Sweat beads sparkled on her sharp but well proportioned nose.

"I have brought the locket." With his hands in the pocket of his rather figure hugging jeans, Ray stood wondering whether to give it to her or not.

"I wait for you," she said, and giggled, displaying a perfect set of small but white teeth. Her expressions and actions were so childlike. "We go inside, now."

Ray glanced over his shoulder. "Why should we go into the temple?"

She shook her head and giggled again. "I take you," she said and turned around. 'Come."

Ray followed without hesitating. They walked right over to the other end, and then she turned right and began walking towards the edge of the cliff. They stopped at the edge, and he looked down. Below it was a sheer drop into the valley, right down to the bottom of the hill; the sight made him go weak in the knees. A rock jutted out a few feet below like a ledge. Deneb jumped down onto it, which made Ray's stomach churn. She bent down and dug her hands into a recess, pulled it hard upwards and then sideways. A portion of the ledge opened up, revealing a perfect oval cut out around three feet wide. She was now standing right at the edge. If she were to move one foot back, she would fall.

"You go first," she said looking up to him and pointing into the opening. She held out her hand as he sat down on the edge and slid down onto the ledge.

"You put head first."

He squeezed himself into the hole and wriggled up the gentle slope, almost flat on his stomach. He hardly had any room to lift his head, but as he progressed inward, the clearance above him increased. Finally he reached the other end, where the tunnel opened up, and there was just about enough room to sit up, when a whiff of jasmine pricked his nostrils. He flipped around and went down feet first.

He shivered involuntarily, as his eyes got adapted to the darkness. Aided by a dull orange glow from an adjacent room, he surveyed the interiors. He guessed he was in some sort of a cave since the ceiling and sides appeared to be made of jagged rock, and the floor was hard black stone. The room was more like a passageway that curved and led into another room, from where the light was coming from. The stone surface was very smooth, but undulating as he felt the sides.

"How did you discover this place?" he asked as soon as Deneb dropped into the cave.

"I transform here. You call this pyramid?"

"Of course not! We built one with our own hands," he said showing his hands to her.

"Where?"

"Oh. In England."

"Eng---," she tried to repeat.

"Oops. Sorry. It is very far from here."

"This place very good. Very high energy." She sniffed and put her nose in the air as if she smelt something. "No people come in here, you see."

"Are you really from outer space?" Ray just stared at Deneb, her golden toupee of closely cropped hair tinged orange in the yellow glow.

"Antares visit here long time ago. He left message, but you don't reply, so I come now."

"Dad did mention something about seeing an apparition in the sky, when I was just born."

Deneb shrugged.

Ray's mind was working in many directions trying to come to terms with what was happening.

"What was the name?"

"Antares."

"That's the bright star in Scorpio." And then his knees went weak, recollecting Dr. Masuda mentioning ANTARES. The very thought of him being haunted by an extraterrestrial was like a punch in the stomach. There were too many coincidences for him to discard her claim of being from another planet. He quickly reached out to the side of the wall, and rested his back against it. Closing his eyes, he squeezed them tightly, and opened them again. She was still there; giggling like a child.

"You are very weak people."

"What do you mean 'weak'?" he said, still leaning against the wall, his hands behind his back.

"Very low energies."

Ray looked at her and frowned.

"That is why I could transform here," she said, wiping a layer of sweat off her forehead. You people lose your own energies. You transfer energy outside."

"Phew! We never imagined aliens to be like us – human beings." Ray thought for a moment. "You are human, aren't you?"

She looked at him blankly, her eyes flickering again. He returned the stare, the conversation with his mother coming forth.

"Why have you come here?"

She walked past him, and disappeared into the passage. Ray followed, and found himself in a similar space as the outer room. On the floor next to Deneb's feet, was an ordinary looking rock, except that it was glowing, radiating an orange incandescence, just enough to bathe the cave in a dusk like brightness. Deneb picked it up.

"Ouch," said Ray. "That thing must be hot as hell?" He went up to her and snatched it away. To his surprise it was not hot. He looked at it intently; trying to figure out the source of its illumination, but in the end gave up and handed the rock to Deneb.

"Did you bring that with you?"

She nodded. "I took stone from up and put my energy as soon as I come."

"Oh I see!" said Ray, trying to be sarcastic.

"Our Masters send message to you to tell you about us."

"Where does the locket figure in this?"

"I have memories of my past. According to my Masters, I come in last life to Earth by mistake, so I die early. The locket gave me energy, which connects me with my past. That is making me uncomfortable all the time. So I come to get it." She looked at him with flickering eyes.

"Why do you keep doing that?" Ray said, trying to flicker his own eye lids.

"My energy level is going down fast here. Now I not able to come out of this place."

Ray just slumped down onto the floor, and sat leaning against the wall, watching the glowing ember. He thought it had dulled a bit.

"Here." He dug his hands into his jeans pocket and took out the locket. "Take this."

She looked at it and suddenly grabbed it and closed her fist tightly over it. She took a deep breath, arched her back and looked up at the ceiling. Then she relaxed, and looked at him, her eyelids flickering even more furiously.

"What was that for?"

"Just telling my Masters about the locket."

"My mother is convinced you are her daughter who was kidnapped. If that is true, then you are my sister."

"I cannot know this. I could contact you, which is good; otherwise I go back without locket." She paused, and opened her fist. She looked at the locket resting in her palm, and, then, picked it up. She held it from both ends and showed it against the light, as if inspecting it. She then tugged at it several times until one end came loose. She threw the cap onto the floor and emptied the contents into her palm. Ray couldn't see what it was, but something powdery did come out as he saw some dust fly around over her palm.

"What are you doing?"

"Removing the power of this?"

"Just take the whole thing back with you."

She shook her head furiously, and her eyes opened wide as if his suggestion was preposterous.

"Look,' she said, sitting down next to Ray and showing what was in her palm. It was a powder, very similar to bhasmam he had seen in the puja room. He took a pinch and smelt it. It was not even bhasmam as there was no smell of camphor. He looked at her, and shook his head.

She took what was in her palm and popped it into her mouth.

"What the hell are you doing? Who knows what this is?" he reached out and tried to pull her hand away, but he couldn't even make it move an inch.

She dusted her palms against her clothes, and got up. "I finish my work. Now you want to ask me something?"

"What if you fall sick after eating this age old powder?" Ray twisted his mouth.

"My internal energy will take care of it." She paused and looked at him as if she was thinking of something. "Was someone close to you about to die?"

"Uhhh –," Ray sat up straight. "Not that I know of?" Then it struck him. "Why do you ask?"

"When I come to know that someone near you is having trouble to decide whether to leave his body or not, I get message from my Master to heal the soul so that it can remain here."

"Is this some kind of a joke?" Ray motioned to get up as he watched the slender figure disappearing into the next room. In spite of the dull fading light, his mind was alert and continuously asking itself whether all this was really happening. He was trying hard to think who this person close to him was.

She came back almost immediately, and continued where she left off. "Our treatment is simple, but very powerful. If you can lift energy levels to higher order, whatever is affecting you is cleaned out of your system. And, that is what I did to that person." She smiled at him as if she had accomplished something. For the first time, a kind of familial connection had been established.

And then it all came forth. She must have been responsible for the drama during Paul's illness. He stood up and wiped his brow, trying to put the pieces together.

"Ah! Now I think I know who this person is."

"We do not make mistakes," she said, in a rather firm and assertive tone.

"What must have happened is: when you transmitted your energy, it interfered with the electronics, making the gadgets malfunction." He paused and looked at her for affirmation. She just nodded. "And once the gadgets were disconnected you had unobstructed access into my Dad's aura."

"You give too much explanation. His blood stream is still contaminated. Once the 'impurities' are flushed out, he will be back to his original state."

"Wow! Why don't we open a small business, together?" He laughed at his own joke, seeing her just look at him blankly.

"It's time you tell me who they are?"

"Who?"

"Your Masters."

"Oh! You must wait for the right moment! They will call us."

Ray took a deep breath and let it out with a loud hiss, completely frustrated by her evasive answers.

"Tut," he clicked his tongue. "At least tell where you from?"

"We are from a galaxy neighboring yours." She looked at him questioningly, her eyelids quivering ever so slightly. "Our planet is called Andrearth."

The excitement in Ray spilled out; his throat went dry as he stared at her; unable to control his bewilderment, he reached out to Deneb, took her hand in his and brought it close to his face as if he was inspecting it. She tugged gently and he let go. Then he tried to cover her face with his palm; before he could withdraw it, he felt a bolt of electricity rip through his hand; in the process, he was thrown back with such force that he fell onto the ground.

"Why do you touch me like that?" said Deneb, kneeling down. She took hold of his arm and helped him sit up straight.

"Huh...?" Ray looked at her in the eye. "You really are from...," he paused and took a deep breath, "Andromeda? Yoouu ... a-a- a- r- r- r- e-e...." He stammered.

"You are not hurt, are you?"

"No…no…. Then Andrearth must stand for Andromedean Earth…. In an identical solar system." He looked at Deneb for validation, but she had a distant look; she seemed to be straining her ears as if trying to catch a faint sound.

"I know we are from a different galaxy. My Masters told me before I left."

"How old are you?"

"Twenty five when I left."

"IT CAN'T BE…!" Ray was at a loss of words. "You don't look a year older. How is it possible? Even if you travel at the speed of light, it would take you two million years to reach here."

"Antares came and went back in twenty-one years," she said, half heartedly. A burst of cool air swept through the cave, making Ray shiver involuntarily. She looked back into the dark passageway as if she was expecting someone.

"T-h-a- t mm –e-a- ns…, Antares… was in contact with me!" His lips quivered as he spoke.

"Must be. He told everyone he took a shortcut."

"You actually came through a Wormhole?" said Ray

"What?" She twisted her mouth in disgust, her high cheekbones rising even higher. "Worms?"

Ray gave a faint smile. *She doesn't know what I'm talking about,* he said to himself.

"A person walking on a sphere needs to travel along the circumference to reach a point opposite to where he started. But he can take a shortcut, if he were to bore a hole through the sphere across to the opposite side." He picked up a stone and showed her what he meant. "Similarly light would travel along the circumference, which is the natural free path, but you would reach there much faster if you took a shortcut like the person, thus beating the light beam. Such shortcuts in space are termed as wormholes." He paused and looked at her, still wondering if she were some projection like Dave Bowman in 'Space Odyssey'

"No one can survive even one millionth of the gravity that exists in those regions of space."

Deneb put her hand to her mouth and giggled like a child. "We are teleported into space, which is the beaming of the human form as energy waves."

"Wait!" Her eyelids began to flicker furiously. "My Masters try to contact me." She closed her eyes and lifted her head. Suddenly she opened her eyes and looked at Ray.

"Who was other person to whom I sent energy?" Her eyelids stopped flickering, and her blue eyes looked into his.

"Other person?"

"He help you."

"You mean, Ross. He went back home. Lost his job trying to help me."

"No. This person died."

Ray froze, wondering whom she was referring to. Then it stuck him. "Oh no. You killed Menon with your energy."

Deneb didn't seem to show any reaction. "He was suffering so I sent energy to heal him. It coincided with his time to go."

"You actually murdered him?"

"One can never be accused of killing someone, even if one is responsible for their death."

"That sounds quite cold-blooded."

"There is limit to this energy level in each lifetime. Once the soul cannot remain in the physical form, it leaves the body, seeking a higher plane of existence elsewhere in the cosmos. This is for our Masters to determine, not for us to worry about. On Andrearth, death is an eventuality, at a predetermined time. At this time, the person is led into a pyramid in which physical matter is converted into energy. The ball of energy floats into space."

"I understand," said Ray, before Deneb could say anything further. "It's similar to what we on Earth term as destiny. If the person is destined to die, he will die, anyway, and if he or she is not destined to die, circumstances and actions of the person and the people around, will facilitate the recovery."

"That's exactly what I mean. The confluence of forces and events will facilitate the course of the person's life in the direction of what is ordained. These gadgets and the doctors have only complicated your life."

"Yes, I get it," interrupted Ray, his eyes widening, as if realization had dawned upon him. For Ray, it was like a wild dream; a dream had come true. He continued to look into her doe like blue eyes, mesmerized by her beauty, captivated by her magnetism, completely overwhelmed by the turn of events. Yet, he felt at peace with his inner self.

Suddenly Deneb lifted her oval head as if she was looking at the ceiling. By now Ray knew the significance of this action. She was in communication with her Masters.

She lowered her head within a few seconds and said, "Very soon they will open the doorway."

Ray stood with his hands on his hips, and chose not to question her. "In the meantime, can you tell me something about your world?"

"I have downloaded the information just now and will tell you." She led him into the outer room. He noticed that she was dragging her feet and she kept one hand on the side wall as if she needed support. The light from the stone was dim, and the room was quite dark, but his eyes had got accustomed to the fading light. She went and sat cross legged next to a rectangular portion of the wall that was smoother than the rest of the wall.

"Come and sit in front of me," she said. Ray obeyed. He could manage to sit cross legged like her, thanks to the yoga training his mother had forced him to undergo whenever they came to Kerala.

"Move a bit forward," she said. "Your body should be inside this area." She pointed to the end of the smooth portion of the wall. "You can ask questions between pauses. Try not to interrupt."

He suddenly felt a draft of cool air, followed by warm air. Then she began to talk.

"Andrearth has regions of varying energy levels that are geographically separated, which form natural divisions in society based on one's state of spiritual evolution; the Thirteenth plane being at the top of the ladder; followed by the Eleventh; Ninth; and the Seventh plane. The frequency of these energies resonate with the faint signals emitted from the human brain, and with progressive spiritual evolution, the quanta of the energy rises; only those who resonate with the particular energy level can survive in that region."

"It's something similar to our metaphysical planes described in scriptures," Ray said, but Deneb didn't seem to react. Her eyes were now closed as if she were deep in meditation. He made sure her thin lips were moving, but was sure it was not her words as the English was very bookish as if she were reading out from a text book.

"The Ninth and the Seventh plane exist contiguously, both situated on an island at the equator; their borders are demarcated by a mountain range. The only means of getting there from the Eleventh plane is by teleportation."

"Which plane are you from?" he again interrupted. She opened her eyes, but her eyelids were flickering, so she quickly closed them.

"Eleventh," she answered.

"And where is the Thirteenth plane?"

"It's contiguous with the Eleventh plane, but at a much higher altitude, where the Supreme Master Sirius and his twelve aides reside. Master Sirius controls the workings of our planet, and ensures that each and every person on it lives life in accordance with what is ordained."

"How does one become a Master?"

"Masters are selected from the Ninth and Eleventh planes – not from the seventh plane -- after undergoing years of study and meditation."

"Then who administers the lower planes."

"Each plane has their administrator who is selected by the respective Master. Aquila administers the Eleventh plane. Under him are a team of four council members, having their individual duties divided among four main areas; food production and supply; water conservation; sanitation management; and education. The overall control wrests with Master Aldeberan, who is appointed by the Supreme Master. Likewise, the Ninth and the Seventh planes have their respective Masters, as well as administrators."

"If you have no desire to progress, there must be no education, and all the Andreartheans must think in the same way."

"Education is not a regimental affair; it is more a means of gathering information, than a challenge and competition among a study group; and, of course, it is voluntary; everyone, on the respective plane, possesses almost the same level of intelligence."

"What field do the Eleventh planers specialize in?"

"The Eleventh planers are scientists, mainly dealing in the study of the cosmos and its interactions with their planet. They limit their study to aspects that have bearing on their lives. Therefore, details such as, celestial mechanics, the laws governing it etc, are regarded as unnecessary, because nature is considered to be a perfect system."

"If you have no books, or any study material how do you study?"

"You are right; we have no tools to study with, except for our mind. Most of the analysis is done by accessing records that are stored as pockets of energy in regions of the cosmos, where souls of the Thirteenth planers float. They have answers relating to just about anything and everything in this universe.

Accessing information is done by drifting into deep meditation, sending signals from the brain to these regions and receiving back an answer. The brain will decode the signals into coherent information."

"The Ninth planers are the creative ones, skilled in art, music and other such vocations. Though the Ninth planers have different frequencies of energy, they have the same energy levels as us. The Seventh Planers, as the name suggested, are at a much lower energy level than the rest of the Andreartheans; they are jealous of the people from the higher planes. Their emotional quotient is the highest among all the planes, which fuels desires, leading to discontentment. Life there is harsh and competitive, each one wanting to overtake the other. Recently, one Master was sent there to prevent any further desecration of mental and material resources."

"Can one move freely from one plane to another."

"One can move down, but not up. For one to move up, one has to evolve to a higher energy level. No one, except for the Masters, can go into the Thirteenth plane."

"How does one evolve?"

"Normally, two life times are needed to evolve to the next higher plane."

"Is it an automatic process?"

"More or less. The soul finds its way to the energy level it resonates with, so the process is almost automatic. Of course, it is dependent on one's conduct in the previous life."

"Suppose someone steps over into the Ninth plane from the Seventh Plane?"

"It's strange that you have raised this question. There is a folklore attached to this:

A Nanon had gone to play music at the Septan administrative head's daughter's wedding. It was a simple ceremony -- an exchange of vows in front of the Master; this was followed by a feast. In the background, the Nanon played his flute, invoking cosmic vibrations, to bless the couple. The flutist fell in love with one of the Septan girls; and they both eloped. This infuriated not only the brother of the girl, but also the whole Septan community. If caught, she would be banished into the mines for the rest of her life, where she would be made to do hard labor. No one would accept her back. The only option for them was to get back to the Ninth Plane, where the Septans would not be able to follow. But, he had forgotten that she too was a Septan. As the story goes, they escaped by the skin of their teeth and crossed over, climbing the mountain that divided the two planes. The moment she reached the foot of the mountain in the Ninth plane, she lost her senses and went into a coma. The higher energies in the Ninth Plane were too strong, the sudden surge leading to short-circuiting of her cortex area — the main neural receiver and transmitter. No one knew the real fate of the couple. Despite several rumors, there was one plausible version, which has been carried down through history:

The Nanon and his wife went to live on the border of the two planes, as his people also did not accept them. Day and night, he played a special composition on his flute to his comatose wife. One day, after many years, on the night of a full Moon, she awoke from her stupor. Ever since, on every full Moon night when the Moon reaches the zenith, the most vivifying piece of music flows into both the planes originating from the mountain top. The flute plays all night until the crack of dawn, which can be heard right down to the base of the mountain. Otherwise, music played in the Ninth plane only flows into the Eleventh plane, and is never heard by the Septans, except on these nights. There still stands an isolated home on the highest point on the mountain, which has been taken to be the border between the two planes. It is now more a grim reminder of the consequences of the foolhardy act, than a symbol of the flutist's endurance.

"It's strange," said Ray, "that this folklore is so similar to our Greek the myth of Orpheus."

Deneb's eyes flickered open. "Why is it strange? We are so sure that our souls have originated from Earth, which means most of our impressions must have been carried forth from Earth?"

"That's by far the most plausible fact I have heard in the past two days," said Ray, stretching his arms out.

CHAPTER 15

The room was now completely dark, but he could see quite well, and got up and went to the other room. He picked up the stone, but it looked just like a piece of rock. It was not even warm. He took it with him and went back to where Deneb was. Surprisingly, she stayed in the same spot looking at the blank wall. Suddenly, a powerful unaccented voice of a man reverberated in the cave.

You have welcomed our Emissary in the true spirit of brotherhood, and have passed the test of trustworthiness. We will reveal our world to you and you only.

The voice faded away, and Ray dropped the stone; he looked around to see where it came from.

"My Masters have signaled readiness," said Deneb.

"You mean to say, that was your Master?"

"Yes." She continued to look at the wall. To Ray, it was just part of the cave, though when he had entered this space for the first time, this rectangular portion did stand out as if it were a marker for a door. But Deneb was feeling the dark black stone, as if she was looking for something on it.

"Are you looking for some hidden lock?" said Ray, half expecting a door to open.

She didn't respond. Suddenly, there was a flash of light, bathing Deneb in a white glow; the rest of the room was dark. He just gaped at Deneb, who was now gesturing him to come to her. A pure white incandescence flowed through the rectangular portion and slowly filled the whole room. A swirl of warm air replaced the cold air. A vestibule of white light streamed out of the wall as if it were a doorway. It stretched far inside and disappeared around a bend. "Oh my---," his mouth remained open. He shut his eyes, tight, and opened them again. She reached out both her hands; he caught hold of them, and held them tightly; then, all of a sudden, she pulled him close and embraced him.

A stream of energy flowed through his body. All his sensations to the outside world seem to vanish; it was as if he was anesthetized.

"Do not attempt to become a part of the action that you will see before you. It is a projection into your mind as far as we are concerned. If at all anyone from that dimension senses your presence, just ignore it. DO NOT, I repeat; DO NOT get carried away; the consequences will be grave and irreversible." Deneb seemed to be warning him, but he couldn't see her or even feel her hands. That was the last he heard, and found himself sucked through, into the vestibule; he felt a bump, and the white incandescence was replaced by complete darkness.

Suddenly, he saw a tiny blue dot in front of him, sparkling like a gem amidst the pitch-dark sublime region of empty space. The dot became larger, and he seemed to be approaching it at lightning speed. Suddenly he found himself touch soft ground, and when he looked down, he was standing on a luscious green carpet of grass, so was Deneb.

"This is the Thirteenth plane,' said Deneb, "and that's where the Supreme Master resides." Ray looked in the direction her finger was pointing. A tall spire, so tall, that its tip was only a speck, reaching out to the sky. But the lower part was a plain square building. It looked more like a church building with an unusually tall spire. There were no windows in the front, and the façade was of exposed brick. And surrounding it was a carpet of deep green grass; further away, the gardens were interspersed with little hillocks and ponds.

Deneb led him up a flight of polished stone steps, through an open archway into a circular room, which he presumed to be a central hall. His eyes roamed the ash-grey stone walls; the windows were rectangular openings, arched at the top. There were three doorways towards the far end of the room. Deneb led him through the middle one into a small passageway, wide enough for only one person; he heard voices as they neared the opening at the other end; the archway opened out into a round bare room with a raised platform at the far corner.

"That's the Supreme Master in his chamber," pointed Deneb, to a man in a white robe, seated cross-legged on the raised stone platform. "The rest of them are the Masters."

There were twelve of them encircling the Supreme Master; each wore a white robe, with hoods covering their clean-shaven heads. Only their round, flat-nosed faces showed.

"I don't think they can see us?"

"Of course not," said Deneb. "We are only projections, invisible to anyone we come across. "I have accessed records of events that are relevant for you and me. I could never be standing in the Thirteenth plane, like this."

"We are seeing through into the past?" said Ray, feeling quite at home.

"Yes."

"Have you come to a decision, yet?" he heard the Supreme Master say.

"No, Master, not yet," said one of the Masters, shaking his head, and so did the rest of the Masters — all in unison.

"That's Master Aldeberan – the Master of our plane, who just answered. This meeting must be in connection with some important decision about our plane."

"Each of the ten volunteers has performed so well in the training program," continued Master Aldeberan, "that it would be injustice on our part to make any exceptions. Give us one more day; after all, it's our very first space mission; moreover, it's a month away."

"No!" said Master Sirius, although his face displayed no sign of irritation. "I will now have to take the decision on my own."

He unfolded his long legs and rose. At his full height he towered above the rest. An imposing figure with large, protruding eyes topped by bushy eyebrows and hung with puffy bags beneath. His bulging eyes contrasted with the sharpness of his other features: the perfect angle of his nose, the thin lips now drawn into a line.

"Now, leave me alone. I shall decide," he said softly, but firmly, as the other Masters quickly got to their feet and huddled out of the round and bare room.

"Ray, I think we witness events that happened even before my birth."

"Nothing surprises me anymore."

Deneb and Ray stayed in the chamber. They saw Master Aldeberan look inside, only to see Master Sirius seated back on the stone platform, once more; he had drifted into deep meditation.

Master Aldeberan shook his head, turned around, and slowly made his way out of the building, followed by Deneb and Ray. He looked into the distance, onto the Eleventh plane, which, though being at a lower energy level than the Thirteenth plane, was a contiguous landmass, at a lower height.

Suddenly Ray found himself float above the Masters and was transported down into the Eleventh plane. He was standing in, what appeared to be, a front lawn of a house with a sloping roof.

"It's my father and mother sitting around the cooking pot, having their cup of hot brew. It is an early morning ritual, followed by most of us on the plane."

"Brew?" Ray was thinking about magic potions.

"Oh! It's only effusion of aromatic leaves."

"Antares, I am so nervous," her mother said, snuggling closer to Antares.

"That's my mother, Ophelia."

Antares put his arm around, and gave Ophelia a tight squeeze. "Don't worry. The Masters would not have allowed us to get married, only months before the launch, if I was supposed to go."

Ophelia nodded half-heartedly. She was trying to get the cooker going again, stoking the little spherical stones, placed under the stone pot.

"What are those shining stones?" asked Ray.

"Those stones emit heat when sunlight falls upon them," said Deneb. The stone pot is filled with seawater, mixed with pulses and rice, to make up our breakfast; it will end up as a soupy gruel, like porridge."

Antares stroked Ophelia's waist-length, black hair with his fingers as he sat, cross-legged, on the well laid out lawn, watching her.

Ray could make out that Ophelia was extremely nervous; she was aimlessly stirring the gruel. He looked away into the distance, over the low bushes and thick foliage that demarcated their compound; the first rays of the sun spread its sheen in the azure, as it rose, hidden from view by the Thirteenth plane. Visible straight ahead, the Palace of the Supreme Master glistened in the sunlight, its outline resembling a Tibetan monastery except for the tall spire that rose into the sky. The forest cover marked the beginning of the willow-lined trail to this forbidden land. The sun made its way over the mountain, and rose above the Palace; it was now almost halfway up above the horizon. A gentle breeze blew across the countryside, rustling blades of green grass.

Ray and Deneb were unable to move from the lawn, as if they were locked in place. The whole region, encompassing the Eleventh and the Thirteenth plane, could very well have been an island in the Indian Ocean, surrounded by lofty hills and undulating landscape. "That's Aquila – our administrative head – walking towards the house," said Deneb.

Ray saw a rather tall well-built man walking towards the house. The characteristic jet-black hair was cut short, not a wrinkle was visible on his taut skin. His sharp features made him look stern. Like Antares and Ophelia, he too was wearing the white top and the sarong, exactly what Deneb was wearing.

"Antares, wake up, it's me, Aquila," he said.

Antares looked at Ophelia and then at Aquila. Ophelia looked distraught; Aquila deliberately avoided looking at her.

"You must be joking!" Antares said, fixing his eyes on Aquila, who was nodding in affirmation. "Tell me, she is going with me." He moved closer, his face turning red. "Please, Aquila… Ophelia; can someone tell me what is going on?"

"I am not going," answered Ophelia; she spoke very softly, like an obedient child. "I knew it all along."

She turned and ran into the house through the main entrance — an open doorway.

"I am sorry, Antares, your partner will be Captain Achernar, not Ophelia. She lacks the experience, and this being our first venture into space, we do not want to take chances," Aquila said it as fast as he could, and with a straight face. "The launch is scheduled for tomorrow afternoon, and you must report before sunrise, on Table-Mountain."

"Ray looked at Deneb; tears were streaming down her face. "If…sniff… sniff… only I knew what had really transpired?"

Ray looked at her quite puzzled by the outburst. "That's really unfair."

Deneb didn't seem to hear him. She continued to stare at her parents.

"I need to see the Master," said Antares. "How could he do this to us?"

"He'll be waiting for you in the administration building," replied Aquila, as if he had expected Antares's reaction. Antares stared at Aquila blankly.

"It's unfair, I know," Aquila said, embracing him. "But I tried my best. There must be a valid reason, which only time will reveal."

Antares hugged Aquila tightly; then he, quickly, released his hold and ran indoors. They saw Aquila making a quick exit.

They followed Antares inside. The main entrance led to an open hallway. On either side were rooms. Except for a wooden stool in each room, there was no furniture in any of them. A few pots and pans hung on the wall of what appeared to be the kitchen. Some were stone dishes and some wooden.

Ophelia was kneeling on the floor of the bedroom. Her hands were on her thighs; she straightened her back, took a deep breath and closed her eyes. Antares walked into the room and knelt beside her; he put a hand on her shoulder, but she remained unmoved.

"You have to go," she whispered, and looked at him. He took her in his arms and kissed her. At this point Ray and Deneb were transported out into the back of the house.

"Antares cannot back out; he cannot go against the Master's dictum," said Deneb, regaining her composure. "After all, it is they who chart the destinies of the Andreartheans. Their decisions are never contradicted, but implicitly followed. They will be now sent for initiation,"

"How do they do that?"

"Initiation is a rigorous cleaning process to overcome emotional stresses that are sapping one's energy levels. It involves the Supreme Master sitting in front of him and transmitting signals into a region of the brain that induces such stresses. These energies erase any abnormalities or aberrations, putting the mind to rest; as a result, they attain resonance with the highest frequency of cosmic energy."

Ray nodded more out of bewilderment than understanding.

"Those are the fields," said Deneb, pointing over the hedge onto large expanse of farmed land.

"The main crops are barley, wheat and maize," Deneb explained, as Ray looked over onto the corn field that seemed ready to pick.

"Who owns these farms?"

"The produce is collected and then distributed centrally to each household. The administrator controls this."

☥   ☥   ☥

Ray saw Antares and a dark complexioned man of medium height, being escorted by Master Aldeberan, along a willow-lined pathway that wound its way up a steep mountain slope.

"Who's with your father?"

"That's Achernar," said Deneb pointing to the man whom now Ray could see clearly; the man sported a moustache and had very short, intricately braided hair. "They are going up onto Table Mountain."

"And, who is the little girl walking with Ophelia?"

"That has to be Carina, Achernar's daughter." Deneb paused. "Must have been five years old, then."

By the time the procession of the thirteen Masters and the two astronauts reached the top of Table Mountain, the sun was approaching zenith. True to its name, the top of the mountain was like a flat round table, as if someone had neatly sliced off the peak. On it, was a raised platform a few meters high, resembling an altar -- a circular stone platform supported by large pillars of stone. The pillars were equally spaced, the gap in between enough to let at least two people through. A pyramid, almost thirty feet tall was standing on the stone platform. Surprisingly there were no trees on the table, except for a ring of high bushes and thick bougainvillea like foliage surrounding the edge of the platform; pink and white flowers in full bloom painted the ring of foliage. The flat and level ground was covered with overgrown grass, a complete contrast to the undulating landscape of the rest of the plane.

"No wonder you didn't recognize my pyramid," said Ray, as he admired the massive hand crafted pyramid. Quintessence of human craftsmanship, the Pyramid, with perfectly straight and smoothly polished sides, made of natural rock, stood solidly on the stone platform, as a symbol of impending loneliness for the witnesses. There were only two of them: Ophelia and Carina. They had come to bid goodbye to Antares and Achernar, who were about to embark on their maiden voyage.

Dressed in pure white flowing robes with hoods covering their baldheads; their robes fluttering in the wind, they stood, with outstretched hands, encircling the gleaming pyramid. There were thirteen of them — the Masters — the eventual conduits of cosmic energy. Facing the hand crafted pyramid, they stood with open palms, as if taking oath before a divine inquisition.

"It is not just the beaming of the human form, but far more complex — the teleportation of two human beings along with the pyramid," said Deneb. "The pyramid is the IGT -- the Inter Galactic Traveler."

"What are the Masters doing?"

"They are imparting their energies onto the IGT, facilitating the conversion of physical matter into energy waves. This ball of energy will be beamed into interstellar space, travelling at lightning speeds, or even faster. On reaching its destination, the IGT would remain energized, becoming a permanent fixture in that region of space, and a home for the two space-farers."

Ophelia and the child had placed themselves on the far side of the table; just behind them was a cliff that dropped down to the ocean. The opposite side sloped down into the Eleventh plane connected by a well-defined pathway lined with willow trees. To the east, the land mass extended far beyond, to the Thirteenth plane, almost hundred meters higher than Table-Mountain.

A pathway, so barren and perfectly straight like a runway, disappeared into a steep climb. Straight ahead, looming above, on the hill, was the silhouette of the Palace of the Supreme Master.

Achernar was already near the Pyramid — their spaceship. Antares had walked down, off the platform, to bid goodbye to his wife. The howling wind was growing in intensity; the tall blades of grass, tinged with a yellow sheen, were almost kissing the ground. Ophelia covered her ears with a scarf and reached her hand out to Antares, drawing him closer. Her long black hair, neatly tied in a high bun, stayed in place, while her slender blue eyes were almost shut to protect them from the wind. He stood with his hands on her shoulders. He gave a boyish smile; with his closely cropped jet-black hair, he looked even younger.

"I do not know if we shall ever see each other again," Ophelia whispered to Antares. "I am carrying our child, my love. Take care."

She broke down, embraced her husband, and cried — sobbed uncontrollably — like a child in its mother's arms, her face resting on his chest. He hugged her tight, but only for a moment, displaying no emotions; his big blue eyes had a faraway look.

Ray thought he heard a low murmur, and, then, the murmur exploded into an ominous roar followed by a beating of drums. Antares looked back towards the high ground. He, then, knelt down and hugged Carina. She was a splitting image of her father; she had his brown eyes; her shoulder length curly black hair was neatly braided and plaited into a ponytail.

"We will be back soon," he said. Then, he abruptly swung around, and walked briskly to the site, without even a second glance at Ophelia.

The tableau appeared so ruthless and cold to Ray, the pyramid looking more like a funerary monument, as he watched Ophelia -- her pensive gaze following Antares into the pyramid.

"The Masters are ready," said Deneb, tears streaming down her cheeks.

"Let's not rake up the past, Deneb, if you are unable to handle it," said Ray.

"Maybe, it's a cleansing process. First, I made peace with my distant past."

Ophelia swung around, probably, to avoid being blinded by the light that was now radiating from the pyramid; she walked away, towards the cliff, with sure, but slow, steps, leaving behind the crimson silhouette. They watched her, as she cupped her hands to her ears and looked over the perilous precipice towards the open sea. A wave was approaching the shores, growing bigger and bigger.

The gigantic wave hit the shores. The ground shook under their feet, and a spray of water dissolved into her tearful face. The beating of the drums stopped abruptly. There was silence; it was as deafening. But the blinding light was gone. The pyramid had also vanished into thin air. She held Carina in front of her and stroked her hair, trying to comfort the sobbing child, who, probably, was more traumatized by the experience than by the departure of her father.

Ray looked up into the sky, with only questions in his mind. Deneb walked away slowly, towards her mother; Ophelia didn't react even when he saw Deneb try to feel her.

This is what the concept of multiverses is all about-- many universes within the same region of space, without any interaction of the forces between the different universes -- each one representing a time span, from creation to, what we call, present-time. But, each universe's concept of time would be different, the fascination of the whole experience drifted into a state of enquiry for Ray as he elucidated what he had just seen.

$$\maltese \quad \maltese \quad \maltese$$

They were now transported back to Antares's home; the sky was dark, rain was pelting down in thunderous abandon. Ray was unsure whether it was day or night.

"Something is about to happen," said Deneb. "Rain and thunder are always a harbinger of either good or bad news."

As the ferocity of the rain ebbed, and the sky began to clear, Ray and Deneb waited expectantly. The sun made its way to the western horizon, and dusk fell, when Deneb saw a clean-shaven head bob out of the sloping pathway. As it approached, a round face — redder than white — supported on a small frame, came into full view. His big ears protruded out, while his small eyes and snubbed nose were hardly noticeable.

"Oh! It is Master Aldeberan," said Deneb. "I have never seen him without a hood."

He walked straight into the house, but came out almost immediately followed by Ophelia who was holding an object wrapped in a cloth, in her arms as if she were cradling a baby.

"It's a new born baby," said Deneb, who had ventured quite close to Master Aldeberan. "Ray…," Deneb paused. "Ophelia has just given birth to me."

"I see it now, said Ray, joining Deneb.

Master Aldeberan turned his face towards Ophelia, and then, took the baby in his arms. He looked at it in the eye, and kissed the baby's forehead. "She has your blue eyes and high cheekbones," he said.

He looked towards the Palace of the Supreme Master. As if offering the baby to this unseen power, he stretched his arms out, and closed his eyes for a moment.

He whispered something into the air, and went back to the house. Ophelia was waiting for him at the entrance; she looked harassed, and confused. Carina stood obediently by her side, looking on with innocent curiosity. She gave a faint smile and took the baby from Master Aldeberan.

"Your daughter, whom I am naming Deneb, will be looked after by the Supreme Master, and so will you," he said, and embraced Ophelia.

He released his hold; looked at Carina, who was holding Deneb; kissed her on the forehead, and left rather abruptly.

CHAPTER 16

Ray felt hard ground under him; all this time he couldn't feel anything around him except visualize and hear what scenes had passed by them.

"Deneb, are you there?"

"Yes. Don't worry."

Suddenly, Ray felt himself being propelled through a vortex. A hazy picture flashed past, and then there was darkness. This went on for a few times, until he was standing on a dusty pathway. Deneb was standing next to him; both looking at each other wondering what was happening. From one bright star in the western horizon, countless stars appeared. They got brighter, as the sky darkened, sparkling like gems, suspended in the background of the limitless cosmos.

"What are those balls on the wooden poles," said Ray, pointing to the football sized spherical balls, mounted on wooden poles, emanating a dull white glow. The entire pathway down to the bottom of the slope was lined with them.

"Those are our streetlights," said Deneb. "The hand-polished balls are carved out of naturally mined rock; they have the property to absorb sunlight, or even starlight, and reflect it."

"Who's that?" said Ray, looking down the slope at a silhouette of a woman approaching them. "This eerie silence; the barren landscape; it is scary."

"It is only my mother," said Deneb.

Wrapped in the softness of her white hand woven attire, like an angel floating in the clouds, Ophelia made her way up towards them.

"She looks much older," said Ray.

Ophelia's doe like, sparkling eyes were deep set, marred by the pain and scars of loneliness; the lines of age and torment distinctly written on her face; her high cheek bones were even more prominent now. Her long black hair was no more tied in a high bun, but was closely cropped. Ophelia stopped in front of the house, looked towards it and then entered the compound, almost brushing past Deneb. The bushes along the perimeter were overgrown; the garden was in shambles with thick undergrowth; creepers covered the walls, hiding the ash-grey stone blocks. She peeped in through the open doorway, but quickly retreated, and stepped out onto the pathway. She turned and then looked up once again towards the Thirteenth plane. Streetlights lined the pathway — a direct route from the Eleventh plane. It was like a shimmering vestibule bathed in pure white light, right up to the Palace of the Supreme Master.

The Palace gleamed in splendor, establishing its supremacy as the seat of highest power on the planet, reflecting its glory into the cosmos. The Palace was lit in its characteristic tricolor — red on the spire, followed by blue in the middle, and green at the base.

"It's breathtaking, Deneb," said Ray following Ophelia's gaze.

Giving one last look into the distance Ray was about to turn back, when he saw a silhouette emerging from the midst of the whiteness. His eyes widened, and he looked towards Ophelia; she had stopped in her tracks and was looking in the same direction. As it came closer, the apparition was taking a human form.

"Am I hallucinating?" Ray asked Deneb.

"Oh my goodness!"

"What is it, Deneb?"

'It cannot be," said Deneb, and her throat went dry. A familiar figure stopped just a few feet away from her. She reached out her hand to feel it, but it just went through the figure.

Ophelia did the same. "Antares, is that you?" they heard her say. "Are you for real?"

And, then, they heard his voice. "Ophelia, my love, everything is so different. I have overtaken time, breaking the bonds that I had left behind."

"It really is Antares," said Deneb. "He looks so young; look at her."

His closely cropped jet-black hair, the longish face blemished with scars of adolescence, was just the same, except that the light tan had faded, giving way to pallor.

Ray looked at Deneb, but Antares spoke again. "You are still as beautiful," he said giving a boyish smile.

Ophelia looked at him inquisitively. "And you too, Antares."

"After twenty-one long years of hibernation, I am out of step with the rest of the world, and will have to start all over again," he said, with a twinge of sadness, while moving a few steps back. "You have aged as we all should, but I am still the same Antares you knew when we married. I have covered two million light years in just ten and a half years. The round trip has taken twenty-one years, which makes me twenty-one years younger than you."

"I can see that. You look more like my son, than my husband. And the best for us is to lead our own independent lives," said Ophelia, with a great deal of maturity and conviction.

Antares looked on blankly, as if he had not heard her.

Ray and Deneb exchanged glances. "Fascinating; mind boggling," said Ray. "We have travelled twenty-one years into time."

"Yes. These were events that took place just before I left." Deneb went back to looking at her parents.

"But…what about our child?" Antares said in a surprisingly calm voice.

"You mean, Deneb!"

"Is that what you have called it?"

"She is our daughter, Antares. I delivered a beautiful and healthy child, eight months after you had departed."

"Why is she not with you? Where is she? Take me to her at once!" he cried out excitedly, and held her by her shoulders.

"Why are you not saying anything? Answer me, Ophelia," he was now almost screaming in desperation.

Ophelia wrenched her petite frame out of his grip. "Calm down, Antares. Give me a chance to explain." Regaining her balance, she straightened her white top and steadied herself.

Darkness had fallen, and the night was well underway; the air was getting cooler; but there was no howling wind; the leaves of the willow trees were still, as if sharing the melancholy of the moment. The Eleventh planers had retired to their homes, and would be asleep soon. But two people were awake, braving the chill of the night, deciding the course of their own future.

"Deneb grew up in my arms. These very hands played with her," Ophelia gestured with her hands, her voice strained with anguish. "She waited and waited for you, but you never came. Finally, she even started to doubt whether I was her real mother. One day the issue precipitated, and she stormed out of the house. Things just went from bad to worse. I tried hard to convince her, but in vain." Ophelia had tears in her eyes; the anguish and regret in her voice evident, but she seemed to control herself. "The Master, too, did not take my side. He had said that it was what destiny had in store for us. Deneb left me long ago, and went to live with Carina. Since then, we have neither talked, nor does she acknowledge me anymore." She paused for a moment. "I do not wish to discuss this any further. It will rake up questions to which I have no answers. I have managed to bury the past and regain some of my equanimity. Good-bye, Antares. Providence is not on my side, but I hope it favors you."

Ray and Deneb looked on, as Ophelia and Antares parted as abruptly as they had met. As the full Moon rose, Ophelia disappeared into the fluorescent yellowish hue of the night, leaving Antares stranded in a time warp.

"I was so unfair to my father," said Deneb.

Ray felt a sudden jolt; there was total darkness, and then, he felt his vision come back, like the first time when he came out of the vortex. He found himself floating, looking down onto a procession of a dozen or so people, led by Master Aldeberan, Antares, Aquila, and the other four functional heads of the assembly; the procession made its way, through an archway made of thick foliage, into a large open ground, more like a stadium. A raised platform was erected, almost ten meters high, in the centre of the ground. The spectators were seated on steps made of stone, which encircled the stage. There was enough space in between the stage and the steps, for free passage. The setting was impressive — almost five thousand people had gathered there.

"I think we are still in the same time period," said Ray.

He got no answer, and he looked around, but Deneb was nowhere to be seen. A scary thought occurred to him, *What if I am stranded in this time warp?*

A loud cheering from the section of the crowd drew Ray's attention. The procession was entering the arena. Antares was waving to the crowd. He, and the rest of the officials were taking — what seemed to be — a victory lap around the ground. Ray followed Antares, who had stopped in his tracks and was staring into the crowd.

Ray took a closer look at the crowd, in the direction Antares was looking. In the front row he saw a familiar face just like Deneb's; the sharp features; those high cheekbones; almost a splitting image of Ophelia; he had no doubt she was Deneb; except that she had hair that fell over her shoulders.

There was another girl next to her — equally beautiful — but she had that extra bit of maturity written on her face. She was a splitting image of Achernar.

Must be Carina, he thought. Her braided hair with tiny curls was now closely cropped; a snubbed nose and big round brown eyes on a round but lean face gave her that tom boyish look; she was a couple of inches shorter than Deneb, and much stockier.

"That's me sitting there," he heard a voice behind him.

"I know; and the one next to you is Carina."

"Isn't she pretty?"

"Cute." Ray paused, and then strained his ears as he heard some musical notes fill the air. "Where is this music coming from?"

"As I explained to you earlier, musicians are from the Ninth plane. Whenever there is a special event in our plane, they are asked to play music."

"You mean we are hearing music being played from the Ninth plane?"

"Yes. Its favorable location, in relation to the Ninth plane, enables the music to be heard over such vast distances, across the ocean.

"What instruments do they use?"

"The flute being the most popular instrument produces sounds that resonate with the cosmic vibrations. But, for special occasions — such as this — the most preferred instrument is a series of different sized wooden pots, filled with water, arranged in a circle. A wooden stick struck on the rim of each pot, in succession, produces the most astounding musical sounds. Resonating with the cosmic waves, a soothing symphony flows into the Eleventh plane."

"You must have heightened sensitivities," said Ray. He was distracted by, what sounded like, the blowing of a conch.

"That is the invocation of the higher cosmic powers," said Deneb. "It also marks the start of the proceedings."

"What is the occasion?"

"Oh! Antares is being felicitated."

Deneb and Ray settled down to watch.

Aquila welcomed them all, and briefly explained the purpose of this gathering. Then, he called upon Master Aldeberan to make the opening address.

"The cosmic bells toll the praise of our hero, Antares," began Master Aldeberan, with his poetic opening line, his voice echoing over the chatter and the music.

The crowd patiently listened to the short and crisp speech. As soon as Antares stood up, it was a signal to the crowd. They began to cheer and whistle.

He just stood and absorbed the praises that echoed in the surroundings.

Ray happened to glance in the direction of the Master, and saw him raise his hand as if he were blessing the gathering. Suddenly, all was quiet.

"It's quite remarkable — a diminutive looking man like him to have such an overpowering effect on the crowd," said Ray.

"At his position, he commands that respect and discipline. For that matter, each of the Master's has similar hold on the inhabitants."

At that moment Antares began his speech.

"A reservation or a proposition is valid as a perception of reality until scientifically proven otherwise, but only when the question is posed do we need to consider the thought. So let me pose a question: Have the Andreartheans inherited the souls of lesser beings from another world? These souls could have evolved to the point of no return to their own civilization. The evolutionary process need not have stopped, and continued to a higher plane of existence. That plane could very well be our own planet. For this, we would need to find a civilization much less evolved than ours. I can tell you with full conviction: there is such a world! But there have to be two worlds -- one, from where we Eleventh planers, as well as the Ninth planers, have evolved from; and the other, from where the Septans have evolved from."

There was a murmur from the crowd. Ray could make out that they were shocked; so was he, continuing to look at Antares. Antares looked at the Master as if seeking approval of continuing further. The Master appeared to nod.

"And beyond our own past there lies a parallel world where the secret of our genesis lies hidden. Let us hope that someday we shall be able to send an emissary to the new world and unravel the mystery of our provenance, enabling us to bridge the gap across the frontiers of space-time between the past and the present. Here it is fellow Andreartheans: the proof of the lesser world."

Suddenly Antares clutched his throat, as if he were choking. He turned towards the Master; the Master had his hand outstretched, and was glaring at him. Ray winced — the piercing stare of the Master was unsettling. Aquila rushed up to Antares, and whispered something into his ear. Antares nodded, and apologized to the crowd of his inability to show any images at the moment. He received a standing ovation from the crowd, as Aquila wrapped up the proceedings.

Aquila stood next to the Master, and began talking to him in whispers.

"We shall meet tomorrow morning at the assembly hall," said Aquila, when he noticed Antares motioning to leave. "You must prepare to show us what you claim to have discovered. Inform Achernar, and receive the images."

Acknowledging the instruction with a nod, he bowed, excused himself, and ran down the steps, out of the grounds.

Ray followed Deneb and Carina out of the arena. He was just in time to hear Carina tell Deneb, "In other words, he is certain there is life in our neighboring galaxy, two million light years away from Andrearth."

"Hey Deneb, your friend, Carina, does not seem very convinced."

There was no answer.

☿   ☿   ☿

The single-storied assembly hall doubled as the administrative building; its architecture was characteristic of an official building with a spire extending out from the tapered roof. The main hall, with several wooden benches arranged in rows, resembled a classroom. This classical style of construction was adapted in all homes and buildings. Large archways without any doors as entrances; and opposite them were square openings for windows. Such windows were there on each wall located exactly opposite each other, facilitating cross ventilation. The ceilings were high, tapered at the top, with wooden beams holding the structure.

Master Aldeberan, Aquila, and the four representatives sat at a desk in the front row. Acknowledging Carina's arrival with a nod, the Master made place for her next to him. Her dark eyes roamed the room. The members were getting restless when a breathless Antares walked in; sweat was trickling down his face and his top was soaked in perspiration.

"You are trying our patience, Antares!" the firm voice of a visibly irritated Aquila echoed in the room.

Antares turned to the Master and bowed. "I beg your forgiveness, Master."

The Master acknowledged it with a gentle nod.

"I was involved in a dialogue with the new world. A little boy came to me in my thoughts while I was connected to the IGT. He said he was from a planet called Earth."

Sweating profusely, he wiped his face with his sleeves.

"I hope you are alright?" asked Aquila with a sigh, as he stared at Antares.

"It is for you to judge from what I am about to reveal," said Antares. He was now more relaxed, having taken a few deep breaths. "Let me first put the matter in its perspective. I am proposing the existence of another civilization, either more advanced or far behind us in terms of harnessing of the power of their mind." Like a schoolteacher standing on the platform, he was addressing the senior-most members of the colony, as Deneb and Ray looked on.

"Let us think for a moment: Is it possible? I am in no position to answer it categorically. But we can, of course, argue: Why not? Our sun is just an average star. Several such *Suns* definitely exist in other regions of our own galaxy, which itself is so vast with countless *Suns*, some larger, and some smaller. What I am talking about is, just another sun like ours, but in our neighboring galaxy."

"How can you be so sure that it was a similar world?" interjected Aquila.

"Yes! I am certain. I was there," said Antares, pointing to the image on the screen. "I beamed myself right into the region from where coherent signals were emanating. Believe me! I couldn't make telepathic contact with anyone. This made me venture closer into the inhabited planet. What I saw was mind-boggling — a self destructive civilization, crowded with humanity!"

"Wow. How do you guys manage to do this," said Ray.

He was witnessing a unique display of mental powers -- the projection of telepathic messages on to a screen; this was tantamount to viewing what was being transmitted, like a movie.

"Our brain is compartmentalized into the left, and the right side," said Deneb. "The right lobe contains the memory and occupational skills; and the left lobe is for routine activities and emotional responses. The central region is responsible for transmitting and receiving telepathic messages, mainly on the instruction of the Supreme Master. The central region is connected to both the sides and receives and transmits to, and from, either side, depending on the frequency of the signal. Antares will use his central cortex to receive the images from Achernar and store it in the right side. Giving a thought will facilitate the process of transferring information to the cortex and then out from the retina onto the screen."

"We can never imagine our minds to perform such a feat," said Ray.

"That's where you are all going wrong," said Deneb. "You are underestimating the power of the mind."

The picture on the screen changed. It was more like a satellite image of little ants crawling on a sphere.

Antares seemed to zoom in. "It's me and my mother, Deneb," said Ray, as the image of an infant sleeping next to its mother, appeared.

"You mean people like us, in flesh and blood, and mind and body!" piped in Carina. Her expression quickly changed; she gave a contemptuous smile. "Chhaa…The mother looks a lot like Ophelia, Antares. Is this your way of communicating your feelings for her? But why waste everyone else's time?" Pointing in the direction of the seated members, she gave another cynical smile. "Master, I think it is absurd; it is a mockery of our faith and understanding."

"Carina, don't jump to conclusions, and drag your personal issues into this," snapped Aquila.

The rebuttal from Carina did not seem to deter Antares. He continued. He had the mandate of the Master, as well as of Aquila, who had gestured him to carry on.

"I should not be telling you this, but I did leave a message behind," said Antares in a sheepish voice. "I hope we get some reply."

"Or, at least an acknowledgement," interrupted Carina with sarcasm and went on. "Look, Antares; if there were intelligent life on this planet you would have made contact. Teleportation can create superficial illusions in our minds, especially while travelling through another realm of space-time. How do you know what forces were acting on you, and what effect they would have had on your mind?"

"Say it, say it, Carina; you don't have to be so polite. I am perfectly sane, and will stand by what I saw. You sit on your glorious theories waiting to disprove anything beyond your comprehension."

"Antares, I think Carina is right," interrupted Aquila. "They should have contacted us, if they really did exist."

"Just look at the screen, all of you," burst out Antares. "This is the region from where the signals were received." He was pointing to the third spiral, roughly one-third the distance from the central core of the galaxy. "I was teleported here, when I saw them. They looked just like us, but were packed so close that there was almost no place to move."

He swung around to see if there was any acknowledgement from the mute spectators; his eyes scanning the room for the slightest reaction, but all were either stunned or just did not care.

"The meeting is adjourned for today. We have seen the evidence, and now it is the decision of the Supreme Master. He has been following these proceedings."

All of them looked along the bench to their left, as if surprised at Master Aldeberan's intervention. Aquila gestured Antares to wait while the rest, including the Master, made their way out. It left only the two of them in the large room.

It was a strange sight — Antares, once, the same age as Aquila, now twenty-one years younger, and looking it, too. Aquila had aged naturally; his graying hair, but wrinkleless face, gave him that suave and dignified look.

"You should have delved further," said Aquila, "and at least got some information about this civilization."

"I did not have the permission or the authority to explore any further. It was most unfortunate," replied Antares.

"You should have informed us of your discovery, before you decided to come back. It would have saved us a lot of time and energy."

"I tried, Aquila. I went to the extent of getting in touch with them. No one answered my signals, though it was received all right. Maybe, by the little child! But there was one more recipient who connected with me, and it seemed to have deflected my transmission. If their mental faculties have evolved and developed to the extent that ours have, we should be receiving a reply."

"It could also mean that there are other beings like us," said Aquila.

"For some reason, as I got closer to the planet my energies depleted rapidly," said Antares. "Maybe, you would have lost me forever, and there would be no debate today. We would be leading our separate lives across galactic frontiers."

"I understand the mess your life is in. Don't forget, you will outlive us all, and your coming back was essential!" said Aquila, and left the room

Antares waited for a while and then walked out of the building.

"Carina…Carina?" called Antares, as he came out of the building into open air.

"Don't scream into my ears," he heard a voice. He looked behind. "You were spying on us, weren't you?"

"I am face to face with the hero of the world. I am honored my dear Antares!" said Carina condescendingly, as he walked down the steps. She now stood just a few feet away from him. "Deneb will be furious with me if she ever finds out that I even spoke to you."

Antares flinched. "It is the Supreme Master who will decide what has to be done next. You are no one in this equation."

"Antares, I know what you dreamt of last night."

"Aaa…. uh. What…? It was only a dream."

"You made love to me last night," said Carina accusingly. She looked at him intently. "I dreamt of you, too, and- had- the- same…"

Before he could complete, she hugged him tight, and then kissed him on the lips. He hesitated; then he took over, kissing her passionately on her lips.

"I believe you, Antares! But I do not want to lose you," she whispered, as he released himself from her embrace, and hurriedly left the scene.

Ray looked at Deneb. "I hope it has not stirred up your emotions?"

"It's no one's fault, Ray. Don't worry; it does not affect me anymore."

"We better get back to Earth," said Ray.

"I don't think we are ready for that. The Master wants you to see and experience more."

"What more can there be than what I have just seen?"

"I don't know," said Deneb. "We just have to wait."

At that moment Ray felt a tug. "I think we are moving forward. The story continues," he said, and everything went dark in front of him.

$$\mathcal{D} \quad \mathcal{D} \quad \mathcal{D}$$

Ray's vision cleared, and he saw Master Aldeberan dragging his feet up a steep slope. Then he saw a very tall spire ahead, as the Master reached the top of the slope.

"Deneb, I think we are back on the Thirteenth plane," he said, when he saw the dome shaped building, from where the spire went up.

"I can see that," said Deneb. "But I hope we have not gone back into time again."

"Let's wait and see what happens," said Ray, as they saw Master Aldeberan take a dip in the spring, just outside the Palace. The water was hot and steamy with a characteristic pungent sulphurous odor.

"There are many such springs across the Thirteenth and Eleventh planes, whose waters are supposed to be therapeutic."

Ray and Deneb followed Master Aldeberan through the central hall, into the Supreme Master's chamber; Ray saw the Supreme Master as a reflection in the polished stone floor, seated cross-legged on the raised platform.

Aldeberan greeted him with reverence -- kneeling down, and bowing until his forehead kissed the floor. He, then, settled himself on the floor a few feet away from the platform -- the two of them suffused in the highest form of energy vibrations.

"Master, I seek permission to send Antares back to the IGT," began Aldeberan. "He should be sent to this new world to seek and find the source of our own souls, which reincarnate on the Ninth and the Eleventh planes. If we can bring about a change in the source, we could possibly have more of the Nanons and the Eleventh Planers on our planet. The Septans are growing rapidly in number, but not evolving fast enough to graduate to the Ninth plane. This is upsetting the balance in the planes. There is an overflow of energies into the Septan plane from the other two planes, as not enough humans are there to harness the energy in the higher planes. This is leading to emotional upheavals even on the Eleventh plane. The Septans are trying to divert those energies for their own selfish means," Aldeberan continued with a note of concern in his voice. "They have set up several small spheres on the borders of the Ninth plane that are absorbing the excess energies. They have attempted to transform matter and create new forms, using the energy stored in these small spheres."

"Enough, Aldeberan, enough!" the commanding, yet soft voice of the Supreme Master cut him short. "I am not here to listen to your complaints. I very well know what is happening in our world, and the new Master in the Septan land has everything under control."

"Sorry Master. I only want to know when we can plan the next mission?" said Master Aldeberan. "We would need a minimum of one month, before Antares is ready to leave. He is drained of his energies, his emotional quotient being high. Along with him, Deneb and Carina are suffering, too."

The Master nodded his head in acknowledgement. "Antares and Carina are my responsibility. Carina, having been nurtured by us, has performed her duties well. She now needs to lead a normal life; so does Antares," said the Supreme Master, his eyes still closed.

After a brief pause he opened his eyes and looked straight at Master Aldeberan. "The next mission will be planned very soon, and I will prepare the candidate. You will come to know who it will be, in due course. Before that there is an important mission to be undertaken."

"Deneb," said Ray. "Can you make out when all this is taking place?"

"Not yet."

"Call upon Altair," said the Supreme Master, "to prepare him for immediate departure to the Septan land. I want him to go tomorrow. The mission is dangerous because he has to restrict the so-called thirst for progress. The Septans have to be dissuaded from proceeding with an experiment, which, if carried out, would have a devastating effect on the environment. It could upset the ecological balance of the whole planet. He would definitely face some resistance. He would be going under the pretext of helping them find more yellow iron, which they have recently discovered."

"Does he go alone," said Master Aldeberan.

"Deneb goes with Altair on this mission. Her presence will ensure that no physical harm comes to Altair. She is sensitive and would be able to judge the mood of the Septans," said Supreme Master Sirius.

"Ray, we certainly have not gone back into time; we are being shown why and how the mission to the Septan land took place."

"Who is Altair?"

"He is Aquila's son. We were born on the same day, and the same time. We were also classmates for almost five years, until I branched out into Mind Analysis. He continued studying the planet and its elements, how they interact, and what lay hidden beneath the crust — a broader form of geology."

☞ ☞ ☞

Master Aldeberan and Aquila were gathered near the pyramid, bidding farewell to the two explorers. The sun appeared as the clouds scattered; the moment had come when the sun was about to reach the zenith.

The pyramid doors did not open. Deneb and Altair just walked through solid stone into the empty and bare space, facilitated by the power of the silent gaze of Master Aldeberan. That portion of the wall reflected a dull fluorescent blue light.

"What's that residual dull glow?" said Ray.

"It's the remnants of the power induced by the Master that had temporarily energized every atom in that space."

Ray saw Deneb and Altair, sitting cross-legged on the floor, facing each other with their eyes closed and their hands on each other's heads. The two bodies glowed, and a reddish halo enveloped them. The halos met and joined to form one large ball; in the midst of it, like being ensconced in a red crystal ball, sat the two travelers. Ever so swiftly, with a grace only Heavens could surpass, the two apparitions blended into one, rose above the ground towards the ceiling. The halo took the form of a donut, transforming the complex biochemical factories into their nascent state. It started to distend, looking like a pyramid with a round base. Like an inverted spinning top, the elongated disc moved up and was sucked out from the apex of the pyramid. The intense heat generated during the process was apparent — the walls from the outside glowed red. The spectators retreated a few paces to avoid the glare.

"That's it; we must have reached the Septan plane," said Deneb.

CHAPTER 17

"Have we been teleported as well?" said Ray, as he and Deneb hovered above, inside a contained space.

"Not exactly; we are just witnesses to events that my Masters want you to see."

"Why are the walls glowing red?"

"During teleportation, every atom around also gets energized."

"Hey look, that's you and your boyfriend, sitting cross-legged on the floor."

Instead of getting any response from Deneb, he only heard Deneb say to Altair, "Are you sure we have come to the right place? The floor is curved, so are the sides. This certainly is not a pyramid!"

Altair shrugged his shoulders. Deneb was now trying to find a way out.

"Is anyone there? Let us out. We have come on the invitation of your Master Canopus," she shouted, banging the walls with her clenched fists.

The sound just reflected back, amplifying into a thunderous roar. The whole structure shook. Altair lost his balance and fell on the floor while Deneb took support against the wall. The reddish glow was now fading, and it was almost pitch dark inside. Suddenly, Ray saw a small portion glow bright fluorescent green. To his utter amazement, the greenish aura began to take some shape; a distinguished looking man in a white flowing robe emerged from the solid wall. For a moment, Ray thought it was Master Aldeberan. The features were so similar; the shape and build very similar; and the gait so very graceful.

"I am Master Canopus. You must be the visitors from the Eleventh plane," he spoke in a soft, deep, yet captivating voice. "You almost rolled the sphere off the hill! It would have destroyed the colony, below," he continued. "The pyramids and spheres are impervious to our thoughts; this makes the process very dangerous. There is no contact with the outside world once you are inside. I expected you Eleventh planers to have more patience. We were very much aware that you had arrived." he said, pointing his finger at the two of them. "Now listen carefully. I will now go out. You follow me after a few moments. This will give me enough time to refocus on the area from the outside."

As gracefully as he had come, he disappeared through the wall. Focusing his vision on the particular area, he directed his energies on that region. Soon after, Deneb and Altair walked through the wall, and out of the sphere.

"The vibrations could very well have dislodged it," said Ray, as he looked on at the spherical ball delicately balanced on a narrow base.

Made of stone similar to the pyramids on the Eleventh plane, the sphere shone like a polished steel ball, perched on the highest point on the plane.

"Wow!" Altair exclaimed, turning to Deneb.

"I wonder how they got it hollow?" she asked, looking at the structure inquisitively. "It definitely is not mined as such. Nature does not believe in leaving empty spaces."

The sun had just crossed the zenith. A blinding reflection off the sphere made Altair turn away. Ray followed Altair's gaze over the other side of the mountain. An alarming sight met his eyes. The Septan colony lay below; it appeared fairly spread out, looking more like a war-ravaged town. There was no greenery, just few scattered trees. In the distance, across the stretches of the colony, the landscape was barren and rugged. There were obvious signs of excavation, apparent from the extensive mining activity in progress.

"It is sad, very sad, indeed," Ray heard Altair whisper. Altair had not noticed Master Canopus come and stand by his side.

"It is a perfect mix of greed, power, and an insatiable appetite to 'progress'. It will destroy the Septans, if it is not curbed," Ray heard the Master tell Altair.

"I am sorry for not introducing the main man on this plane," said the Master, pointing to a dignified looking man with sharp features who was sitting on a log of wood. "He is Dorado, the administrative head. He will be in charge of you, during your stay on the plane."

Dorado made his way towards them. "I have the privilege to welcome you to the Septan Plane," he said. "We have a lot to learn from you. But don't try and impose your ideas upon us."

"You, Altair," Dorado said in a rather contemptuous tone, "the son of my counterpart, Aquila, have come to help us with our search for a new form of iron. It is yellow in color, and has captivated our women folk; now it has become a matter of prestige to own a piece of this. Men are prepared to fight for it, as there is so little that we have managed to find. Therefore, for the sake of the happiness of our people, it is imperative that you help us find more of this yellow iron."

Dorado ended his rhetoric, and he started walking downhill, towards the colony.

"This yellow iron could spell disaster for the Septans. Dorado must be made to understand that greed and passion is a ticket to hell for the human race, contrary to what he thinks that it could bring happiness," Deneb said, voicing her fears to Altair, as she caught up with him.

"Such qualities are cleaned out of the system," said Master Canopus, having overheard Deneb, "if found to be manifesting themselves in any person on the higher planes. The higher planers have the power to distinguish between the essential emotions and the emotions that reduce their energy levels. The energy quotient, a measurement to determine the general health of a human being, is recorded every year. The Septans seem to have evolved from a much lower form of human beings than those reincarnating on the Ninth and Eleventh planes."

"That means my father was right in proposing the existence of two more human civilizations," said Deneb.

Master Canopus nodded in agreement.

Altair nudged her. Dorado had stopped and was looking at the three of them suspiciously. He received a piercing glare from the Master, and quickly started off again. The rest of the journey, downhill, was completed in silence. When they reached their destination, the Master, all of a sudden, bowed and said, "Treat them as your honored guests, Dorado," and walked away.

The landscaping was similar to the Eleventh plane. There was a sizeable garden going right around the house, and the neatly trimmed bushes marked the boundary. But the architecture was different. They were seeing a two-storied home for the first time.

"We will now leave you both to rest in the afternoon," said Dorado breaking his silence. "In the evening you shall be introduced to our fellow Septans. There will be an exhibition of our developments on this plane. When the sun sets, and the sphere glows red, one of us will be here to lead you to the grounds." Dorado nodded half heartedly, triumph clearly marked on his face, and left.

Having got Dorado off their backs, they went into their new home. The ground floor had the pantry and the dining area. They went up the stairs, and found, what appeared to be the bedroom. Deneb went to the window and looked out. She saw the gigantic sphere looming majestically at the top of the mountain, glistening in the sunlight, resembling a beacon; to Ray it was a symbol of miraculous human accomplishment. He too was captivated by this awe-inspiring sight.

The sun had just disappeared below the horizon. From the bedroom window, they watched the sphere change color, from yellowish white to orange, and now, it was turning red. At that moment, Ray heard the beat of drums, in the distance, and so did Altair and Deneb.

"That must be a call for the Septans to make their way to the exhibition," said Altair, gesturing Deneb to follow him downstairs.

As they made their way out of the house, Altair saw a man walking towards them.

"At least these people have a sense of time," he was telling Deneb while pointing to the approaching man. "Our escort is here."

Altair looked at the man closely, as if he had never seen someone like him. Ray, too, found him distinctly different looking. He was much taller and heavier than an average Andrearthean man; his hair was closely cropped; his longish face with pointed ears sticking out; all this definitely cast doubts on his origins.

Suddenly, Deneb gestured to Altair, and pointed to her own finger.

"Deneb, Deneb," he called out and tugged at her hand. "What is the matter with you? Are you afraid of something?"

"Yes... No! Altair! Look at his left hand index finger," she said. "It has got the yellow band. This must be the yellow iron Dorado was talking about."

"They can do us no harm. I am with you," said Altair.

Ray looked around for Deneb; her absence didn't surprise him, as he, by now had noticed her absence whenever she was in the scene on Andrearth.

𝕯   𝕯   𝕯

Goldie — the nickname that Deneb had given to the yellow iron man — escorted the two of them under the darkening skies, towards the *exhibition*.

"Altair, I am sensing trouble this evening!" whispered Deneb. "Do you think it is wise for us to interfere?"

"Master Aldeberan would not have sent us here only to be silent spectators," said Altair.

Ray continued to follow them. There were no pathways lined with trees and greenery. Instead, dilapidated wooden facades, resembling a Hollywood set of a western movie, cluttered the surroundings. Stumbling over wooden planks and pothole-ridden roads, the three neared their destination; it was apparent by the ominous beats of the drums getting louder. Turning into a narrow lane, Ray was amazed at what he encountered: a makeshift stage towered above the ground.

They were led up the steps, onto the high platform. The moment they were visible to the crowd, applause and cheer filled the air. It was an awesome sight, just the sheer number of people. Over ten thousand men, women, and children had congregated for this special occasion. They had assembled in a semicircle on wooden platforms that went far back, sloping upwards in steps. This ensured an unobstructed view for the person behind.

Master Canopus was seated on a stool, which resembled an archaic throne. Altair and Deneb stood to the left of the Master along with Dorado, while the three other assembly heads stood to the right. They all faced the crowd. There was another raised platform in-between the stage and the spectators. Ray made it out to be a single slab of stone at least ten feet square. It rested on four legs — more like tree stumps — a couple of feet high.

"Are the Nanons invited to play the drums?" Ray heard Altair ask Deneb.

"We do not need any outside help to create noise, for that matter, for none of our needs. Soon we will be teaching the world!" the reply came from Dorado.

Altair shuffled and then turned his face to avert Dorado's sharp gaze. Deneb was too engrossed in her own observations, busy scanning the mass of humanity, to have heard what Dorado had just said.

At that moment, Ray witnessed an incredible display of the powers of the Master. The Master was standing up; his right hand was raised, pointing in the direction from where the sounds of the drums were coming. A reddish glow emanated from his palm. The light extended out, as if it was being transmitted towards the sound of the drums. At the next instant, the drumbeats stopped. There was a murmur in the crowd, befuddled by the sudden silence. Before anyone on the stage could realize what had happened, the Master settled back into a meditative posture, his countenance displaying a picture of equanimity. It almost seemed as if it were a signal to start the proceedings.

"He is not just a mute witness to the proceedings," Deneb whispered to Altair. "I think he is on our side,"

Altair sighed. "Only time will tell."

Dorado wasted no time, and had already begun his speech.

"Master Canopus, assembly heads, and fellow Septans, I welcome Altair and Deneb. They have come from the Eleventh plane to help us in our quest for progress."

He was speaking through a horn shaped contraption that had a protrusion in the centre with several small holes in it. It looked as if it were carved out of wood.

"It facilitates the amplification of his voice so that the crowd sitting right at the back will not miss his rhetoric," Ray heard the voice of Deneb, but couldn't see her.

"Now, I request the fellow Septans to show our guests the progress we have made," continued Dorado. "Every community has an inherent desire to progress, to display their strengths, and achieve supremacy in the world." A loud round of applause followed, but he still had more to say.

"And, in the process, discover and invent instruments and processes that we can use in our daily life." Dorado had raised his voice to almost a scream. "It is not magic, only the judicious use of the power of the mind. Fellow Septans, show the world what we can do."

"He was mobilizing the Septans to steer away from the natural course," Ray heard Deneb again.

What Ray heard next was unbelievable. A melodious symphony of flutes pervaded the surroundings. But the music did not last long; it faded away in no time, as if it were an intrusion. Then the real display began. Two men appeared in the ring, and the crowd egged them on. One of them had two stones in his hand; the other had a bundle of dry leaves and twigs. The man with the stones raised his hands showing off the two stones as he walked around the periphery of the grounds. He came in front of the stage and began furiously waving the stones at Altair and Deneb.

"The stones are small, but are different from what we get, Altair. They look more like the spheres we cook our food with," Deneb whispered into Altair's ears.

"Look Deneb!" cried out Altair, but in a whisper. "It is Goldie. Can you see his shiny yellow band?" He was looking down at the man with the two stones.

The arena was now illuminated with the shining spheres. They emanated a yellowish incandescent fluorescent glow, almost turning night into day. Ray looked around and found Deneb, a few meters away, looking down with a faint smile on her face.

"The Septans, in their quest for progress, have processed a lacquer extracted from a plant," said Altair. "When this lacquer is applied to any surface, it absorbs starlight and glows yellow in the dark. They have overlooked the fact that the lacquer does not store any light. It only works when there was an active source of light falling on it."

Before Deneb could respond or ask any further question, Goldie had returned to the ring. In one hand he had the stones, and in the other, he had the voice box. He was now shouting at the top of his voice, oblivious of the fact that the voice box was distorting his words. He romped around the ring, whipping up frenzy amongst the spectators.

"He is screaming like a wild man," whispered Deneb.

Dorado overheard her. "He is going to show you an experiment that will change our lives forever," he interjected. "It is a matter of pride; look at the yellow man. He has come as a messiah to show us the pathway to progress."

Dorado gave a devilish smile, showing his yellowing teeth.

"Well, that is if we survive to reap the benefits of your fantastic ideas," said Altair.

"We Septans have discovered the latent power of nature. We just need to harness it and transform it. For that, we have to work hard, unlike you souls. You are such inefficient and lazy people. Just wait and watch the fun." Altair was the only one who heard him, as Goldie's rhetoric reached a crescendo.

He suddenly stopped screaming, handing over the voice box to his accomplice.

"The time has come! Tonight is the night, from when, our lives will change forever, leading us to a brighter and more comfortable tomorrow," announced the accomplice. He had a sober voice, his speech audible through the voice box.

"Look at these twigs. Everyone, please look here carefully," said the accomplice. "These are two stones, which he will rub together. When he strikes one stone with the other, you will see the miracle."

Tut, Tut, Tut, Tut, Tut…. Goldie was trying to rub the stones against each other. Nothing happened in the first try. As soon as he struck the stones again, Ray noticed a reddish flame erupting from one of the twigs.

"Look, Look!! Altair!" Ray heard Deneb exclaim, distracting everyone, including the Master, on the stage.

Altair held on to Deneb and squeezed her hand. "Don't panic. We have to handle this with great care," he said and turned to Dorado. "May we go and observe this closely, Dorado."

"Hmm ...hmm, alright," said Dorado, and led them down the steps, towards the ring.

As they came closer, flames were leaping out of the twigs. The fire was raging, but was contained in the little spot. Deneb began to cough, the smoke almost choking her.

"The air is black and unsafe for us. If we do not get out of here NOW, we will never be able to go back to our plane," she managed to warn Altair between her gasps for breath.

Deneb was clutching her throat, but Altair still did not react.

"Stop this nonsense," Deneb screamed, finding her voice.

She turned and looked towards the stage; the Master was still in his meditative posture with his eyes shut. Altair was continuing to watch the two men in the ring. As if asking for alms, they gaped into the sky, the sweat on their bare chest glistening in the firelight. Altair's gaze followed the rising black smoke.

"Will you tell them to stop, Dorado, please, please; our race will be wiped out from the face of this planet. It is suicide!" Deneb had turned to Dorado, pleading with folded hands; her eyes smarting.

Dorado stood staring at the two men in fascination, ignoring Deneb's pleas. His eyes were smarting, too, and he kept wiping the tears. Goldie was fuelling the fire with more twigs, as the spectators watched in complete silence.

Ray surveyed the crowd; he saw most of them looking on, dumbfounded. He noticed some commotion from the corner of his eye, and quickly turned.

To his horror, he found Deneb picking herself up from the ground; and Dorado was hurriedly making his way to the stage. Altair ran to help her.

"You fool!" said Deneb, gritting her teeth, and flung his hands off.

"Calm down! I had warned you not to go after him!" said Altair.

Dorado was back on the stage. He stood with his assembly heads, in one corner, pretending to be busy in a conference. Ray noticed that the Master had shifted his position. He was sitting right at the edge of the stage, facing the scene of the '*crime*'.

"Get two pots of water. Quick!" Altair told Deneb.

Without any hesitation, Deneb ran in the direction of the stage, but went under it and out through the little lane. Goldie, the yellow iron man, saw Deneb disappear into the lane. He followed her out, but kept a safe distance.

Suddenly, flashes of lightning streaked across the sky, followed by thunder. It was the heaviest rain that Ray had ever experienced, as it came down in sheets.

He saw Deneb drenched to the bone, as if she had stood under a waterfall.

"It's as if the Heavens revolted against this blatant desecration of the delicate balance it maintains on our land," Deneb told Ray, as the lights faded away.

It was now pitch dark, but Ray could still hear voices in the distance; he found himself coming closer to them.

"Master, why didn't you stop all this nonsense?" Ray heard Altair say.

"I am here to maintain harmony among people, and not to resist them. If you restrict them, there is conflict within. I keep 'throwing water' on what could lead to a life threatening catastrophe, testing their patience until they give up. After all, the Septans are impatient human beings. It is easy to divert their minds. The Septans consider themselves as the deprived souls. For them, the only way to hide their sense of inferiority is to be different and get noticed — a purely human problem arising out of their own insecurities."

The rain seemed to have stopped, and Ray was beginning to see the lights come on. He saw the Master standing with his arms folded — an epitome of calmness and fortitude -- in conversation with Altair.

"Conflict is the worst antidote for facilitating change. You try and bend a fresh branch; it will spring back and hit you harder," the Master said.

"So you knew all along about the fire experiment. When it became life threatening, you powered the cosmic forces to create the thunderstorm!"

"Yes, my son, I also want you to know that being from a higher plane, your reaction was out of line, especially of your girlfriend."

Canopus walked away leaving Altair alone on the stage. Dorado and his team members had made a quick exit, and with them the crowd had vanished, too.

"Altair, I am lost," Deneb's voice echoed into the expanse.

Altair looked around him, when he heard Deneb, again.

"Look at the sky, Deneb," he shouted into the night. "Can you see the Moon?" After a brief pause he shouted again, "It is to my right."

"I see it," Ray heard Deneb's reply.

Scanning the sky, Ray found the heavenly marker looming over the wooden huts on the opposite side of the road. It looked like a fluorescent orange balloon rising over the dilapidated structures.

Altair waited, craning his neck, expecting Deneb to emerge from over the elevated landscape.

"Deneb," he called out sharply, when she didn't appear. He cupped his hands and repeated, "DENEB," in a much louder voice, but there was only silence.

"Deneb…. Deneb…, this is not the time to play games," he shouted into the night. He looked all around, his eyes searching far and wide.

By now the lights were bright enough for him to see the lay of the land. To his left was a thick forest; to his right was dense foliage; and right ahead was a large body of water. He couldn't see her anywhere around the field.

Ray followed Altair back home. Altair stopped halfway and appeared to be listening to something. Ray heard faint voices, too.

"That's the council hall," said Deneb.

"Oh! So you are still around," said Ray, as he turned to look. "I was so engrossed in what was happening down there that I almost forgot we are just mute witnesses to events that have already taken place."

"Wait, there should be more to come."

The council hall was similar to the one in the Eleventh plane — an empty square room, devoid of any furniture. Occupying a raised platform, the Master sat in a meditative posture. But he was alert, watching the council members who sat on the floor in a small circle. Goldie, the yellow iron man, was seated to the right of Dorado. The rest of the members were pointing accusing fingers at him, while Dorado appeared to be shielding him. Dorado raised his hands gesturing everyone to remain quiet.

"I decide who does what," his authoritative voice echoed in the hall. "The yellow iron man is our future. He holds the secret of our glory. The girl is out of our way, and now we can use the boy to achieve what we want."

Altair was just in time to hear the last two lines. Before any of the members could respond to Dorado's statement, Altair saw the Master raise his hand.

"As an emissary of the Supreme Master, I have the discretion to overrule the council, especially when things have gone too far. I hereby declare this assembly dissolved with immediate effect!" It was no miracle, but a straightforward assertion of the Master's authority. The words hit them like a bolt of lightning. All the members stood up. Dorado was the first to raise his hand in protest.

Before he could say anything, the Master spoke again, "The decision is final. In consultation with the Supreme Master, I will fix a date for re-election. Dorado, you have undermined our authority and thrown accusations at our Master Aldeberan; this disqualifies you from standing for elections."

Ray saw the Master's eyes. They were red. His face was flushed with anger. Suddenly, the Master closed his eyes again and slipped into meditation. During those few moments, Dorado attempted to leave the hall. Before he could reach the door, he was thrown back with such force, that he staggered back and almost fell over.

"I have a difficult task to perform," said the Master, as soon as he came out of meditation.

He paused, looked at Dorado, and saw him recovering from his fall.

"I, Master Canopus, confine you to three life times on the Septan land. The Supreme Master orders me to sentence you to death. This lifetime has ended. I hope you will evolve into a better human being in your new life, which will be in the world you had come from. You will be executed at noon tomorrow. Until then, you will not leave this room. The rest of you may please leave now!"

Dorado's countenance was expressionless. He did not stir from where he had landed. The rest of the members, including Goldie, quickly huddled out of the room.

Altair took one last look at Dorado. The ferocity on his countenance had vanished. The greed and the contempt had given way to a helpless look.

"Son," began the Master putting his arm around Altair's shoulders, as they both walked out into the open, "it is your duty to overcome the magic of the yellow iron man. I have the power, but it will be looked upon as aggression."

"I must admit one thing. The yellow iron is very powerful. It emits radiation, which counters our own transmissions to the extent that if one wears such a band on the head," Canopus drew a circle in the air around his own head, "he would be completely out of our control. Therefore it is imperative that you find the source of this yellow iron. After which, I shall energize the area around it to prevent anyone from accessing it."

"But, what about Goldie?" said Altair.

"He is no threat. It was Dorado, who really was the mastermind; and Goldie was only a pawn in his hands. However, you will have to pretend that you are helping him. And the rest, we shall take care, when we need to."

There was no further mention of Dorado and Goldie while Canopus and Altair walked in the direction of the sphere.

Canopus held Altair firmly by his shoulders and embraced him.

"You have terrains to explore while she has light years to travel. Both of you have to keep the tryst with your destinies," the Master whispered these parting words, and started downhill.

$$\mathcal{D} \quad \mathcal{D} \quad \mathcal{D}$$

"Deneb, we are back in the Thirteenth plane, aren't we?"

"Yes, it's the last leg of my journey," she said.

"My child, welcome back to the civilized world." Ray heard the voice of the Supreme Master, and looked down.

The Supreme Master had embraced Deneb.

"Aldeberan!" Deneb cried out, and tried to break away from the hold of Master Sirius.

"Get hold of yourself, Deneb," he said firmly, as she broke into sobs. "Master Sirius is only protecting you from the high energies of the Thirteenth plane."

"What happened to me, Master? Why am I here?"

You were treated very badly by Dorado and his gang, so we had to pull you out of the Septan plane, before any grievous harm was caused to you."

Ray followed the three of them to, what he assumed to be, her room — a wooden-roofed hut. There were, precisely, twelve huts, each with their own garden. The lone window, at the far end of the barren room, opened out to reveal the most breathtaking sight -- lush green grass spread across the expanse interspersed with neatly groomed bushes in clusters. Like miniature spas in the midst of the greenery, the hot springs bubbled. The rising steam floated over the green pastures, creating a misty hue. A cluster of trees that shaded each spring, doubled up as curtains. A garden of vegetables and fruits stretched far down the mountainside, contiguous with the white sandy beaches that disappeared into the crystal clear blue waters of the ocean.

They didn't stop at her room but went straight to the Palace of Supreme Master Sirius. Deneb was told to wait outside in the central hall. After a few minutes, Master Aldeberan came out and called Deneb in. Seated on the stone platform, Master Sirius seemed to be in a casual mood, playing a kind of a game with some sticks and a ring shaped object.

"Where did you get this ring from, Master?"

He immediately stopped playing the game and looked up. "You are very sharp, but not sharp enough." He paused, as if waiting for her to reply.

"You brought it with you," he told Deneb. "That was the real purpose of your mission to the Septan land. Canopus slipped it on just before you entered the sphere. He had coaxed the yellow iron man to give it to him on the pretext of Altair wanting to analyze it before he could start his search. When you got out of the pyramid here, I slipped it off your finger," continued the Supreme Master with a triumphant look in his eyes. "Why do you think you survived the entry into the Thirteenth plane? The yellow ring absorbed most of the surrounding energies, which reduced the shock on your cortex area."

"You mean I was used as a specimen for your experiment," she said calmly. "And, if it had not worked?"

"We do not play with lives and certainly do not take chances," replied the Supreme Master.

Deneb just shook her head.

"It is a very serious matter," said Master Aldeberan. "Now that we have a sample of the substance, we will have to find out how to nullify its power. This secret must never go out. It should remain between the three of us and Canopus."

"You are implying that by wearing this ring anyone can invade the Thirteenth plane," said Deneb.

The two Masters ignored her question.

"Now coming back to you, dear Deneb, we have come to a decision. You are the ideal candidate for the next mission to the IGT!"

The Supreme Master paused. Both, he and Aldeberan, looked at Deneb closely, as if, expecting a reaction; she remained unfazed.

"You have the perfect balance between your emotional and energy quotients. Your mission is far more complex than just observing and sensing the signals, which your father had already done," continued the Supreme Master. "Once you find the inhabited planet, you will have to teleport yourself there. We know it will happen, but you have to figure out the rest, which shall unfold as you go along."

"This Mission will also help wipe out the disturbances from your past," said Master Aldeberan.

"But, on one condition, Master...." No more words seemed to come out.

The two Masters stood unmoved and unconcerned.

"That will be all. You leave at noon tomorrow."

"You will now undergo a cleaning regime," said the Supreme Master, as he unfolded his legs. "Master Aldeberan will escort you to the chamber."

She was taken to the adjacent room, and made to sit in the centre of a pyramid-shaped enclosure, which looked more like a tent.

Very soon, Master Sirius joined them with five other Masters. They stood around the tent with their hands raised, their palms facing Deneb.

All Ray saw was Deneb seating herself with the Masters in position, and then, the next moment, he saw a blinding, white light illuminating the space; she was covered in an aura of white light, which seemed to last for a long time. The very next thing he saw was her walking out of the room.

Ray watched the procession arrive at its destination – on Table Mountain. The Masters quickly took their places around the pyramid.

Ray noticed Ophelia admiring her daughter, as she walked towards Deneb, who was talking to Antares.

"Antares, I do not know whether I will come back," Ray heard Deneb say.

Deneb moved a step back while Antares stood his ground. "I now bid goodbye to you, Papa. If you meet Ophelia..." Deneb broke off, sensing the presence of another person nearby.

Deneb turned, and found Ophelia staring into her eyes. "It is too late," she said under her breath, smiling to herself.

"Here, Deneb, my baby. Let me hold you just one last time."

Holding her arms out, Ophelia looked at her daughter in hope.

Deneb embraced her mother and whispered, "Mommy."

"Goodbyes are for parting souls. But, for a mother, the soul of her child is very much her own," said Ophelia, and slowly walked away.

Antares stood transfixed.

"Deneb, it is almost noon," Aquila called out. "Antares, please come and join us in her farewell."

The finality of the moment had arrived.

Deneb embraced each of the twelve Masters, Aquila, and finally the Supreme Master, who stood close to the pyramid. He was ready to 'open the doors', paving the way for Deneb to venture into the sublime vastness of darkness and vacuum.

She turned, taking one last look at the Masters, and surveyed the surroundings, absorbing the last moments on her planet. Bending down to kiss the ground, she took a deep breath. As she lifted her head, she saw Ophelia wave to her in the distance. She waved back. But a familiar figure caught her eye. It was Carina; she'd suddenly appeared, and was coming towards her. She stood as if waiting for Carina to approach her; then, she turned around and walked into the Pyramid.

"Tell father, I miss him," Ray heard Carina's voice in the background just as Deneb was about to walk into the pyramid.

The red glow at the apex signaled the beginning of the journey. And then, Deneb was gone!

The next moment, sheets of rain thundered down, but Ophelia continued to look skywards. The Heavens seemed to be celebrating their triumph! Ophelia squinted, as the sun suddenly peeped from behind the clouds. With divine grace she waved her hand, looking towards the pyramid, which, now, stood only as an edifice glistening under the clearing skies.

The very next moment, everything in front of Ray went blank.

CHAPTER 18

"Huh...," said Ray, struggling to stay on his feet, feeling very drowsy and light headed. He tried to readjust his vision, as he felt hard ground.

"Open your eyes," he heard a voice, but it sounded very distant. "RAY, the journey is over; we are back on Earth."

His eyes flickered open and he spread his hands out to feel what was there. His hands felt cold stone; he withdrew his hand, suddenly, as a thought came to him, *Have I gone into another dimension.*

"Oh Master, bring me back to Earth," he repeated several times, until he felt a sudden jolt. He opened his eyes, only to shut them again, blinded by the glare of a very bright light.

"Ray," he heard the voice call his name. "It's me, Deneb."

The name Deneb struck a familiar note, and he opened his eyes slowly. A dull yellow glow filled the space he was in; he surveyed the surroundings; to his relief he was still in the cave. Deneb was standing in front of him, holding the stone that seemed to have been reenergized, while he was still seated cross legged in the same place.

He took a deep breath. "Phew! We're BACK," he spoke aloud.

"Yes," said Deneb, putting the glowing stone on the floor. "You're very much on Earth; in the same place."

Ray took her hand and pulled himself up. "Was it all a dream?" He stretched himself, but didn't feel any stiffness.

"NO! We have power to access records of the past, only if our Masters wish to."

"The conversation I had with you during this séance -- at least that's what I would call it -- all what I saw and experienced, indeed, was your life story. I have more or less relived your life on Andrearth."

"YES"

"Why are you shouting?"

"It is your energy level that has increased your sensitivity."

"By the way, what happened after the big show?"

"What show?"

"On the Septan plane."

"OH!" Deneb raised her chin and laughed. "I remember being dragged and thrown into a pit. An invisible force pulled me out of the pit. When I opened my eyes, I found myself seated in the sphere! I didn't even say goodbye to Altair."

"You were in love with him, weren't you," said Ray.

"Not anymore," she said, shaking her head.

"Meaning?"

"I don't feel anything for him, now."

"You must hate Dorado?"

"Dorado and Goldie's acts of aggression were just reflections of their own insecurity," said Deneb. "Looking back, I think, my own reactions during those two days, were childish."

"I fail to understand your way of thinking," said Ray. "It's hard enough to come to terms with the fact that I am sitting with an *alien*."

He rubbed his eyes, and looked at Deneb in the eye.

They are so human, he thought.

"We are definitely human, but in control of our destinies, and not having the thirst for progress."

"I should have known, you can read my thoughts," said Ray, and smiled. "Our scientists formulated laws that govern the universe and had comprehended the vastness without really experiencing it. Your story fits perfectly into the scheme of things. Einstein must have had a vision as expansive as yours. What you have experienced in terms of slowing of time, energy waves etc, were understood by him through complex mathematical equations. If only he could have met you."

"Who is he?"

"He was a one of our great scientists, and could just as well have reincarnated on Andrearth."

"I have not told you."

"What's more to tell?"

"Master Sirius knows about Earth. He is very concerned about you all."

"So what's he doing about it?"

"He is in touch with the other person I connected with. And our contact is just the beginning."

Ray was recollecting the conversation with his mother about brighter worlds, and he suddenly felt very excitable inside.

"I AM THE LUCKIEST SOUL ON THIS PLANET," he screamed. Deneb cupped her ears and closed her eyes.

Suddenly, his equanimity was restored, and the sadness inside had disappeared as if someone had lifted a huge weight off his chest.

Ray looked at Deneb. Her eyes were now flickering furiously. "I have to go."

"You mean, all the way back to Andrearth?"

Deneb giggled – again like a child. "I have to rebuild my life; make peace with everyone there."

He raised his arms in defeat. "It's beyond me!" he said, shaking his head. "You talk of emotional bonding. In your evolved state, is it not contradictory, and against the very essence of spiritual progress, to have emotional ties?"

"I don't know your system, but I can tell you one thing: Emotional bonds are very much part of our existence." Deneb gave a shallow laugh. "The Master has shown us what we needed to know; the duty to spread the message across this world is yours, now."

"You are not here for the locket are you?

She shook her head sideways. "I didn't have any idea until I transformed here."

"I guess so, because there was nothing that happened on Andrearth that had any connection with the locket."

"Only the Master can tell us that. But I get these bouts at a particular time of the year, and today seems to be that day. My mother used to think I was pretending; just to seek attention." She looked at him as if seeking affirmation. Ray just nodded and waited for her to continue. Nothing baffled him anymore. "Whenever this happens to me, I see myself trapped under water. Suddenly, I am confronted with this brilliant white light; it is the end of my dream, when I get lost inside this light."

Ray was listening, wide eyed, one foot resting on the wall. Suddenly, he stood erect. Something more bizarre and scary dawned on Ray. "No, it cannot be," he muttered under his breath, shaking his head.

"Yesterday was the day Anahita died, or rather, disappeared."

"Yes," Deneb nodded. "The memories are images from my previous life. We, on Andrearth, have evolved from a lesser world, to where I have come -- back to my past. Anahita was a special child, who must have been very near to the energy levels required for her to evolve on Andrearth; but she was reborn here, and then died very early."

"But she should have been on the Seventh plane," said Ray. "You are from the Eleventh plane?"

Deneb looked at Ray thoughtfully. "I have found answer. Your world is from where the souls come to Ninth and Eleventh planes. People who are more inclined towards science and technology come on the Eleventh plane; and those who are creative, are born on the Ninth plane."

"Yes Master." Ray chuckled. "This fits into the profile of people living on each of the two planes. But what about the Septans?"

"They must be from the other world that my Masters are talking about."

"The fact that you took ten and a half years to come here does not match with your being born soon after Anahita had died."

"Once we die, the soul is free to travel anywhere; they can be anywhere, or, everywhere, at anytime. But, when we are transformed to enable intergalactic travel, we do not attain that level of freedom and energy levels of a free soul. We are still bound by the impressions of our current life."

"I think I am beginning to find a deeper connection," said Ray. "We are connected in spirit, and can feel the pain of one another. That could explain the strange dreams I had, when I was small."

He began to narrate one of his dreams, which had been engrained into his mind. "I first had a nightmare, as if I were being attacked by some bad people. They were just like one of us, but the surroundings were unfamiliar. I was standing in an open field, which overlooked into a lake. Someone was trying to push me into it, when I heard someone call out to me. It was a girl, but she called me by another name. I cannot remember it," as Ray spoke his eyes widened with earnestness. "Again, I dreamt of the same place, but found myself running towards a huge ball that shone very brightly in the sunlight. That is when I saw the girl disappearing into the sphere. A man in a long white flowing robe stopped me. Then, the dream ended with a blinding flash of light."

Deneb had a look of complete bewilderment. "It seems to be the time when Altair was looking for me, on the Septan plane. The girl you saw was me being teleported into the Thirteenth plane."

Suddenly Ray sat up. "I am sitting with my sister, who died almost thirty years ago."

Deneb looked at him and frowned. "Why is it bothering you so much?"

"Actually, nothing. It's my mother whom I'm worried about."

"The Master has taken care of it. The locket made a connection between me and Anahita, which will bring peace to mother and I will not have those headaches."

"How are you so sure?"

"Are you not at peace? You had a rough life, full of hurdles, and now you have achieved all that you dreamed for. The Master's have taken care of it."

Ray thought for a moment. "I guess so." He actually was searching for the sadness and emptiness within, but it had vanished; he felt much more positive about life ahead.

"Can you tell me how you died?"

Deneb shook her head. "How will it help us?"

"I want my parents to know you really died, because they only know you disappeared never to come back." He looked at her expectantly. "They need closure."

Deneb closed her eyes and stood still for a few moments and then opened them again. "I was drowned in a small pond."

"Were you alone?"

"Wait I am receiving this information in bits and pieces. The Master does not really think it necessary."

"No, there was one man but they refuse to reveal his identity."

"Was he responsible for your drowning?"

"Umm…They are not very sure if it was deliberate."

"Would they have any idea what happened to your dead body?"

"You are very funny people; worrying about dead bodies when there is so much else to think about."

"It is not that. You cannot let people get away with murder."

"Death is inevitable. My Masters will not reveal anything else." She suddenly closed her eyes. "Near the coconut tree on the Eastern bank of the pond….."

"Did you hear that?" Deneb asked.

"Yes, but what does this mean?"

Deneb shrugged and shook her head. "That's all they will reveal."

Ray suddenly felt very cold; Deneb's clothes fluttered as if a breeze was blowing through the cave.

"It is a call from my Masters to go back."

"You can't just disappear," said Ray, staring at the rectangular slab of stone that was not solid anymore; it fluttered like a curtain, slowly dissolving into individual dots as if it were disintegrating. Soon it turned into a translucent film as if it were a mouth of a tunnel from where a swirl of steam was coming out. Ray could make out the interior through pockets of transparency. The walls of the tunnel swayed like a rope bridge.

Deneb stood at the edge, holding onto both the sides of the wall to maintain balance. "You have been chosen to spread the message." She staggered back.

He took a step forward and then another. As soon as he took the third step, a surge of electricity struck him squarely on his chest. He was thrown back, but something checked his fall, and he managed to stagger back a few paces.

"YOU CANNOT COME NEAR THIS. Now it is fully energized. This can crush you to pulp," she said. "Look." She took a stone from the floor and chucked it inside. "It is gone, POOF, smothered into plasma."

Ray gaped in complete bewilderment. "Wow ---"

"I was just looking for aliens, like, probably, a million other astronomers. And you choose me?" Deneb turned around without responding, and walked into the elasticized vestibule. He suddenly felt tiny vibrations under his feet.

Through the dull translucence, he saw her glance back and wave. Instinctively, he raised his hand. He thought she smiled, and the next moment she disappeared around the bend. As if someone was sucking air out from the other end of the tunnel, the doorway suddenly moved in, tapering into a line of darkness. The rectangular face became darker. Suddenly, a burst of hot air shot out of it, and, then, everything went dark. This was followed by a tremor so strong that the ground underneath shook, bringing Ray to sit down. He dug his head between his folded knees and clutched it with both hands as if to stop it from spinning.

Oh my God, this is the end, he thought aloud, waiting for the ceiling to cave in. Everything was happening so fast; the tremor dissipated into a rumbling noise, like that of a tube accelerating away from the platform. He slowly rose from his position, and wiped a shower of sweat streaming down his face. He opened his eyes wide, peering into the pitch-black calm, while his mind tried to piece together the events.

He waited for a while, but nothing happened. The orange glow from the stone also had gone out. He picked up the stone and turned it over and over to see if it were any different from what was around. Seeing no difference, he just threw it to one side, and quickly exited the cave.

As soon as he came out, a cool breeze blowing across made him shiver involuntarily. He looked into the sky only to find the darkening azure painted orange. He was not sure if it was dawn or dusk. All 108 wicks were alight, and the temple door was open, with a dull orange glow inside. The sky was getting darker as he walked towards the temple, and the evening star appeared, shining brightly just above his line of sight, when the sky suddenly turned grey and the *kirr* of the crickets started. It seemed as if time had stood still all this while.

He chose not to peep into the temple, and went home. On the way, back, the village temple was adorned in a necklace of oil lamps that he had seen on his way up to the hill. The inhabitants of Verkath were just going to bed when he entered.

His mother looked at the clock on the wall and said "You took a long time, Ray. I expected you at the temple."

Time had really stood still!

𝕯   𝕯   𝕯

When he looked back, it seemed just perfect that he was not going into the SETI program, but into the new course that Dr. Lowe had taken up. It still dealt with space and astronomy. The fascination for extra terrestrial life had just vanished.

Revathi's rather nonchalant attitude was enough for Ray to figure that she was out of her depression; she didn't even mention the locket, and Ray also chose to leave that part out. He was more curious as to what was going on in his Mother's mind, but he didn't have the heart to rake it up, lest she went back into her shell. It was almost as if she was waiting for Deneb to appear and ask for the locket. But the hint Ray got from Deneb about the pond and the coconut tree, was enough to set Ray searching. He finally dug around every coconut tree on the eastern bank. He found a few remains quite deep down, but chose to keep it to himself since Revathi had accepted closure. He performed a prayer and covered it back, putting some flowers on the grave. He had now guessed what must have happened: Shashi must have left Anahita near the pond and left. She must have fallen into the pond and drowned. Shashi must have come back and seen her in the water. He would have panicked and buried her near the pond itself. Soon after, he would have left for Dubai. The only doubt he had was whether Menon – the museum curator in Salisbury -- was Shashi? He didn't want to confront his mother on this as she had accepted closure.

He knew what he had experienced was true, at least for him, which was a vindication of his own convictions as well as his Master's whispers! And that night, when he happened to peep into his parent's bedroom, Revathi was reading 'Whispers' and smiling to herself!

"Has Anahita left?" he heard his mother say.

"After a brief sedentary hiatus, we are resuming our nomadic way of life. Our remote descendants, safely arrayed on many worlds through the Solar System and beyond, will be unified by their common heritage, by their regard to their home planet, and by the knowledge that, whatever other life may be, the only humans in all the universe come from Earth." ... ***Carl Sagan, Pale Blue Dot, pg 405***